TED TAYLER

LAST ORDERS

VINCI

BOOKS

By Ted Tayler

The Freeman Files

Fatal Decision

Last Orders

Pressure Point

Deadly Formula

Final Deal

Barking Mad

Creature Discomforts

Silent Terror

Night Train

All Things Bright

Buried Secrets

A Genuine Mistake

Strange Beginnings

Dead Reckoning

A Normal November

Into the Sunlight

Tame the Storm

One True Friend

Whispered Truths

A Morning Murder

Quick to Anger

Vinci Books

vinci-books.com

Published by Vinci Books Ltd in 2025

1

Chapter One

Sunday, 15 April 2018

THE BEST-LAID plans can often go astray.

Gus Freeman woke early and showered and dressed before eight o'clock. He stood ready for the day ahead. A glance through his kitchen window confirmed the weather remained cloudy but mild.

As the clock ticked round to the top of the hour, he decided on healthy oats and yoghurt for breakfast. Those suit trousers in his wardrobe only had one waistband extender button, and he'd already taken advantage of that. There would be plenty of opportunities to check out the other taste sensations amassed in his storage units.

Gus had restocked his fridge and freezer ahead of weeks, searching through a maze of questions posed by the ten-year-old murder of Mrs Daphne Tolliver. Finally, after three years of retirement, he returned to the job he had performed successfully for forty years. Gus Freeman merited his reputation as an excellent detective.

Assistant Chief Constable Kenneth Truelove persuaded him half a dozen cold cases had his name on them. Then, in a moment of weakness, perhaps blinded by the beauty of the ACC's PA, Vera Jennings, Gus put aside his gardening tools and re-entered the fray.

In his absence, the ongoing fight against crime had become an even more uphill battle. Cuts in the number of front-line officers were the most visible evidence to those who suffered as a result. Austerity cut deeper wounds in support staff, too; the police service that faced Gus on his return was lower on morale than when he retired. Something he didn't believe was possible.

Gus reflected on the speed of events in the past week. The knack for asking the right questions of the right people paid dividends. The old methods proved helpful yet again.

Even though he had only met his Crime Review Team members on Monday morning, they unmasked the killer by late Friday afternoon. Detective Superintendent Geoff Mercer arrested Leonard Pemberton-Smythe, the local MP, in front of the Manor House, the imposing country pile Leonard shared with his wife, Joyce and their staff.

Pemberton-Smythe was touted as the next Home Secretary and shortlisted for the highest office in the land. Gus and his team examined events surrounding the evening of Saturday, the twenty-eighth of June 2008. They discovered that the disgraced politician had committed not one murder but two.

Gus spooned the last of his breakfast from the bowl. He grimaced as he swallowed the healthy concoction. First things first, he popped into the bedroom to set the alarm for the following morning. Even if it meant forgoing fifteen minutes in bed, fried egg, bacon, and sausage was a better start to the day. Why support the producers of Scottish oats and Greek yoghurts when he could find locally sourced fresh food from farms within three miles?

If the worst came to the worst, he could always drive into town after meeting with the ACC in the morning and get a new suit.

Yesterday had been a busy day. He and Neil Davis, one of his two Detective Sergeants on the team, drove to London to interview Vanessa, the sister of the second victim, Mark Richards. Richards and Pemberton-Smythe were lovers. A relationship that proved fatal for the younger man when Daphne Tolliver disturbed the two men in Lowden Woods.

The old lady had to die to protect the Secretary of State for Justice's reputation. Richards died because he was a witness. The volatile nature of the relationship convinced the MP that two deaths were more acceptable than leaving himself open to blackmail.

Gus returned from the capital with vital information to strengthen the case against Pemberton-Smythe. An early evening visit to the Manor House produced more damning documentation from the MP's wife, Joyce. Gus could add that to the impressive pile of evidence for the prosecution later this morning.

It had been a grand day out. Even the sad duty of calling on Megan and Mick Morris felt cathartic. Gus told them they had closed Megan's sister's case at last. They had arrested her killer. Gus sat with them for over an hour, hoping the news might bring them closure, but the truth was far worse than they imagined. The killer was someone they knew. An important person in the public eye killed two innocent people. Daphne had worked at the Manor House for six years. It was hard for them to comprehend.

Gus knew there would be shock and dismay when the

news reached the media. There would be disbelief and questions asked. Had the police got the right man? Could Wiltshire Police run as sensitive an investigation as this? Who was in charge? He was thankful the buck stopped with the ACC and Geoff Mercer. Those two had broad shoulders. One thing was guaranteed; the Corporate Communications and Engagement people would earn their crust in the coming days.

Gus was one hundred per cent sure that the man DS Mercer would interview again later this morning was guilty. Two counts of murder. Bang to rights. It was time for the Crime Review Team to move on to its next case.

Gus gathered the documentation and his phone with the messages Vanessa had kept for a decade and left the bungalow despite the early hour. He locked the items in his Ford Focus glove compartment and drove through Urchfont village to the allotments. Ten minutes spent catching up on how his plants were coping wouldn't put a significant dent in his day.

There was no sign of Bert Penman. He'd be working here this afternoon after attending morning service at the church up the road. The bells hadn't started to ring yet. The silence on a morning such as this was a blessing. Few cars were on the road, and the birds grasped the opportunity to fill the temporary gap. Gus sat outside his shed for a spell.

He enjoyed two minutes alone with his thoughts.

"Mr Freeman?"

Irene North, Frank's wife, arrived beside him. Gus thought she could work for the SAS; he hadn't heard a sound.

"Good morning, Mrs North," he said.

"Frank hasn't been home," said Irene.

Gus gave her his full attention. Irene North was not

trying to catch Frank smoking a crafty ciggy. Nevertheless, the deep concern etched on a face lined with age and the worry of being married to a habitual offender was genuine. Gus had a terrible thought.

"When did you last see him, Mrs North?"

"Frank said he was coming here last night to check he'd locked his shed. He reckoned he was gardening for four hours yesterday afternoon. Frank spent it smoking and chatting, I'll bet. Don't think I don't know what he gets up to when he's here. I wouldn't mind if he brought armfuls of fruit and vegetables home, but Frank's got light fingers, not green."

"So I understand, Mrs North. He assures me that's in the past, though, and he's mended his ways. I couldn't get to my allotment yesterday, so I can't confirm if he was here. Frank's shed is locked, as you can see. What time did he leave home?"

"Just before ten,"

"Did he wear a coat, carry a torch? Did he go prepared?"

"Frank didn't go out late at night without a hat and coat, not with the state of his chest. I don't know if he took a torch. Knowing him, he'd strike a match to see whether that lock was secure. Then he'd just as likely light a blessed fag with it so as not to waste the match."

Gus understood Irene North's concern. Both were in their seventies and stayed together through thick and thin. Frank was as skinny as a rake. His long-suffering wife made three of him. Irene might give her old man a hard time over his smoking, but if their marriage had survived this long, a deep affection was involved. Even if it lay hidden.

Gus considered the situation. Frank North was old, not in the best of health, and missing for twelve hours. He knew Frank could have been taken ill or had fallen in the dark and lay hurt somewhere. But he and Irene walked past the likely spots when they came to the allotments. There was just one road through the village. Frank and Irene's place stood four hundred yards away.

So, where else might he have gone? Ah, the glorified shed belonging to Monty Jennings, Vera's estranged husband.

Geoff Mercer had told Gus that initial surveillance of the land behind Cambrai Terrace began last night. Plain-clothes officers had watched the lane entrance for strangers. The plan was to gather information to add weight to Frank's argument someone was living there. If people were living on the property, then that posed a problem. Nobody had ever applied for planning permission.

Gus told Frank not to stick his nose into the matter after he'd passed the issue on to the proper authorities. What if the silly old sod ignored his warning and wandered along the lane behind Cambrai Terrace for a quick peek? With his reputation, the officers on watch would have thought he was up to his old tricks. Frank North was housebreaking yet again. Irene's best chance of finding her husband might be at the local police station.

"I don't think you need to fret over Frank," said Gus. "If he'd had a stroke or tripped and broken a hip, we would have found him somewhere between your home and here. Telephone the police. If he's wandered off somewhere, they could keep an eye out. He's had his moments. Although he swore he'd stopped the thieving nonsense, we must accept he might have lapsed. In which case, the police could have him."

"I'll swing for him if that's what he was up to last night."

"At least you'll know where he is, Mrs North," said Gus.

Despite the potential seriousness of the situation, Irene North treated Gus to a gap-toothed smile. She soon returned to her standard disparaging tone.

"He can kiss goodbye to me visiting him this time," she said. "Our pensions barely put food on the table. There won't be spare cash for half-hour bus trips to Erlestoke."

With that, Irene North made her way home. Gus gave up working on his allotment. He relied on Bert Penman to sort out any urgent problems. The sooner he got the evidence he collected yesterday to Geoff Mercer, the better.

The trip into the valley was a pleasant one. Everything was coming together. The sun shone, and their first case went well. Alex, Neil and Lydia had the makings of an effective team. He'd taken the first step towards having a social life again with Vera Jennings. Where it might lead, Gus didn't have a clue.

He swung his Ford Focus into an empty parking spot outside the new custody suite on the outskirts of town. Gus was coming to terms with the layout of his new working environment. He welcomed the opportunity to see inside this modern addition to the Wiltshire Police family. The compound held several Bobby Vans and signs that the Neighbourhood Policing Units were well-represented. Even on a Sunday morning, there was a buzz about the place. Of course, it may have been a swarm of flies or a dodgy streetlight.

Once inside the building, he asked to speak with Super-intendent Mercer.

"The DS is interviewing a suspect. Perhaps if you take a seat?"

"I suggest you get a message to him," said Gus, "the items I have here are evidence. He should have enough for a result, but if the suspect's lawyer still retains a faint hope, this should shatter any illusions of a miracle."

Gus only needed to wait five minutes. Geoff Mercer came out to greet him.

"Good to see you, Gus," he said. "That QC he's engaged is keeping us on our toes. We're well ahead on points, though. Another session, and they should see sense and throw in the towel."

"I bear good tidings," said Gus, "we have text message conversations between Mark and Vanessa Richards from 2007 that confirm he was in a relationship with a senior politician. We have details of the location of the Minister's apartment. We identified the nightclub where they first met. There's a postcard sent to the sister from the village where Pemberton-Smythe had his holiday home. Mark was supposed to have sent it, but he was already dead and buried in the grounds of the Manor House. An expert can examine the handwriting, if necessary."

"This is dynamite, Gus, thanks," said Geoff. "I want to listen to these messages before I go back. They asked for a fifteen-minute comfort break. I plan to be lenient on time-keeping. It will suggest we're on the run. The impact of this additional evidence will be even greater. What else do you have there?"

"Joyce Pemberton-Smythe produced diary details of Leonard's activities on the Saturday evening of the murder. Based on entries in both Joyce and Crompton's diaries, he was not at home. Although he *was* out in the rain long enough to catch a chill, he delayed his return to Westminster until early on Wednesday morning. That was a complete change of routine. It was unique, based on the evidence in the diaries. He left the house at lunchtime on Monday and didn't return until after Joyce went to bed.

The murder and the subsequent burial of the body took place during those missing hours."

"This will help speed matters," said Geoff, rubbing his hands in anticipation. "Many thanks for this, Gus. I'll get these items processed. Do you want to observe? There's a spare chair next to Interview Room One."

"I'm not bothered," said Gus, "I can leave things in your capable hands. Even you couldn't fail to score from this distance."

"I knew you hadn't changed, deep down, you bugger."

"Did the surveillance crew spot anything or anyone last night?"

"Ah, sorry," said Geoff, "we pulled so many resources out to the Manor House that we left ourselves stretched. Then there was an incident on the M4 between Chippenham and Bath. A youngster jumped from a bridge. We postponed the whole thing. I've been too busy here to organise another try."

"Damn," said Gus, "I may need to look up there myself."

"The shed's not going anywhere; surely whatever Monty's involved in can wait?"

"Frank North is missing. He's the old chap who first gave me this tip. He's got the patch next to me on the allotments. His wife told me this morning that Frank left home at ten last night and never returned."

"Look, I need to get back inside with this evidence," said Geoff. "Call Suzie Ferris. The counter staff will give you her number after I've convinced them you're one of the good guys. Go with her to see what's what. Then, Suzie can start the ball rolling if it needs an official investigation."

Gus nodded. He watched Geoff Mercer pause at the desk as he rushed through to carry on the interview with

Pemberton-Smythe and the expensive QC he'd called. In the old days, Gus would have driven up to Cambrai Terrace, nosed around and thought nothing of nicking a suspect if he uncovered criminal activity. Instead, as a consultant, he needed a serving officer to help him do the basics.

That was the negative side of things. Suzie Ferris was young, attractive and on a fast track to the top. He could think of worse ways to spend a Sunday afternoon.

The young constable on the counter handed over Suzie's number, and Gus entered it into his phone. His contact list was growing apace after three years of inactivity.

"Suzie?" he asked, "Gus Freeman here. Sorry to bother you on Sunday morning. Can you spare an hour?"

"I didn't expect to hear from you, Gus. I told you to put your feet up and relax. Re-charge the batteries after a busy week."

Gus wondered why Suzie imagined he needed a long bed rest after spending a few days in the office. He was only sixty-one, for heaven's sake.

"Geoff Mercer is interviewing our man here at the custody suite. He volunteered your services. How long will it take you to get to Urchfont?"

"Fifteen minutes," replied Suzie, "isn't that where you live?"

Gus sensed another question left unasked.

"I live in the village, but that's not where Geoff volunteered your services. It's above board. We're searching for a missing person, so I'll fill you in when I get there. I'm leaving the police station now, and we'll meet at the end of Cambrai Terrace. It's on a hillside at the edge of the village."

"I've ridden past there," said Suzie, "the lanes there

aren't ideal for hacking, but it's a light exercise for my horses and good relaxation for me. Drive safe."

Gus wasn't surprised to learn Suzie was a horsewoman. There were plenty of them in the area. The Avon Vale branch of the Pony Club was on her doorstep. Her accent wasn't broad enough to place her as Wiltshire, born and bred. If she grew up near Devizes, her love of horses probably started before she went to school.

"Drive safe, indeed," he muttered as he left the custody suite and drove along Crook Way. He hadn't forgotten her unmerited swipe at his elderly Ford Focus on Friday evening. Suzie was waiting in her Golf GTI in a passing place on what amounted to little more than a single-track road.

Typical, she must have broken the speed limit to arrive ahead of me, thought Gus.

Suzie watched Gus park, then got out and walked towards his car.

Gus had admired the smart-looking officer in her uniform at the Manor House. Today Suzie's hair hung loose on her shoulders, not pinned in a bun under her hat. Her black blouson jacket covered a navy-blue polo shirt. Jodhpurs and riding boots completed the outfit of a girl at home in the country.

"Where are we off to?" she asked.

"Let's stroll along Cambrai Terrace, to begin with," he said, "I'll bring you up to speed on the story so far. We're interested in anything beyond the houses rather than the houses themselves. I hope we can tell whether anyone is hanging around in the fields above us on this first recce. It might be dangerous to get too close."

"You didn't tell me this might be dangerous," said Suzie. "It's okay; I carry my expanding baton and pepper spray in the car. I'll pick it up when we walk back. That's why we girls carry these huge handbags. I bet you thought it was just because they were trendy."

As they strolled along Cambrai Terrace, Gus told Suzie of the strange goings-on Frank North had reported. Her eyebrows shot up when he mentioned Monty Jennings owned the land which contained the glorified shed.

"So, this poor old chap has been missing since late last night? What would they do if something illegal was happening on the premises and he stumbled on it?"

"That's exactly why I told Frank to stay away," said Gus. "Monty Jennings flies close to the wind, according to Geoff Mercer. Violence doesn't appear to be in his make-up."

"He may have leased the place to someone else," said Suzie, glancing over Gus's shoulder as they turned into the cul-de-sac at the end of the road.

"I couldn't see anyone," said Gus, "how about you? Any sign of smoke?"

"Nothing at all. We can't be sure there aren't vehicles in the lane behind the houses. We'd have a better view if we walked up to the brow of the hill and cut across the field. It won't attract as much attention if we pose as ramblers looking across the valley."

"Smart move, dressing the way you did. You blend into the scenery."

"You decided on smart-casual this time."

Her laughter was infectious.

Gus knew at once she'd learned about his first meeting with the ACC. So, after three years of dressing as he pleased and spending most of his spare time on his allotment, he drove to the London Road HQ in his gardening clothes.

Suzie trotted ahead of him to collect her baton and pepper spray from the boot of her car. She dropped the items into her shoulder bag, together with her warrant card. Suzie paused as she passed the strap of her handbag over her head to prevent it from being ripped from her by an attacker.

"There's no telling to whom Monty might have leased this place," she said, "Vera says he'll do anything to make a quick profit."

"That worried me too," said Gus, "we've got three sizeable cities within twenty miles. County lines gangs have been growing in strength and numbers. If they're involved in this, Frank North could have walked into a heap of trouble."

The winding lane took them ever upward to the brow of the hill and disappeared into the valley. From the ridge, they could see the lane running along the backs of the houses on Cambrai Terrace. At the far end stood the outbuilding. It was too substantial to call it a shed. The chimney was only an ornament today, but why would anyone need to add a chimney to a property designed to store tools and equipment? A vast expanse of greenery below them was broken by a scattering of housing throughout the valley. Hard to imagine there was anyone else alive in the world. The place was so quiet.

"No cars or people. No sign of Frank North," sighed Gus.

"What do we do now?" asked Suzie.

"The logical place to look is inside that outbuilding."

"We need a warrant to get inside without an invitation."

"If they're up to no good and we walk down the hill and knock on the door…."

"They'd tell us to go away and disappear before we returned with a warrant."

"We'll leave it for today," said Gus, "Geoff Mercer can

arrange surveillance tomorrow. If he's not back, I'll bend the ACC's ear until he does the necessary. I don't like the look of it, Suzie, but we can't jeopardise what might prove a major operation by jumping in too early. There could still be a simple explanation for Frank's disappearance."

They made the walk in silence. Gus stopped to stand on the bottom rung of gates at the entrance to the fields for any signs of Frank. A lone car passed them as it struggled up the incline.

"Two little old ladies out for a sunny Sunday afternoon drive," said Suzie.

"Seasoned criminals in Agatha Christie country," said Gus. "Sorry to interrupt your day with what turned out to be a waste of effort. Do you want to follow me back to my place? I can offer you a bowl of soup and a crusty roll."

"If you're sure I'm not keeping you from something important. Yes, please, the walk and the fresh air have made me hungry."

For the first time in a long time, two cars pulled into the driveway of Freeman's bungalow. They parked on the right-hand side, under the climbing roses.

"They're beautiful," said Suzie Ferris.

"My late wife Tess planted those. She hoped to trail them across the whole side of the bungalow in time."

"There's a long way to go, Gus, but they look sturdy enough."

"Bert Penman, one of my neighbours on the allotments near the church, reckons every plant has two choices. Live or die. Those roses are no different. I hope they continue to thrive because digging them up will mean one more memory of Tess gone."

"I haven't lost anyone close to me," said Suzie, "both my parents are going strong. We lost my maternal grandmother when I was eight. She lived in New Zealand with my grandfather. I was old enough to understand what had happened, but I'd never met her in person. So, it didn't have the same impact. Mum and Dad didn't take my brother and me out for the funeral, either. Too expensive. Gramps and my Dad's parents are in their eighties now and beginning to look frail."

They had moved inside the bungalow, and Gus showed Suzie into the lounge.

"Give me twenty minutes in the kitchen," he said, "see if there's anything among my record collection you fancy."

Gus got to work on the soup. Suzie called through from the next room: -

"Vinyl's making a comeback," she said, "you were right to hang on to these. You're in fashion again. My Dad's got a live Yardbirds album from the early Sixties he reckons is valuable. He treats it better than he treats my Mum."

"Not the one from the Marquee Club?" asked Gus, who stood in the doorway. "I've always wanted to find a copy of that. Clapton murdered the vocals on 'Good Morning Little Schoolgirl', but the album was sensational."

"It was a mono recording, so it sounds tinny compared to today's stuff. None of that was my scene, as you can imagine. Boyzone, Westlife and Britney Spears never got me hooked. I was only interested in horses."

"I guess it's not a surprise if you live in this area. Where do you stable your horses?"

"I keep forgetting; you're new to this part of the county. We have a large farm near Worton, and the stables are a stone's throw from the main house. Horses have been part of my family for years. My Mum was a national champion, and my Dad rode point-to-point until recently. After that, music and several other things have taken a back seat to my horses and career."

"You're not related to Vera's family, are you?" Gus asked.

"Distant cousins," Suzie replied, "so you've delved into her background, have you?"

Gus grinned.

"I like to know who I'm working with," he said and returned to the kitchen to continue preparing lunch. Eva Cassidy's voice accompanied his labours. Eva was one of Tess's favourites.

"Is this too gloomy?" asked Suzie as she watched Gus pour the soup into two bowls. "I didn't think, sorry. My Mum loves listening to this album."

"We oldies can still pick them, then?" said Gus, inviting Suzie to sit. They ate in silence as the album moved track by track to the end of side one.

"That soup tasted great, Gus," said Suzie, "just what I needed. Do you want a hand with the washing-up?"

"Leave it. I'll put everything into the dishwasher. Are you rushing away?"

"What did you have in mind?

Gus missed the raised eyebrow. Instead, he was engrossed in getting the dishwasher stacked, as Tess insisted.

"It's still a pleasant afternoon," he said, "we could wander along to the allotments. You can thank my patch in person for its excellent vegetables."

"Exercise is always beneficial after lunch," said Suzie, "my Dad falls asleep in the chair by three o'clock. It's his age, I suppose."

"I never have that problem, young lady," said Gus, "now, are we ready?"

As they took a brisk walk through the village towards the allotments, Gus noticed neighbours in their gardens stand and stare. Other couples he didn't recognise strolling home from the pub nodded and said 'Hello'. Nobody took a blind bit of notice of him any other time.

Suzie Ferris slipped her arm through his.

"Now they'll have something to talk about," she laughed.

She let go of his arm when they reached the gateway to the allotments. Someone waved, eager to catch their attention.

"That's Bert Penman," said Gus, "the chap I mentioned. He's looking after my patch while I'm working on these cold cases. I wonder what he wants?"

"Afternoon, Mr Freeman," said Bert, removing his cap in the presence of a young lady. "afternoon, Miss."

"What's the matter?" asked Gus.

"There's something over yonder you need to see," said Bert, pointing to the far side of the allotments. Gus could see a young man who appeared to be comforting a woman, maybe his wife.

Gus started to run. Suzie chased after him. They saw a dark shape lying under the cemetery wall in the top corner of the field.

Gus recognised the overcoat and the worn-down soles of his shoes.

"Frank North."

"That degree of damage can only mean one thing," said Suzie Ferris.

"Two shots to the back of the head, execution-style," said Gus.

"I'll call it in. You know where Frank lives. Tell his wife, and for God's sake, dissuade her from coming here. Whoever Monty Jennings has got involved with this time is bad news."

Chapter Two

Monday, 16 April 2018

THE ALARM BROUGHT a welcome interruption to the dream he'd been having. Gus rolled out of bed, padded to the shower, and was dressed before the events of yesterday crowded into his head once more.

What a mess.

Gus watched the sausage and a rasher of bacon frying in the pan. An egg lay in wait to the side.

Poor Frank North. No matter how many times he got nicked for thieving, he didn't deserve that. A defenceless man murdered for what? It wasn't for money or his mobile phone. He carried neither that night.

Suzie Ferris switched from Sunday afternoon companion to Detective Inspector in seconds. She took control of the situation, and a host of police personnel descended on the allotments within the hour. Some would still be there. Gus knew he must leave well alone. There was nothing there for consultants. All civilians, move along, please.

The last thing Suzie said before he left to visit Irene North was the amount of blood indicated the killer had dumped Frank's body. They needed to look for the actual crime scene. His only thought was to ask her to discuss the matter with the ACC. If Monty Jennings's shed was the first place they visited after discovering the body, any future surveillance was pointless.

It was a mess, alright.

Gus cracked the egg into the frying pan. Bloody typical. A double-yolker. It was supposed to be lucky, but it didn't feel it today. He tried to recall what he'd been dreaming about just before the alarm rang.

Vera Jennings was driving that yellow Alfa Romeo through the village as Gus and Suzie Ferris strolled past the Community Shop. It was a perfectly innocent scene. Then Gus remembered a squeal of brakes and the roar of an engine. He had looked round to see the bonnet of the Spider closing on them. The alarm bell came in the nick of time.

"Perfect," said Gus, and he wasn't referring to his cooking skills.

Gus dished up his breakfast and flicked the switch on the kettle. A mug of coffee would be the ideal complement. The fry-up proved what he hoped it would be. Better than oats and yoghurt.

Later, a warm and sunny morning greeted him when he stepped outside the bungalow. Gus wondered whether the ACC might postpone their meeting. The drive to London Road took longer every day. As he stopped at yet another set of temporary traffic lights, he thought back to Irene North.

Gus lost count many years ago of the number of times he'd informed family members of the death of a loved one. It was never easy or pleasant. He had walked from the allotments to her council house, trying to get a grip on the words he wanted to say. He'd done the same thing on every previous occasion for his benefit. Of course, the person receiving the dreadful news never heard the specifics of what you said, anyway.

As he walked up the path, he spotted Irene rising from her chair and hurrying to the front door. She understood what was coming. Gus walked straight in, closed the door behind him, took hold of her arm, and walked back to her chair.

"Where did you find him?" she asked.

"On the far side of the allotments. We think Frank was there since last night."

"My Frank was there this morning?"

Yes, thought Gus, one hundred yards away from where we chatted, thrown in the corner of the field with his face shot off.

"We believe so. Do you know anyone who wanted to harm Frank, Mrs North?"

Irene North's hand shot to her mouth.

"Oh, my Lord. Are you telling me it was murder? Frank didn't have a heart attack or something."

"No, it was murder."

Irene started to get up from the chair.

"I must go to him," she said.

"That's not a good idea," said Gus.

"What do you mean? What did they do to him?"

"They shot him, Mrs North. They'll take Frank's body away later this afternoon. We'll look after him. Maybe, you can say goodbye to him later. Do you have family members to contact? Is there someone who can come and stay with you?"

Irene North sat and considered for a moment.

"There are only a few family members to ring," she said. "Not many have cars. The buses are useless, especially on Sundays. I could ask my neighbour to sit with me. Her old man won't be back from the pub until closing."

Gus popped next door to ask the neighbour if she'd mind keeping Irene company. He'd left the two of them drinking a glass of sherry. It was a new bottle, so with luck, Irene North would sleep well despite everything.

When he returned to the bungalow, he noticed the red light flashing on his landline.

Geoff Mercer had left a message.

"Thought you deserved to hear the good news. When we resumed the interview, I just placed the postcard on the table, then the diaries. I told them we were waiting for a transcript of text messages extracted from Mark Richards's phone. We sat in silence for two minutes. His QC could see he was about to crack, and when Pemberton-Smythe leaned forward to speak, he tried his best to stop him. The brief could tell we had him bang to rights. It's done and dusted. The penny dropped later that we hadn't got anything so far from the two phones found with the body. We may get lucky in time. Perhaps I should have said we were waiting for a transcript of text messages extracted from Vanessa Richards's phone she said came from her brother. A slip of the tongue."

Gus had been amazed to learn Geoff Mercer could be a devious bastard; they might make a decent copper out of him yet. They had the right bloke. That case was done and dusted before the coup de grace yesterday afternoon. As for Frank North, that was a different matter.

Gus wasn't surprised to find parking spaces scarce at HQ. It was Monday morning. There had been a shooting in a village a few miles from Devizes. The media would be swarming over that and pressing for information on what the police activity had been about at the Manor House on Friday. How the ACC kept a lid on it throughout the weekend, he couldn't imagine.

The reception staff were more used to him now. He signed in and stood outside the ACC's office in no time. That probably meant the ACC wasn't there. Gus never trusted operations that ran like clockwork.

"Good morning, Gus. Hope I didn't wake you when I left."

DI Suzie Ferris was back in uniform and looking terrific. Very young, striking, and with a wicked sense of humour.

Gus spotted Kassie Trotter over Suzie's shoulder. He could have sworn her chin hit the desk when she overheard that remark. But, wherever Suzie headed, she looked to be in a hurry. Gus didn't have the chance to reply, so he stopped by Kassie's desk to limit the damage.

"Before spreading malicious gossip, may I point out that DI Ferris and I worked together yesterday? We found a dead body near the cemetery wall on the allotments. Suzie parked in my driveway until released from her duties, and then she drove home."

"Whatever you say, Mr Freeman," said Kassie, "was this another thing I need to keep quiet, then?"

"As long as you tell the truth, that will be fine."

"Mr Truelove's in with the Chief Constable, in case you wondered," she said, nodding towards the ACC's door.

"I can wait," said Gus. "Until he gives me another case to crack, the Crime Review Team have nothing to do, anyway. I suppose DS Mercer is still off-site?"

"He's finished with that politician. The ACC gave him twenty-four hours leave; I reckon they're keeping those closest to the job as far away from the media as possible."

"For which I shall be eternally grateful," said Gus.

He knew there was someone behind him. If his sense of smell was still intact, the woman had worn the same perfume on Friday night.

"Good morning, Vera," he said.

Kassie's eyebrows tried their best to rise, but they were at an implausible height already.

"You *are* a detective," she cooed.

"Hello again, Gus," said Vera, handing him a file. "The ACC asked me to give you the details of your next case. He apologises for not being available to recap last week's success. There's a press conference in fifteen minutes where he will confirm we've charged Leonard Pemberton-Smythe with two counts of murder relating to events from June 2008. The ACC doesn't expect to escape the media's clutches for a while."

"Keep calm, and carry on, I guess?" asked Gus.

"That's the size of it. You'll hear this soon enough, but the Police and Crime Commissioner called the Chief Constable for an urgent meeting yesterday afternoon. The best way to describe the outcome would be to ask him to consider his position. We expect his resignation within the hour."

"At least he waited until the poor chap finished his round of golf. A harsh decision, but fair enough in the circumstances," said Gus. "They'll need another picture to commemorate the opening of the Hub now. Two of the smiling faces have fallen from grace."

"Trust you to point out something as trivial as that," said Vera with a smile.

"It is a big picture," said Kassie Trotter, "It will leave a gap. I'll contact the Publicity people to see what they've got in stock. An image of the Stones would be good."

"Not sure the Rolling Stones can claim any Wiltshire heritage, Kassie," said Gus.

"Stonehenge, I meant," she replied, giving Gus a pitying look.

"That's a great idea, Kassie," said Vera, "or Salisbury Cathedral spire, given the latest news headlines."

Kassie trotted off to hunt for a replacement photograph for the Hub wall. Vera and Gus could chat in peace.

"Friday was fun, and you had a hectic weekend, I hear," said Vera.

"I had a delightful Friday evening, too, thank you. I spent most of Saturday in Camden Town or at the Manor House collecting the final pieces of the jigsaw. I planned to relax for an hour before dropping those pieces over to Geoff Mercer yesterday morning, but one of the villagers came to inform me her husband was missing. As soon as I'd finished briefing Geoff, I drove to Urchfont to meet Suzie Ferris."

"I heard a whisper," said Vera.

"Nothing escapes people around here, does it?" he said. "As Geoff pointed out, I can't go wandering around sticking my nose into active cases or reports of suspicious activity. Not as a consultant. Geoff Mercer volunteered Suzie Ferris as my official police presence."

"Responsible adult might be better," said Vera.

Gus could tell she was winding him up, but it felt good to spend time with her. If he held his nerve, he might ask her out again this week.

"Did you hear we found the missing man's body in the allotments?"

"That was terrible," said Vera. "Suzie said the killer shot

the poor man in the head. She didn't know how she held on to the vegetable soup you prepared for her."

"I've only met Suzie twice, but she has the makings of an outstanding officer. The sky's the limit for her. As for inviting her to lunch, it was the civil thing to do after dragging her away from exercising her horses. Or whatever else she planned to do with her Sunday," said Gus.

Vera stroked his upper arm.

"No need to explain, Gus. I understand; you're a gentleman. Good detectives and gentlemen have something in common; both are very much a dying breed. We need to treasure you as long as we can."

Now could be an excellent time to ask her out, thought Gus, but Peter Morgan, the Police Surgeon, arrived at the top of the stairs. He was heading for one of the outer offices but stopped as soon as he saw Vera.

"Good morning, Vera. Did you have a good weekend?"

"Quiet, Peter and yourself?" she replied with little warmth.

"I finally reached the Brecon Beacons. Walked bloody miles, overate as usual, and undid the good work."

"It's the thought that counts," Gus offered. Morgan turned as if noticing him for the first time. Gus thought that Morgan and Vera must have known one another for a while. Perhaps they had a history.

"Freeman? Friday's episode was a shocker, eh?" said Peter Morgan.

"Good police work. I shall be interested to learn what you discover from the items removed from the ground at the Manor House. There's another body for you to look at, I'm afraid. This one was unconnected to the Manor House case. A gruesome start to the week."

"That's life," said Peter Morgan without a hint of irony.

"It appears I've missed a lot by motoring to Wales for the weekend. On the way, I heard that the Chief Constable had fallen on his sword. One has to vet one's friends carefully for skeletons in the closet. Although that may not be the best metaphor."

"There's no suggestion the Chief Constable knew what his golfing chum had done," said Gus. "Ten years ago, they hadn't even met. Of course, the Minister's sexual preferences wouldn't preclude the two men from becoming friends in many walks of life. But public confidence and trust in his role must be maintained at all costs. His position was untenable."

Peter Morgan shrugged and left for his appointment.

"Don't mind, Peter," said Vera, "he's a pompous prat."

Gus smiled. What a relief.

"Suzie mentioned you searched for this missing man near Cambrai Terrace," said Vera, "she didn't say why you thought he might be up that way."

"Frank North had a reputation for housebreaking. Those cottages up on the hill are holiday homes. I wondered whether he might have had an accident trying to gain access to an empty place. Frank's wife didn't believe he would have left the village, so we covered as much area as possible on foot."

Vera seemed convinced. Gus decided to take a risk.

"Would you have dinner with me later in the week, Thursday or Friday?"

"I'm meeting the girls on Friday," said Vera, "but Thursday sounds good."

"Chinese or Italian?"

"I love both. Surprise me."

"You're paying."

"Sorry?"

"Well, you said to surprise you. Also, I noted your concerns over being seen too often in public before your final divorce. I hoped we could eat in a restaurant off Market Square near the Old Police Station. After work, we can meet for a drink, and I'll book a table for around half-past six. How does that sound?"

"Perfect," Vera replied, "you had better run along before your team sends out a search party."

"See you on Thursday in the Ring O'Bells. It's across the road from the office."

"I know it; we girls have visited it once or twice. It's better than the Crown."

Gus was too wise to refer to the last of the FEW, Kassie Trotter's unkind quip referring to them being members of the frustrated ex-wives club. He restricted himself to a brief wave as he left her.

Vera returned to her desk in the administration area. As he descended the stairs to the Reception desk, Gus met Kassie struggling with a large package.

"Can I help you with that?" he said.

"I'm alright, Mr Freeman," she said, "this was a print they bought at the time. I reckon it's great, but Takashi Murakami got rejected by Japan's Got Talent Committee."

Gus left Kassie to carry the modern artwork to its new home. He could understand why Kassie found an affinity with it. Her sleeve tattoo came from a similar palette. However, he had no clue what the staff in the Hub would make of it.

Gus drove from the London Road HQ car park just as the Press Pack descended on the building. It was like watching sharks in a feeding frenzy. He wished Kenneth Truelove every bit of luck in the world.

His arrival back at the Old Police Station didn't go unnoticed.

"The wanderer returns," said Neil Davis as the lift rose from the ground floor.

Gus's team had followed his instructions and finished entering data into the murder book. The team had decided to call it the Freeman File. It contained collated documentation relating to the Tolliver and Richards cases.

Their charts and whiteboards were cleared, ready for a new challenge. If an office could look pristine, then the CRT office fits the description.

"Morning, guv," said Neil, "what was the atmosphere in Devizes?"

DS Alex Hardy and Lydia Logan Barre turned their heads to hear their master's voice.

"Where's my coffee?" asked Gus. "black, no sugar. How can I work without sustenance?"

"I'll go," said Alex.

He raced across the room, negotiating the door into the restroom in his wheelchair without a bump. The Gaggia whirred into action, and mugs and spoons clinked on the worktop.

Gus flicked through the murder file Vera had handed him while he waited. Coffee was the last thing he needed, really, but he wanted the team alert and focused. They performed well last week, but complacency soon set in in this game. It was a tricky fault to eliminate. The murder of Trudi Villiers, which he was looking at for the first time, could prove a difficult nut to crack.

Lydia thought Alex would struggle to bring four coffees back into the office. She got up to help him with the tray.

"Alex will work it out," said Gus, "each team member puts in an equal share. I told you that last Monday."

Lydia hovered, unsure whether Gus was serious; then, realising he was, she took her seat.

Alex emerged from the restroom with four mugs of coffee in a plastic tray moulded to accept four containers.

The tray looked safe and sound, securely positioned on his lap. Hands-free, Alex never spilt a drop.

"Black without, guv. Black with one sugar for Lydia. Two white with one sugar for Neil and me."

"How much did that cost?" asked Neil.

"This beauty cost under a tenner," said Alex, "I use it at home when people visit. I decided it was stupid not to bring it to work."

"Only one design fault that I can see," said Neil, "there's nowhere for the Hobnobs."

"Right," said Gus, "while we drink this coffee, I'll tell you the latest. Neil will have told you what happened on Saturday until I dropped him off at home. I received more useful evidence from the lady of the Manor in the evening. Then I passed everything to DS Mercer at the custody suite on Sunday morning. Geoff got a full confession yesterday afternoon."

He paused while Alex, Neil and Lydia clapped, punched the air or did a little dance.

"There's been another casualty this morning," Gus continued. "The Chief Constable has resigned. The PCC has seen his friendship with the Minister as a lack of judgement. Although, how he could have known the bloke killed two people from the way he swung a golf club, heaven knows."

"Another new face at the top, then," said Alex. "How will that affect us, guv?"

"The ACC and DS Mercer championed this CRT initiative. As far as Geoff Mercer's concerned, if we keep getting results, it won't matter who's in the Chief Constable's chair. They'd look stupid if they pulled the plug. The PCC appoints the Chief Constable anyway, so I'd be more worried if a new face took over that role and decided they'd prefer cold cases remained unsolved."

"Is there anything else you want to tell us, guv?" asked Neil.

"If you mean, did DI Ferris and I discover the body of a murdered man yesterday afternoon, then yes, we did. You don't need to know what we worked on as it doesn't impact our work on cold cases."

Neil realised they wouldn't learn more regarding events late on Friday evening after they left the Waggon and Horses. The boss had moved on already.

Alex wondered how Gus had got involved in something dangerous. When he agreed to return as a consultant, it was to tackle cold cases. Suzie Ferris was a Detective Inspector at the sharp end of live criminal activity. It sounded far more than a chance discovery of a body and more interesting than gossip about the boss's love life.

The team spent the rest of the day poring over the details of the Trudi Villiers murder.

JUST AFTER ONE o'clock Sunday morning, the fifth of October 2003, Trudi Villiers left the Ring O'Bells pub where she worked as a barmaid. Her route home took her through Market Square and along Riverside Walk. Her destination lay at the north end of the Greenwood Estate, a vast network of housing, small shops, two schools and the community hospital.

Trudi was twenty-six years old, single and left school at sixteen. Her first job was at Graceland's, the care home on the outskirts of town. Eighteen months later, she switched to Woolworth's on the High Street. Trudi never stayed anywhere for long. As soon as she saved enough money for a holiday, she jetted off to the hot spots of Magaluf or Aya Napa.

By the time she reached twenty-one, Trudi had changed jobs five times and been on twenty Mediterranean holidays. There was no accurate number of the men in her life. Her reputation was nothing to be proud of, and the landlord at the Ring O'Bells would never have employed her unless they hadn't needed her physical attributes to sell beer.

The girl had pulling power, and the punters loved her. Her low-cut tops, short skirts and outgoing personality seemed to be what male pub goers expected to see on the other side of the counter. Trudi never disappointed them.

Krystal Warner, Trudi's flatmate, started working alongside Trudi three months after pulling her first pint. Although Krystal was attractive enough, she didn't possess the same sparkle as Trudi. Nevertheless, she followed Trudi's lead in whatever she did, and her wardrobe and banter with the paying public gave the pair a formidable presence.

The other local pubs soon became aware they faced competition for their trade as the Ring O'Bells drew an increased regular clientele throughout the week. They offered live music on Friday and Saturday nights, and the bar areas were even more crowded.

The town still had its fair share of petty crime and pub fights. Someone might get their wallet lifted from a jacket, or a handbag could be sneaked away under a coat. It wasn't unheard of for the community hospital to have late-night visits from people needing a stitch or two.

As long as they enjoyed themselves, it seemed a reasonable price to pay. Everyone in town hoped that the bad times lay behind them. The days when two rival gangs ruled the roost. There were too many recreational drugs in circulation, but they shared that menace with every other town in the country.

Soon after midnight on the fifth of October, Krystal Warner went home by taxi with her current boyfriend, James Bosworth. Trudi Villiers was saving for yet another holiday and volunteered to stay on at the pub. The usual routine was to collect the glasses, empty the ashtrays and leave everything for the cleaners in the morning. After a series of wild weekend nights, that became a significant issue with the day staff.

So, Trudi and Gary, the bar manager, tackled the glasses, washed and dried them, and then put them back on the shelves. They replaced the beer mats and stacked the bar stools on the tables. The bar areas were cleared by one o'clock so the floor and carpets could be swept clean and ready for the Sunday lunchtime rush.

After Trudi left for home, Gary locked up and went upstairs to join his wife in bed. He was a happy man. The extra ten pounds he paid Trudi would stop the moaning from the cleaners and save him from looking for someone else to do the dirty job for peanuts.

Riverside Walk was a pretty stretch during the day; the path wound between weeping willows and plane trees alongside the river. There were benches and fishing points. In daylight hours, it received plenty of visitors. However, it was poorly lit at night and not recommended for a young woman alone in the early hours.

The Imperial Dragon Chinese restaurant owner, Steve Li, spotted a young woman on the opposite side of the road, heading for Market Square at one o'clock. He was preparing to drive home in his Jaguar. He recognised the person as Trudi Villiers. She was a frequent visitor to his premises. Trudi was always loud, often drunk and with her arms around a young chap, more out than in her dress.

Steve had thought of calling out to offer her a lift but knew his wife would give him hell if she ever found out. Nevertheless, Steve hadn't seen anyone following Trudi or on the streets when he drove home minutes later.

There were no reports of further sightings.

Dawn broke on the riverside, and the chill of the morning kept many residents indoors until a pale sun warmed the streets. Ten o'clock struck on the church clock before anyone entered the pathway heading into town. It's remarkable how often a poor dog walker is first on the scene at such times.

Tony Virgo, a thirty-seven-year-old hairdresser, exercised Bubble and Squeak, his Yorkshire terriers. As he walked down the slope onto Riverside Walk from the street where he lived with his husband, Tristram, Tony spotted Trudi's partly clothed body dumped on a patch of ground behind a bush, five yards from the path.

Trudi's body was only visible from the higher ground on the edge of the Greenwood Estate. She had been stabbed in the throat and chest at least a dozen times.

Police found no weapon at the scene.

Her skirt, underwear, mobile phone, purse and shoes were missing.

Wiltshire Police reacted with haste once they received a report of the body's discovery.

The pathologist took several swabs, and subsequent forensic examination confirmed semen in the vaginal and anal orifices. The blood type was determined to be 'O' positive. Trace evidence was gathered, including fibres underneath Trudi's fingernails.

There was little evidence the barmaid had made any sustained attempt to fight off her killer. Given her well-documented promiscuity, she may have been a willing participant, at least at the outset. The ferocity of the sexual assault might have made her change her mind. Perhaps she told the man involved to stop, resulting in an argument. However, there were no reports of shouting or screaming in the early hours. Something had prompted the frenzied attack.

Did Trudi have rough sex with someone she knew? Her history didn't preclude it.

Did she meet a stranger on Riverside Walk and take one risk too many? That was something to consider.

The wounds to Trudi's throat grouped closely together. Although the blade was four to five inches long, it proved impossible to specify the weapon.

There were two wounds to the chest, made by a similar weapon. The pathologist determined one of these had been the fatal wound.

The repeated onslaught destroyed so many wound edges in the throat that he couldn't say whether the same weapon made them. So different weapons may have caused throat and chest wounds.

The pathologist noted a marked difference between the force used in the two areas. The chest received a greater degree of force.

The news of the murder spread around the town like wildfire. The cleaners arrived at the Ring O'Bells to find a third of their work already done. As they stopped for a mid-morning coffee and cigarette, their good mood faded as they heard passers-by querying the significant police presence on Riverside Walk.

The rumour spread of the discovery of a body. A young girl had been murdered. Gary, the bar manager, went to investigate. He had a sick feeling in his stomach. Gary prayed it wasn't Trudi. Gary's wife and the cleaners gathered by the side door to the pub when he returned. One look at his ashen face told them the truth.

The Ring O'Bells closed at lunchtime out of respect.

The slip of paper pinned to the barred front door notified their regulars they would re-open at seven in the evening.

There would be no last orders tonight. Many of Trudi's customers and several of her lovers would enjoy a lock-in to remember the busty barmaid with the beaming smile.

Chapter Three

FEW ADDITIONAL CLUES emerged during the rest of Sunday. The hunt for suspects began on Monday morning, the sixth of October 2003.

DI Dominic Culverhouse had recently assumed control at the Old Police Station. It was his first major case. So he turned to one of his long-serving detectives to do the grunt work. DS Terry Davis took WPC Debbie Turner with him to interview Krystal Warner.

The officers found Krystal still in her bedclothes. Her fluffy pink dressing gown wrapped around her like a comfort blanket. Krystal's eyes looked puffy and red; the twenty-four-year-old barmaid didn't appear to have slept much. She was drinking a mug of coffee. The two police officers didn't get an invitation to join her.

Krystal was heartbroken. Trudi, her flat-mate and best friend, dead. They had planned to spend two weeks in San Antonio next Spring. She told them she arrived home at a quarter past twelve with her boyfriend, James Bosworth. The taxi dropped her off, and James carried on to his place on the Westbourne Estate on the other side of town. Krystal had been shattered after their busy shift in the Ring O'Bells and slept through until ten o'clock.

Krystal hadn't worried when she realised her friend hadn't made it home. It wasn't unheard of for Trudi to jump in the back of a van with band members that played in the pub. When pressed, Krystal admitted that she had joined her friend more than once on a Friday or Saturday night before she met Bosworth.

Davis and Turner then crossed town to interview James Bosworth during his lunch break. Bosworth was thirty years old and a self-employed electrician. Bosworth was tall, swarthy-looking and his hair curled over his shirt collar. Debbie Turner could see why women were attracted to him. His dark-brown eyes and designer stubble gave him a good look, even if that look held a hint of danger.

Bosworth's story differed from his girlfriend's. According to him, when they reached her place, she begged him to stay until Trudi got home. Bosworth told them Krystal became angry when he refused. He hadn't wanted a quick shag and then walk two miles across town. If their relationship was serious, then he wanted to spend the night. On the other hand, he wasn't happy with them shooting off to Ibiza together either because he knew Trudi. She'd jump into bed with anything with a pulse.

WPC Turner noticed scratch marks on Bosworth's forearms, plus a bruise on his cheek. When she asked how he came by them, he said Krystal had done it after they stepped out of the taxi. He kissed her goodnight. She begged him to stay. When he refused, she laid into him. He got back in the cab, and the driver left her standing on the pavement outside her place, cursing him.

DS Davis traced the taxi driver later that evening, but he

reckoned he had so many fares that night that he couldn't remember. So he suffered his fair share of domestics inside the cab, youngsters puking on the back of his seat and punters running off without paying.

"How the heck can I be expected to remember a girl slapping her boyfriend when they weren't even in the taxi? I was probably listening to the radio."

The following morning, Davis and Turner drove to Salisbury to visit various addresses. Four band members who played in the bar that night admitted having had sex with Trudi Villiers on previous occasions. However, she was still working when they finished packing the gear on Saturday night.

When DS Callum Wood had interviewed the bar manager, he told him he called 'last orders' ten minutes early. His wife dealt with a few stragglers reluctant to be separated from their glass, but everyone left before midnight. After that, he wanted to crack on with the clean-up operation. Gary and Trudi got stuck in, and his wife went upstairs to the flat.

The band had been in and out of their van with equipment until a quarter past twelve. When the guys called out their goodbyes, Trudi locked the door behind them. The two of them worked on until five to one, and then he'd let Trudi out of the front door, locking and barring it behind her. He saw nobody in the street as she left.

Gary's wife told Callum Wood she was asleep when her husband joined her in bed. The last time she looked at the clock before she drifted off to sleep, it was twenty-five to one.

"ANY THOUGHTS SO FAR?" asked Gus. There were two puzzled faces in front of him. One person looked more troubled than puzzled.

"Are you okay with this, Neil?" he asked.

"Yes, guv, there was bound to be a cold case involving my Dad. The police didn't have much to go on, did they?"

"Did they follow up on the witness report from Steve Li?" asked Alex.

"Well, either he was the last person to see Trudi alive, except for the killer, or he followed her into Riverside Walk and attacked her," said Lydia.

"Steve Li has lived and worked in the town for a long time," said Gus, "his wife confirmed he arrived home at twelve minutes past one. He's also a regular blood donor, type B."

"Could the bar manager have followed Trudi after Steve Li drove home?" asked Neil.

"His wife said he came to bed after twenty-five to one," said Lydia, "but if she was sound asleep, it might have been two o'clock or later. She wouldn't have known."

"They interviewed the cleaning staff," said Gus, looking for the details, "here we are."

'No way was there any funny business between Gary and either of the two barmaids. His wife would have killed him if he'd tried it on with them.'

'Gary's a lovely bloke, but he only employed Trudi and Krystal because they were game for anything. He knew the pub had to appeal to the working man to survive the recession.'

'Pubs are closing all the time. Gary protected his livelihood. Bonking the barmaids would have seen him out of house and home in weeks. If half the punters got extras with their drinks, it wasn't his problem.'

"That's a no for Gary's involvement, then?" said Neil.

"I reckon so," said Gus, "of course, as Jimmy Cricket used to say - there's more."

"I won't enjoy this next bit, will I guv?" said Neil.

TRUDI'S MURDER occurred ten days after a rape in Glastonbury. This earlier assault followed reports of sex attacks across Hampshire, Dorset and Somerset. The attacks showed a degree of escalation in violence and took place in Ringwood, Blandford and Yeovil. The gap between each of the assaults had been getting shorter.

DI Culverhouse was under pressure to get a result.

Not just because this was his first murder case, but after the events two years earlier, residents wanted reassurance the police had wrested control back from the criminals who blighted their lives for the past decade.

The news came through that detectives from Dorset Police had liaised with officers at the Portishead Headquarters of Avon & Somerset Police.

Dennis Lewington, a delivery van driver for a major transport firm, had been arrested in Minehead for actual bodily harm.

An analysis of the company's records showed Lewington near each of the recent attacks on the days they took place. There was enough circumstantial evidence to support a theory the twenty-eight-year-old had been responsible for a string of unsolved cases of indecent exposure, molestation, attempted rape and rape.

A pattern emerged when they scrutinised his delivery schedules for the last two years. He covered Hampshire, parts of Berkshire to the east, and Devon to the west.

Unsolved cases in the counties involved stretched back six years.

Within a month, five police forces in the South of England eyed the prospect of wiping a catalogue of historical cases from the books.

Research showed that escalators were younger men who attacked strangers with increasing severity. These men often have a previous psychiatric history. Dominic Culverhouse looked at Trudi Villiers's case details and wondered whether the violence had continued to escalate, culminating in murder.

DS Terry Davis went to Portishead. The first thing he discovered was that Lewington was 'O' positive. The same blood type as the semen recovered from their victim. Davis also learned that 'O' positive was the blood type of over twenty per cent of males in the UK. So, this was not conclusive proof Lewington was their man.

Lewington had a history of mental illness. His parents said that, as a teenager, their only child had been held in psychiatric facilities on two occasions and prescribed anti-psychotic and anti-depressant medications.

Terry Davis reckoned the increased frequency of attack and escalation in violence made it possible for the murder to be a natural progression from attacks in Ringwood, Blandford, Yeovil and Glastonbury.

The Avon & Somerset Police believed the Minehead attack to be an aborted attempted rape. However, Terry Davis considered the ABH the first step in Lewington's subsequent sex attacks. If they didn't stop him, Lewington would go on another rampage, leading to another young woman's death.

Davis convinced his boss that Dennis Lewington had

escaped justice for six years, and now it had caught up with him.

Once Lewington's name was in the frame, the narrative from the file suggested Davis fit the crime around Lewington rather than prove he did the crime. Again, there was an element of time-shifting to suit the picture he wanted to paint.

Lewington insisted he was in Bristol on the night of Trudi's murder.

Davis countered that by checking the route, Lewington took on Saturday, the fourth of October, from the transport company's records. He made deliveries in five towns within a ten-mile radius of Riverside Walk. There were no witnesses to prove the van driver's assertion he stopped in Bristol overnight.

Davis argued that Lewington could have driven through the town early Sunday morning to hunt for his next victim. Trudi Villiers might have appeared at just the right moment for him to satisfy his urges. It was circumstantial, but his past gave this conjecture credence.

There was no semen or degraded semen found in the other assaults. Davis offered a plausible explanation for the semen discovered inside Trudi Villiers.

Dennis Lewington was inadequate, said Davis. He intended to assert his dominance and power. In his earlier assaults, he relied on verbal threats, intimidation with a weapon, and increasing levels of force to subdue his victims.

Lewington's brand of rapist fantasised about sexual conquest and rape. They believed that even though the victim resisted them initially, once they overpowered their victim, they eventually enjoyed the rape.

Lewington's attacks had become more violent. It was only a matter of time before he killed someone. Unfortunately, in choosing Trudi Villiers as a victim, he miscalculated. She was highly active sexually, and no doubt challenged his fantasy of dominance. If Trudi had laughed at him and told him he wasn't enough for her, he could have lost control in more ways than one.

The police hadn't recovered a weapon from the murder scene. Again, Davis provided an answer.

Lewington had punched and kicked his other victims and threatened them with knives but never used them. He carried a toolkit in his van containing items such as screwdrivers and Stanley knives. The chest wounds didn't show a close match, but the throat wounds were so ragged that a frenzied attack with a screwdriver could have caused them.

Why would Lewington attack another woman in Minehead so soon after an attack had ended in him killing someone? Wouldn't the murder have satisfied his rage?

Davis argued that because it was only a fantasy, Lewington never felt reassured for long by his performance or the victim's response. He had to find another victim, convincing himself the next one would be the right one. Offences by rapists such as Lewington became repetitive and compulsive, and they often committed a series of rapes over a short period.

DI Dominic Culverhouse was convinced. He argued the case for Wiltshire Police to take this case forward. He thought the circumstantial evidence was compelling enough to present to a jury.

"HOW DID they swing that one, guv?" asked Alex Hardy. "Surely, the other county forces were keen to pursue the attacks that Lewington had committed on their patch?"

"In cross-border cases, an offence must have a substantial connection to have jurisdiction," Gus replied. "Best practice is for prosecutors and investigators of the relevant jurisdictions to meet face to face to consider how to proceed. They need to balance the different factors when deciding where to prosecute."

"I presume the same thing happens if crimes occur in different countries?" asked Lydia.

"It's essentially the same process, but there could be other factors in play. Prosecutors must consider whether they can divide a prosecution into separate cases in two or more jurisdictions. They consider the location and interests of victims. Where the witnesses are based and how easy it is for them to travel. Believe it or not, they must take the accused into account too. Where is it more appropriate to hear the case?"

"So, in the end, they passed the ball to Wiltshire and prayed they didn't drop it?" said Alex.

"A guilty verdict carried a life sentence," said Gus. "Rape is customarily punished by a maximum of fifteen years of criminal imprisonment. That can rise to twenty years if the victim is under fifteen. Wiltshire hoped for something in line with the outcome of the Huntley trial only months after the Trudi Villiers murder. Instead, he received a life sentence with the judge's recommendation that he serve a minimum of forty years. A verdict that saw Lewington locked up for thirty years would have been acceptable to the other forces."

"Why was so little DNA recovered at the scenes, guv?" asked Neil.

"This wasn't like CSI on television, where samples reach the lab and are instantly analysed. They conjure up a picture of the suspect in minutes on a TV show. We've moved on since 2003, but we're still unable to work miracles. We can't always collect perfect samples from a crime scene. Victims are often left exposed to the elements before someone finds their bodies. It rained on the night that Trudi died. In several related cases, the victims didn't report the attack at once. Evidence could have been washed away through bathing. The fact they didn't find semen on any of the other victims isn't unique. Lewington could have used a condom on every other occasion. As DS Davis suggested, if he did lose his temper with Trudi Villiers, then it was feasible that he carried out the brutal rape without protection. The police had no weapon in the Villiers case. Half a dozen people might have handled a possible weapon if they recovered it. There are a hundred reasons why DNA wouldn't have been the magic bullet."

"The file mentions degraded DNA samples too, guv," said Lydia, "if they collected those and they're still around, could we get more from them with our advanced techniques?"

"Degradation of DNA at crime scenes can occur for many reasons. Environmental exposure is the most common. Water and enzymes can degrade biological samples. In the old days, it was almost impossible to analyse degraded samples. The Hub has specially developed software to compare the forensic profile to profiles taken from the main database. The Hub can generate a list of those offenders already in the database and produce a very close relative of the individual whose DNA is in the forensic profile. Lewington was an only child. His parents were squeaky clean. It's not always possible to have a start point for a search. We often use other leads, such as witness statements, to identify suspects. There were precious few in this case. Once they identified the suspect, they sought a legal DNA sample. If your luck's in, you can compare it to samples found at the crime scene. None of the other forces could do that until the suspect was apprehended. Once Wiltshire assumed overall responsibility, there was no hurry for the other forces to hunt for a match, even if they had samples in their possession."

"The case took a long time to get to court, didn't it?" asked Alex.

"The defendant underwent a psychiatric evaluation to determine whether he was fit to stand trial. The defence applied for a change of venue, arguing it would be impossible for their client to get a fair trial in the jurisdiction where the crime occurred. A judge denied this request. He stated that the defence barrister had adequate preparation time and was playing for time."

THE TRIAL TOOK place at Swindon Crown Court on the thirteenth of January 2005 before Mr Justice Henderson.

Dennis Lewington maintained his innocence throughout the trial.

As the case relied only on circumstantial evidence, he and his legal team doubted it would result in a conviction. The prosecution couldn't produce compelling forensic evidence against Lewington.

In their wisdom, the jury believed the prosecution's version of events and found him guilty of the rape and murder of Trudi Villiers.

The judge sentenced Dennis Lewington to life imprisonment.

An application for leave to appeal against the conviction was rejected in June 2005.

The judge who heard the appeal said he found no reason to think Lewington was anything other than guilty.

"IN NORMAL CIRCUMSTANCES, that should have been that," said Gus.

"I never questioned why my Dad retired and emigrated when he did," said Neil, "he was in his early fifties at the time of the trial. Dad celebrated his sixtieth birthday in Marbella and has never returned here."

Gus could tell from his slumped shoulders that Neil struggled with the knowledge his father fitted up a suspect. Terry Davis had earned a reputation as a 'plodder' who would never rise above Detective Sergeant. His superiors always described him as 'consistent'. He was consistently late and consistently lazy. If a short-cut existed to complete a task, Terry Davis found it.

"Neil must have skipped a few pages, guv," said Lydia, "and I'm not sure why he's got a problem with this. Lewington *was* guilty of loads of crimes, wasn't he?"

"He never admitted his guilt," said Alex.

"If he didn't kill Trudi Villiers, why should he?"

"The innocent prisoner's dilemma is a downside of our legal system, Lydia," said Gus. "Admission of guilt can get you a reduced sentence or early parole. If you are convicted of a crime wrongly, the system can punish the innocent person for his integrity and reward the person lacking in integrity."

"That means an individual could die in prison rather than admit to a crime they didn't commit."

"That has happened," said Gus. "But you must balance that against research suggesting prisoners who freely admit their guilt are more likely to re-offend than those who maintain their innocence."

"How did Lewington get to be pardoned then, guv?" asked Neil

"Oh, now I understand why we've got this case file,"

said Lydia. "I thought we would use modern techniques to prove Lewington guilty. I hoped it was so that Neil's Dad didn't get in trouble."

"Thanks, Lydia," said Neil, "but all the rumours couldn't be false. A reckoning has been a long time coming."

"Modern techniques were to the fore," said Gus, "plus Lewington pleaded guilty to around sixty separate assaults back to 1997. However, he insisted that he never killed anyone. So, they re-examined the evidence. Finally, a long-distance lorry driver who had spent the past eight years on the continent driving for a German car firm came forward. He said Dennis Lewington parked next to his truck and trailer in the Asda car park at Cribbs Causeway."

"How could he be sure it was Lewington?" asked Alex.

"One night, eight years ago? It must have been memorable," said Lydia.

"You don't have to be sceptical to work here, but it helps," said Gus. "Driving vans and lorries isn't everyone's ideal career. But those that spend a lifetime doing it find a camaraderie that many other occupations lack. Dave Broomham had seen Lewington at truck stops and roadside cafes across the south of England. They often chatted over a mug of tea and a bacon sandwich."

Gus found the relevant sheet in the file.

"Here's part of Broomham's statement,"

'I didn't particularly like the bloke. There was something off about him. When only you two stood at the counter of Joe's Café by the side of the A303, beggars can't be choosers. What did we discuss? What do drivers always discuss? The volume of traffic, the number of potholes, and how roadworks always crop up when you're behind the clock. The weather. Football. Women we've seen driving in

TED TAYLER

short skirts and see-through tops that day. You wouldn't believe what you see at traffic lights. I've clocked women touching themselves, giving the male driver hand relief. It's a wonder there aren't more accidents.'

"Gross," said Lydia, "this Broomham bloke sounds as creepy as Lewington."

"There's more," said Gus, "when questioned about the night of the murder, Broomham said this,"

'I'd been up to Worcester in the morning and made two drops in Gloucester Quays in the early afternoon. Rules on breaks mean you must take a break of at least forty-five minutes after no more than four and a half hours of driving. I had a big breakfast in Worcester before heading to Gloucester. I made half a dozen drop-offs in the Bristol area that took me up to five-thirty. Because I lived in Chiswick then, my hours had rocketed. The main EU rules on driving hours meant that you must not drive over nine hours daily. No more than fifty-six hours a week. I didn't have enough hours to get home on Saturday night. So, I stopped in the Asda car park. It cost nothing at the time, very handy for several delivery drivers. It never got overused back then, either. We never caused trouble, so the supermarket didn't give us any grief. I rang the wife, told her I'd be home in the morning and took a taxi to the city centre. I went for an Indian meal, drank two pints in a pub next to the Hippodrome and returned to Cribbs. Just after nine o'clock, the taxi dropped me off by my rig. Dennis pulled in next to me forty-five minutes later. I stood by my cab, having a fag. He was full of it, as usual. Dennis was one of those blokes who spent so long chatting to women at every drop of his run; he had to rush to get through his schedule. I'll never know how he never got a ticket or wrapped his van around a tree. His tachos must have been a nightmare for his firm to unscramble. Anyway, he first told me about a coloured bird in Westbury with legs up to her backside. Then a middle-aged woman in Bradford-on-Avon was gagging for it. He went through every detail of what they looked like, what they wore, how he'd imagined everything he'd do to them while he stood there chatting. He thought of driving back to Bradford in the morning before he drove home to Portsmouth. I reminded him it was Sunday and the offices closed. It didn't seem to phase him. He convinced himself she fancied him. I was ready to turn in after an hour of this idle chit-chat, but Dennis was still hyper. I let him ramble on and smoked a cigarette, then I got in the back of my cab and didn't see him again until seven in the morning.'

"When asked what time he got into his cab," Gus added, "he said it was a quarter past eleven."

"Lewington could have left at midnight and still been at the murder scene," said Neil, "maybe my Dad didn't have it so wrong."

"Dave Broomham said he didn't 'see' him until the morning," Gus emphasised. "However, while Broomham tried in vain to get to sleep, Dennis Lewington watched videos until at least two o'clock. The volume was loud enough to annoy Broomham but not so loud he could hear what they said."

"So, Lewington's van never moved before two," said Neil.

"Afraid not, Neil," said Gus.

"What were these tacos Broomham mentioned, guv?" asked Lydia.

"Not tortilla wraps, that's for sure," said Neil, "tachos, short for tachographs."

"This led to the most damning piece of evidence to prove Lewington had been fitted-up," said Gus. "All drivers like Broomham and Lewington must record their journeys on a tachograph under EU rules. Most tachographs produced before May 2006 were analogue. Lines were traced on a wax-coated paper disc that rotated through a twenty-four-hour period. These tachometers have gone digital now. They have to retain discs for twelve months. It's a little more complicated than taking a glance, but seasoned transport managers can interpret the data and tell whether a driver has broken any of the rules.

"Why didn't they grab these tachograph discs from Lewington's van?" asked Alex.

"They did," Gus replied, "and those records got logged in evidence at Portishead when the initial joint investigation began. The records formed an integral part of the case compiled by the Dorset and the Avon & Somerset teams. If you remember, Lewington's company schedules confirmed him in the right places to commit the assaults in the weeks preceding his arrest in Minehead."

"So, he drove to the towns, and the clients received their goods. They signed for them, confirming the times," said Alex. "His breaks would be logged too, wouldn't they?"

"That's right; activity showed as either drive, other work, availability or rest. In those days, GPS wasn't commonly fitted to cars or vans. Lewington was devious, and he knew that the 'V' trace needed to match the mileage figure, but it wouldn't record exactly where he drove. As long as he made the deliveries, he was okay."

"He parked in free spaces such as the Asda car park to avoid incurring a record," said Neil. "He chatted with fellow drivers who wanted a way to save a few quid on parking costs. For Lewington, it was more than that. He never wanted to register at an official truck stop or pay for a ticket; anything that placed him in a particular spot, particularly one that piqued the curiosity of his transport manager. The tachograph showed his vehicle not moving for hours. We know what he was up to with hindsight. He parked for the night, taking the tools of his trade and hunting his prey on foot."

"When Terry Davis analysed the evidence they gathered, he cherry-picked the items that suited his rationale," Gus continued. "Somehow, after the case passed to Wiltshire Police, certain items got misplaced."

"Please tell me he didn't destroy evidence, guv," pleaded Neil.

"I said misplaced, Neil. First, it got separated from the main body of evidence and other pieces that didn't fit the narrative and filed somewhere safe. Then, during the re-investigation in 2013, those discs surfaced. In court, an expert witness demonstrated that Lewington could not have been in Wiltshire that night even if Dave Broomham had made a mistake. He calculated the distance travelled and showed the start and end mileage for the day and the number of hours the vehicle was at rest. When the expert compared this data with his string of deliveries, the only reasonable conclusion was that he visited the five Wiltshire towns as stated on his schedule. He then drove through Bath for two more deliveries and travelled along the M4 to reach Cribbs Causeway from Junction 32. The tachograph record for Saturday, the fourth of October 2003, showed his vehicle stationary from around nine to seven on Sunday, the fifth."

"That was that then, Dennis Lewington was not guilty of Trudi Villiers's murder," said Alex, "it says here he got released in 2013. If he pleaded guilty to sixty sex offences, why didn't they keep him in prison?"

"They arrested Lewington during October 2003," said

Gus, "held on remand until January 2005 and then in prison for a further eight years. The judge decided the sex offences fell into a sentencing band of nine to thirteen years. If the murder charge had never been on the table, Lewington would have served half that sentence in prison and the remainder on licence. His name will appear on the sex offenders register for an indefinite term, but with his murder conviction quashed, he was set free."

"Wow," said Lydia, "what a story. How can we even start to work out who did it after this long?"

"Sorry, Neil, but we can't trust any of the information in that file," said Alex, "times altered, material evidence left out altogether; we'll have to start from scratch."

"I'll have to stand down from this case, guv," said Neil.

"You stay, Neil until the ACC or Geoff Mercer says otherwise. We're a team. Alex and Lydia will play the public roles on this one. You will stay in the office and do everything above and beyond to retain my trust. One slip and you're out. I think I can rely on you to do what's right. Remember this; your Dad left these shores the year before the shit hit the fan. In 2018, he's still a free man. Why do you think that is? There have been many changes in how the police operate in this country over the last five years. One thing that we've always been good at is sweeping mistakes under the carpet. That hasn't changed. There was a furore over the county force's handling of the case in the media. But it soon got overshadowed by the murder of Lee Rigby. Then the Edward Snowden affair hit the headlines the following month. Lewington became a ten-minute wonder. Nobody's asking where he is now. If you care, he's unemployed, living in a caravan deep in the countryside of North Wales. He's as keen for it to resurface as you are. Terry Davis wasn't the only one guilty. Dominic Culverhouse sanctioned Terry's handling of the case. He argued that Wiltshire should pursue the murder charge above the other offences on the table. Where is Culverhouse now? He's one of the ACCs at Avon & Somerset. I think they will let sleeping dogs lie, Neil. Do me a favour, though."

"Whatever you say, guv," said Neil, "I want us to solve this one properly."

"We'll try, Neil. Just don't mention what you're working on to your Dad."

"Scout's honour, guv,"

"It's been a long day," sighed Gus. "Let's get off home. We'll start unpicking this lot in the morning."

Chapter Four

GUS HAD a lot on his mind when he drove back through Devizes to Urchfont. He pulled into the allotments and parked the Ford Focus. It was time to pause for thought—no better place than outside his shed on a warm summer evening.

This new case had thrown up a lot of problems he didn't need.

Gus fetched his chair from inside the shed and made himself comfortable.

Could he, in all conscience, keep Neil Davis involved when his father had royally screwed up the investigation? How had Terry Davis filtered and manipulated the evidence without Culverhouse's knowledge?

Gus knew Culverhouse was still in the force and occupied a lofty position. It might be worth a quiet pint with Geoff Mercer this week to discover where other superior officers at that time were currently serving. Some would be retired, but they might live locally and be active in the Police Federation business.

News of his team's focus on the Villiers case would soon reach their ears.

Gus had agreed to come back to delve into unsolved cold cases. He had no interest in being used to sully the reputations of senior officers into the bargain. Was the ACC selecting these cold cases on purpose? Had his team been set up as fall guys?

The Crime Review Team only saw one murder file at a time. There was no clue what the next one would contain. Vera Jennings had handed him this latest file, not the ACC.

Gus had readily accepted that Kenneth Truelove was entertaining the press. It made sense revelations regarding the Minister, and the Chief Constable took precedence over meeting a retired Detective Inspector only recently recruited as a consultant.

Gus wondered whether conspiracy theories were alive and well here in the West Country.

"A penny for them?"

Bert Penman stood beside him. The eighty five-year-old former butcher held a wooden tray in one hand and his walking stick in the other. Bert laid the stick against the shed and placed the tray on the upturned crate next to Gus.

"The last two people to sit there to chat with me were Irene and Frank North," said Gus, as the memories of the past weekend flooded back.

"Nasty business that," said Bert, "I've heard rumours about who was behind Frank's death. I ignored them, of course, until I learned the facts from you."

"Wish I could tell you something, Bert," said Gus, "DI Ferris is leading the investigation. As a consultant, I can't interfere. You'll hear any news at the same time as I do when the police issue a statement."

"What's the world coming to, eh? Frank wasn't a bad

lot, even if he'd been inside a few times. None of us thought we needed to watch him when he worked here on his allotment. I never took special precautions to keep my tools safe. I feel bad taking advantage of him as I did."

Bert had taken a few vegetables to save them from rotting in the ground. Frank wasn't the best gardener by his admission. He had bowed to Bert's experience that he'd been unlucky his crop had failed.

"Don't blame yourself, Bert. You can make up for that now. What say we talk to the other allotment holders and agree to deliver fruit and vegetables to Irene North in the future? She'll need the support of the community from now on."

"That's a great idea, Mr Freeman. Leave it with me."

"I'm conscious that I'm leaving plenty with you these days, Bert. I can tell by the freshly dug ground and that tray on the crate you've been busy on my behalf. Thanks to you, these April days are getting ever warmer, and my patch might not be as far behind as I feared."

"The allotment will always catch up in the end and reward your patience with a bumper harvest," said Bert. "If I hear a whisper of a frost, I'll hold back and wait a day or two rather than take the risk. I still plan to get those onion sets in by the weekend. Then I'll follow on with the beetroot, carrots and as many greens as you wish."

"I'm ever so grateful, Bert. Keep up the good work. I didn't drop by to check up on you. I had a difficult day at work, and the fresh air helped clear my mind. Although, with the number of thoughts I have to ponder, I reckon it will take more than a penny to settle the debt."

"You strike me as a deep thinker, Mr Freeman. Who would have thought such a dark secret hidden behind our local MP? You uncovered that, I expect. Why is it so often that the innocent suffers? Daphne Tolliver all those years ago and now Frank North. Retired people are entitled to live the rest of their days in peace. It's wrong."

"I can't argue with you there, Bert. Look, I need to go home and get a meal inside me. Another busy day tomorrow. Maybe, I'll pour a glass of single malt later to aid my deliberations. At least one of my problems needs resolving before I leave for work in the morning."

"Whiskey can help," said Bert, "but a good night's sleep will work wonders. The single malt might be less beneficial in that regard."

Bert picked up the tray and his stick and made his way up the allotment.

Gus smiled. That was rich. Bert Penman suggesting drink wasn't the best medicine. His first port of call after he left here would be the Lamb. He never left until closing time. Bert didn't need the stick. Except when he staggered home. Gus watched as Bert set to work on his allotment. He hoped to be as agile at eighty-five.

Gus decided the conspiracy issue could wait until he met with Geoff Mercer. He had other things to sort out. Neil had been warned not to contact his father, but Gus thought it only right the former Detective Sergeant had the opportunity to defend himself. He would call him at the earliest opportunity.

The drive to the bungalow allowed him two minutes to consider Alex Hardy.

Lydia appeared to get on well with him. Both in the office and when they had socialised together. She could be an ally in helping Gus ease Alex back into the action. The former motorcycle pursuit rider had consistently pushed for a chance to show he was ready. However, this case might mean having no choice but to use Alex for interviews.

The last thing he mulled over as he swung his car into the driveway was the lack of suspects for the Villiers case. Lydia had posed an excellent question. Where the heck do we start? He wondered the same thing.

Gus sat in the car with the engine running.

Something didn't look right. A curtain in the lounge had moved. Gus knew he hadn't left it that way this morning. Someone had been inside the house. Perhaps they were still there?

Gus sat and waited. Who might have done it if there had been a break-in at his home? What were they after? The age profile of the villager was above the national average. There were a few teenage kids, but word had spread since he moved here. Everyone knew he was an ex-copper.

He couldn't think of anyone on his doorstep who might have decided this was a good time to steal from him. They had to have transport if they travelled to the village from a local town or further afield. Where could that be? There were no apparent signs anyone had used his driveway since he pulled out into the lane this morning.

So, they had to be people with enough guile to drive past the bungalow and park out of sight. Then they waited for the coast to be clear and walked into the driveway. The front door looked secure. The back door was screened from the road and not overlooked from the rear. That's how I would gain access, thought Gus. He hadn't been aware of any strange car parked between the bungalow and the allotments as he'd driven through the village — time to do a recce.

Gus reversed quietly out onto the lane. Not the safest option, but he didn't want to alert anyone inside the bungalow. He drove further up the lane but saw nothing there. He turned around and went back towards the Lamb and the

Community Shop. The car park would be a good place to hide a vehicle in plain sight. The eight cars he spotted gave him no cause for concern — time to do the sensible thing.

Gus called the police.

"Suzie? Are you still at work?"

"I'm heading home. I'm five minutes away from your place. What's the matter?"

"Do you carry your baton with you?"

"Of course,"

"I think I've had burglars. In case they're still inside, I could use backup."

"Sit tight," said Suzie, "are you near the bungalow?

"Not far away, I'm parked outside the Lamb at present. I'll drive up the lane and wait."

"I can appreciate why you're cautious. Keep this line open."

Three minutes later, Suzie spoke again.

"I can see you ahead of me. Let's park to the side of the driveway and go inside together."

They crossed the gravel, and Gus slid his key into the lock and opened the front door. Suzie brushed past him with her extendable baton at the ready.

"Police!" she shouted. There was no response.

Gus took a few steps inside the hallway and prepared himself for the worst.

"The kitchen isn't too much of a mess," said Suzie, looking into the rooms off the hallway. "Everything looks to have been moved. Drawers and doors open halfway. They came in through the back door. We can make it safe until you get a glazier out here. I'll report this. Don't touch a thing. Sorry, Gus, force of habit. You know the drill."

As Suzie made the call, Gus inspected the lounge. It wasn't as bad as he feared. Nothing broken. His precious record collection was intact — photos of him and Tess were still in their picture frames. The drawn curtain prevented the intruder from being visible from the lane.

The bedrooms weren't much different. Gus's wardrobe doors were open. Every drawer was inspected, but the damage he had expected hadn't materialised. What had they been looking for, and why? These weren't common-or-garden burglars. They would have trashed the place just for kicks if they had been and found nothing of value.

Gus joined Suzie in the kitchen.

"A forensic team are on the way," she said, "anything missing?"

"Not from the brief look I've had. Well, we've preserved the scene. Unfortunately, I don't have a spare set of keys in the house. Tess's keys are in my garden shed at the allotment. So, they're not able to wander in here whenever they fancy. I'll get that door fixed and then invest in extra security. Cameras at the front and rear of the property are linked to my smartphone. It will ruin my perfect rural idyll, but it will help keep me safe."

"We need to mull this over, Gus," said Suzie, "take care and switch on the kettle. We've got ten minutes before the guys arrive."

They took the mugs of coffee outside into the garden.

"We must face the possibility this break-in has links to Frank North's murder," said Suzie.

"Just because they dumped his body in the allotments field doesn't mean that much," said Gus. "It could simply have been a convenient spot. Somewhere the body wouldn't be discovered at first light."

"I'm not so sure," said Suzie, "they may have forced Frank to tell them you knew what he'd seen up on the hillside. Whatever's going on warranted killing an innocent senior citizen. I've badgered my superiors throughout the day, trying to prevent any more bloodshed. We have to stop the operation, whatever it is. The top brass say their hands are tied."

"So that means the National Crime Agency or the Organised Crime Task Force is interested in that shed. Which suggests this affair *has* to be far larger than Monty Jennings and a hare-brained get-rich scheme."

Suzie's phone vibrated.

"The guys should turn into the driveway in a moment," she said. "Sorry, Gus, the neighbours will think the reputation of this placid village has gone to hell."

One van and a car whipped through the gateway, and five personnel were ready for action in seconds. Suzi directed operations, and Gus stood in the warm evening sunshine with two empty mugs.

Gus knew that Suzie was right. The buggers that broke in here today meant business. They had destroyed nothing, taken nothing, and left no message. Yet they had demonstrated that they believed they could do what they liked, and he couldn't stop them. But, maybe, they thought that was message enough.

Fifteen minutes later, Suzie came back outside. She smiled at him, sitting on his car bonnet with the two mugs leaning against the windscreen.

"It won't be much longer. Another few minutes, and you can have your kitchen back."

"I was starving when I left the allotments," Gus said, "the first thing I planned to do when I got home was cook something."

"Do you want company? I can always eat a meal that someone else cooks for me."

"When do I get the run of the rest of the house?"

"Within the hour. Don't worry; you've suffered a trauma. That will explain my staying on after the others leave. I want to make sure you're safe."

Gus looked at his watch. There would be precious time to work through the issues troubling him. They didn't seem important somehow. It dawned on him what Suzie had said.

"Make sure I'm safe? I'll be OK."

A forensic guy called out that the kitchen was free. Gus and Suzie made their way indoors.

As he started to prepare the food, he nodded towards the wine rack.

"I reckon I deserve a glass of wine. There are soft drinks in the fridge."

Suzie poured two large glasses of Merlot.

"I've already texted my mother to say I won't be home," she said.

"Bugger," said Gus.

He'd cut himself, slicing the vegetables.

"That just goes to show you're not safe to be alone," said Suzie, "let me see. It's not too deep. Wash it under the tap. Where do you keep your plasters?"

They finished preparing the meal together. Gus found Suzie easy to talk to; the Merlot helped. When Suzie dished up fifty minutes later, Gus poured them a second glass. What was going on? Was she staying because she thought a police vehicle next to his car outside would deter any night visitors? Or was she interested in blokes thirty-plus years older than her? The papers were full of them. Of course, those men tended to be rolling in it. They weren't clapped-out coppers with a bungalow, an ageing Ford Focus and an allotment. Forget that thought. Suzie's just considering your safety.

Gus looked at Suzie Ferris as she tucked into her food.

This relationship malarkey had been hard enough when he and Tess went through it forty years ago. Gus sure as hell didn't understand how it worked these days. Even though they had been engaged and were refurbishing their first place together, Tess had steadfastly refused to sleep there. Fast forward to 2018, and he had a young woman sitting in his kitchen, sharing a meal and a bottle of wine. He'd met her for the first time on Friday. They spent two hours together on Sunday and found a dead body. Today was Monday, and she was investigating a break-in.

It was obvious they would soon finish the first bottle.

Gus checked the wine rack. He had another bottle.

If Suzie had an ulterior motive, he would need that. He hadn't slept with anyone other than Tess. Suzie looked up and caught him staring at her. She didn't speak. She smiled and took a sip of her wine.

The girl had rung her mother, for crying out loud.

If he and Tess had spent the night together before they were married, they would have died rather than tell their parents, even if it was because they were too shattered to drive home after decorating all evening.

"Not long now before the forensic crew will be out of our hair," Suzie said, "this meal was great. What do you have in mind for dessert?"

Gus decided it was time to find out whether Suzie was serious or pulling his chain.

"I saw Vera this morning at the London Road offices. We're meeting for dinner on Thursday. Do you think that because you stayed over, it will upset her?"

"Vera knows you've got two bedrooms," said Suzie, "why should she be upset?"

Gus looked to see what he had to offer her in the fridge.

He was off the hook. Suzie was here for his protection, nothing else.

"I've got low-fat yoghurts, a strawberry cheesecake…."

A knock on the kitchen door interrupted the menu.

"Sorry, Ma'am, we've found something."

It was one of the forensic teams. The man passed Suzie an evidence bag.

"Where did you find it?" asked Gus.

"In a drawer in the main bedroom, Sir, under a scarf covering several personal items."

The bastard had been in the drawer where he kept Tess's hairbrush, necklace and other souvenirs.

"It's an Order of Service," said Suzie. "No doubt they wore gloves, but the card and its content might tell us something about who sent the message."

Suzie Ferris held up the evidence bag so Gus could read what it said.

"Very touching," said Gus, "*In Loving Memory - service will be held in the near future for Augustus John Freeman, policeman and gardener unless he leave well alone. No more messages will be given.*"

"Augustus? I hadn't thought about what Gus was short for; I reckon they're foreign, don't you? Not illiterate, though. British thugs would never spell your name right, for a start."

"They spent more than a few minutes here, too," said Gus, "that photo they've used is from one in the lounge. Tess liked it. She took it when we holidayed in Weymouth. We watched the 2012 Olympics sailing events in Portland. I was fifty-five."

"You look happy. It suits you. Could the intruders have used your computer to produce this card?"

"No idea. Tess used it for various work-related things. I never felt the need. I muddled through whatever I needed to do my job in the office. These days I use a smartphone to access everything I want."

"The guys will have dusted the computer for prints, of course. After they've gone, I'll fire it up. Maybe these thugs were looking for something else. Files relating to their shady operation. They created this card to put the frighteners on you."

"Do you still say that?" asked Gus. "I thought that phrase went out years ago."

"I'm an old-fashioned girl," laughed Suzie. "I was right to stay. The whole thing is turning nasty. I'm calling in this threat to the higher-ups at HQ. We need increased surveillance on Monty's shed and the area surrounding this place. It's late, but if we can organise armed support, that would put my mind at rest."

"They didn't mess about when they got rid of Frank North," said Gus, "a can of pepper spray and a baton won't be much of a deterrent. I can see I won't get much sleep tonight."

"Vera told me you arranged to see her again, by the way," said Suzie.

"Do you tell each other everything?"

"Not everything. Cheesecake would be nice, and there's only half a glass each left in this bottle."

Gus uncorked the second bottle, plated two slices of strawberry cheesecake and carried them to the lounge. Suzie had kicked off her shoes and unpinned her hair. Her uniform jacket lay neatly folded over the back of a chair.

"Do you want to listen to music?" she asked, standing by his record deck.

"I'm not sure I have much that suits the mood. Did you call for additional support?"

"Yes, while you struggled with that cork. Let me see that finger of yours. Has it started bleeding again?"

"No, Mum, it's fine. Stop worrying about me. I'm not decrepit."

"I know. Let's eat, and then I'll wash while you dry, and we can relax with another glass of that scrummy wine."

"My evening was supposed to be quite different to this," said Gus. "I planned to get home, cook something simple and sit here listening to Mahler or Greig while I puzzled over our latest CRT case."

"You called me, don't forget. Geoff Mercer or the ACC wouldn't have offered to stay with you. They would have shipped you off to a hotel, no doubt."

"I'm not complaining. In fact, on the two occasions that we've spent time together, it's been as if we've known one another for years."

"We've got a lot in common," said Suzie, "both involved with the police, both single. We enjoy good food and fine wine. I don't believe we have the same taste in music, but there are not many big differences."

"I haven't had much to do with horses," said Gus.

He couldn't think of anything else.

"There you are then," said Suzie, "that's more ticks in the positive box than most married couples I know. We get on; it's simple, nobody else's concern but ours."

Gus took their plates through to the kitchen. Suzie joined him.

"We can get this done by the time you stack everything in that dishwasher," she said, "I noticed you yesterday afternoon. You have a method."

"It was Tess's method. A lot of things feel unnatural to me. So I keep taking stuff out and trying another way to find which matches the picture I carry in my head."

"It's more fun this way," she said, as she ran hot water into a bowl, "we can talk while we work. I can watch where you put it away, so I'll know for another time if I come over and you've cut off a finger altogether."

"You invited yourself, young lady. I might not ask you to stay for dinner again."

"I hope you do. We have lots in common, remember?"

They soon returned to the lounge. Suzie sat in the chair next to him and tucked her feet under her bottom. Gus began pouring from the second bottle.

"What problems cropped up with this new cold case today?" Suzie asked.

"They gave us the Trudi Villiers case from 2003,"

"I had just left school and was heading for university," said Suzie, "I know nothing, I'm afraid."

"Have you heard of Dennis Lewington?"

"Oh, the man they pardoned not long ago. Was that the Villiers case?"

"Yes, the DS who put the evidence together for the original trial is the father of one of my team. He fitted up Lewington, even though he was guilty of multiple sexual offences. I want to keep the son with me but exclude him from talking to any witnesses. There were no other suspects because as soon as Terry Davis linked the murder to Lewington, they stopped searching."

"You should be okay, Gus. You're not re-investigating the Lewington case. Your job is to find out who killed your victim. Was this Terry Davis brought to book over the evidence tampering?"

"No. It got buried. Davis's superiors are either dead, retired, or promoted far enough up the ladder to be untouchable."

"Hang on, are you saying they knew what he'd done before the case went to court?"

"I've no proof, but Terry Davis is in Marbella. He hasn't returned to these shores since he left. A year before Lewington's pardon."

"That does smell, doesn't it?"

"Do you reckon I may have got this case to bring that smell into the open?"

"The ACC plays with a straight bat, Gus. He's a good copper. I don't believe he'd stitch you up and drop you into the role of a whistle-blower."

"Perhaps it's coming back into this world after a three-year break," said Gus, "I see conspiracies around every corner. As soon as I saw Terry Davis's name on this case, I thought back to last week and wondered whether someone had heard a whisper about our local MP."

"I'm positive you're making too much of things, Gus. The Crime Review Team were kept as far away as possible from the media when the shit hit the fan over the weekend. They wouldn't do that if they wanted to get your name attached to a witch hunt."

"You're probably right. Anyway, the Davis problem created another potential headache. Alex Hardy is my other DS. He's in a wheelchair. I told him today he'll be my wingman on interviews. Alex is recovering from a massive motorcycle accident. I don't want to push him to do something that will delay or prevent a full recovery. What if we come across a situation where he's at risk?"

"If you were thirty years younger, you'd sort the criminal out yourself. With one man down and Alex recuperating, you don't have a young hunk like Neil Davis to protect you. That isn't an easy one to answer, Gus. Geoff might find you a rugby-playing DC to join your team for the short term."

"Male or female?" Gus asked.

"Cheeky. That's enough wine for me. Can I shower before I go to bed?"

"Certainly, you'll find plenty of towels in the airing cupboard. No female soaps or shampoos, though. Sorry."

"I'll cope," said Suzie and strolled off to the other end of the bungalow.

Gus took their empty glasses into the kitchen. He returned to the lounge until the spare bedroom door closed. It was the only door that needed a push to click it shut.

He turned off the lights and went into the main bedroom. Tonight was another first; nobody else had stayed here since Tess died. A quick visit to the en suite, and he stripped off and slipped under the duvet. He promised himself he wouldn't lay awake for hours fretting over the Villiers case.

Or the break-in, or what Vera Jennings would think if she knew Suzie Ferris lay in the room along the corridor.

Gus fell asleep within minutes, dreamed of Bert Penman, and row upon row of spring vegetables.

Chapter Five

Tuesday, 17 April 2018

THE ALARM WOKE Gus at seven o'clock. He heard someone moving about, and at first, he panicked. Were the intruders back?

Then he remembered Suzie Ferris would be about to head home to her parent's farm. A Detective Inspector needed a change of clothes. No way could she turn up ruffled and careworn; there was something to be said for being semi-retired.

The country girl he admired would have a horse or two to tend to before driving to Devizes to start a new day fighting crime.

Gus reflected on the events of yesterday evening.

The break-in posed an ongoing threat. His team's new case had thrown up new problems. The meal with Suzie and the conversation that followed helped settle things in his mind on the latter. Any repercussions of the intruders' visit were another matter altogether.

That second bottle of Merlot last night may have been overambitious. Gus headed for the shower. It was time to face the fact he couldn't handle it as he did in the old days. Fifteen minutes later, he left his bedroom, fully clothed and eager for a fried breakfast.

Gus found a note on the kitchen table. Not so much a message but more a novella.

'Had to dash, sorry. Your daytime protection detail is in place. Don't crack a stranger over the head and tell him he's nicked. He's one of ours. I'm pushing for a meeting with whichever agency deals with Cambrai Terrace. The ACC must find out whether Frank North's murder was preventable. I hate to think Frank North was collateral damage. If the ACC hears that we should consider the bigger picture, that won't sit well with me. So that you know, twenty minutes after we said goodnight, I opened the bedroom door without making too much noise. Then I stood outside your door, listening to you snoring. What happens on protection duty stays on protection duty in my book. I won't hide the fact I find you attractive. But I decided it wouldn't be right while you and Vera decide whether there's something long-term in your relationship. I'll ring tonight to update you on the break-in and my face-to-face with the ACC. Suzie xx

Gus wondered how he would have reacted if Suzie suddenly appeared next to him under the duvet. Gus shook his head. Yet again, she'd proved that he didn't understand women. He'd convinced himself he was off the hook last night, and Suzie was just a friend concerned for his safety. Surely, he was too set in his ways for a friend with benefits.

The weather outside his kitchen window looked sunny and warm. Indeed, when he switched on the radio while he cooked his breakfast, the forecast was said to be 'unseasonably' warm.

The rest of the week would see temperatures shoot up to twenty-five degrees, and the region would enjoy wall-to-wall sunshine. How long would they continue with these stupid references to the seasons he'd known as a child? In his youth, the four seasons were as distinct and different as night and day.

Climate change altered that forever.

He had been six when snow fell on Boxing Day 1963, and the country was in winter's icy grip for months. Mild winters were more the norm now, with a covering of snow on two consecutive days bringing the country to a standstill.

Summers contained more hot days than when he was a boy, and individual records bettered regularly. Yet, in 1976 he sweltered on a camping holiday on the Isle of Wight. Day after day of that fortnight, there was no relief.

Snow had fallen at the start of June. It was only a month before that holiday, but once the hot, dry weather took hold, it continued without a break until September. If you got four days of high temperatures these days, you could guarantee a storm was brewing that brought high winds and rain, usually at the weekend.

Those were unseasonably wet and windy too. It was all bollocks; there were no seasons anymore. Gus thought they should scrap the computer-generated forecasts and ask Bert Penman what weather to expect for the next twenty-four hours. He rarely got it wrong, and looking further ahead was pointless when the new seasons became so changeable.

Gus finished his breakfast, drank a second mug of coffee and started to feel human again. Time to make a move. As soon as he stepped outside the bungalow, he spotted the pool car. He turned into the lane, gave the driver a friendly wave and drove towards Devizes.

His shadow followed him until the roundabout near the Crammer. The pool car driver flashed his lights and turned right towards the London Road headquarters. Gus turned left and made for the nearby town and the CRT office in the Old Police Station.

Gus parked at the rear of the building at ten minutes to nine. He was the first to arrive today. When he got upstairs, he remembered he needed to phone a glazier. After a brief chat, he admitted defeat. It would cost him more than he hoped, but at least the guy agreed to fix his back door. Gus just needed to make sure he got home by half-past six tonight.

Alex, Neil and Lydia emerged from the lift at one minute to nine. Gus made a point of looking at his watch. The team was still in its infancy, but Gus wasn't about to let timekeeping become an issue. He had never been one to wield a big stick. He preferred to lead by example. His arrival in the office in the weeks ahead would be as close as possible to ten minutes to nine. The others would soon get the message that he didn't enjoy being up here alone.

"Where do you want us to start with the Villiers case, guv," asked Alex.

"First things first," said Gus, "look, I said you didn't need to know about the business that cropped up at the weekend. However, two things have happened since then. One, some bugger broke into my place yesterday and left me in no doubt that I would come to harm if I stuck my nose in where it wasn't wanted. Second, DI Suzie Ferris reckons that either the NCA or OCTF monitor activities on the hillside above my allotments."

"Bloody hell, guv," said Neil, "this consultancy malarkey

is more dangerous than you thought. Do you need Alex and me to ride shotgun?"

"DI Ferris has taken care of that matter, Neil. That reminds me, I've got someone coming tonight to mend a glass panel in my back door, but I need cameras installed. The sort I can have linked to my phone. Anyone local you can recommend?"

"I don't think there's a firm here or in Devizes," said Neil, "but one of the nationwide companies has a place in Bristol. It's a false economy to get something cheap and cheerful just because it's on your doorstep. When your life could be at stake, you may as well pay for the best."

"Thanks, Neil. That's made me feel a whole lot better."

"Sorry, guv. Just trying to help."

"So, this friend of yours everyone is talking about, but we're supposed to ignore, died because he knew too much," said Lydia.

"Frank North was an acquaintance. I wouldn't say a friend. He worked on the neighbouring allotment. Frank pointed out the suspicious goings-on above a place called Cambrai Terrace. I walked up there with Suzie Ferris on Sunday afternoon after Frank's wife reported him missing. We saw nothing untoward above the houses on the hillside, but when we passed by my allotment later in the afternoon, someone attracted our attention. They'd just discovered Frank North's body."

"Do you reckon it was drugs, guv?" asked Alex.

"Odds on, given the circumstances," said Gus, "the National Crime Agency or the Organised Crime Task Force don't get involved for a minor offence. It has to be people or drug trafficking. Either way, whoever's behind it has a lot at stake. Frank North took a closer look at the shed they were using late on Saturday night. They could only have discovered my connection to Frank by questioning him before they shot him in the head. I want these bastards. As a mere consultant, as you so delicately pointed out, Neil, my input is restricted. I have to leave it to Geoff Mercer and detectives like DI Ferris. Geoff has cancelled surveillance on the lane leading to the shed. That's now screening visitors to my bungalow. I don't intend to antagonise these bastards more than I already have. I like living. The other option isn't appealing. DI Ferris is trying to determine which agency is running the investigation to press them to bring it to a swift conclusion. As far as possible, I want us to concentrate on the case. The ACC will inevitably want to discuss this matter with me. Until then, let's set out our programme for the next four days. Neil, can you please prepare a list of the people we might interview? Remember how Alex approached it last week? Think outside the box. I don't care if we have to chase people across the country. Short of digging them up, we'll follow every potential lead."

"Yes, guv," Neil replied. He had accepted the step back from the front line in this case. It made sense. He'd not mentioned the matter to Melody. She wasn't his Dad's biggest fan. His wife wouldn't be pressing him to ring his father to see how things were on the Costa del Crime.

Alex Hardy spent a fair bit of last night considering his role change. It was what he hoped would happen, but it had come much sooner than he'd expected. He knew he could play a full part in this team. After all, he'd come a long way to get here.

ALEX HAD BEEN mad about motorcycles ever since he could remember. His mother hadn't been keen, but his father rode trials bikes as a young man. That was enough incentive for Alex. He first rode a moped at fourteen. It belonged to the older brother of one of his schoolmates.

After many hours of fun, he caught the bug racing around a patch of waste ground, well out of sight of his parents. His first official bike was a Honda 50cc moped his Dad bought him on his sixteen birthday. He rode it every day to sixth-form college. So when he joined the police in 1998, he had his heart set on joining the dedicated Motorcycle Section.

Eighteen years of trouble-free motoring lay ahead. Alex had owned various cars without ever falling in love with them. They were convenient for hanging out with friends and shifting items too large for motorcycle panniers. On the other hand, nothing beat the sports-touring-orientated bikes he owned. Since his early twenties, he toured mainland Europe on various Honda and BMW models. He had a bucket list of challenging routes to tackle. Each year he spent his holiday time ticking one more country and one more mountain pass off his list.

Alex had his fair share of girlfriends but always took his biking holidays alone. The girls were okay with a week in Spain or the Canary Islands. A weekend in New York for Christmas shopping was perfect. It was out of the question if he suggested the Pyrenees or Norway's Atlantic Road. In the end, he found fifteen thousand miles a year touring preferable to the hassle of searching for that elusive soul mate.

When he joined the force, his career path led him towards the CID. Alex spent two years in uniform in Swindon, where he undertook the standard Traffic Police motorcycle courses, plus specific courses aimed at covert riding and driving. He demonstrated a much higher level of anticipation than the others on his course. His superiors sat up and took notice.

Alex had achieved his ambition of joining a covert policing team and trained as a surveillance motorcyclist. He followed people involved in organised crime and suspected terrorism offences. He encountered several life-threatening situations. Riders like Alex conducted high-speed pursuits but still had to negotiate red traffic lights and congested roadways without endangering the public. Every day brought a new challenge. He loved his work. Even the hours he spent escorting abnormal loads along country roads or ridding the M4 of boy racers with no sign of a licence, tax or insurance. It had all been in a day's work on a motorcycle.

Alex remembered the Monday of his accident. The thirtieth of October 2017. The day before Halloween. It started sunny, but the cloud built up by noon. There was a breeze, but the temperature hovered in the low teens of centigrade.

Alex had been after another bad guy: blue lights, bold manoeuvres, at ton-plus speeds. Out on the Shrivenham bypass, the chase ran for over three minutes. A wail of sirens followed him as colleagues in cars raced to catch him.

The pursuit began when Alex pulled up at traffic lights behind a car he thought seemed familiar. He was sure he recognised the registration. The control room confirmed the vehicle belonged to a serial offender with an outstanding warrant. Alex switched his flickering blue lights to signal the car in front to pull over. When the traffic lights changed, the car accelerated away.

"Vehicle making off," Alex radioed to his station's control room.

"Speed five-zero. Fifty miles per hour."

He gave chase. Everything escalated after that - 60, 80, and 100mph.

As they approached the next intersection, the red light turned green. Alex turned left to follow the car. Both vehicles accelerated back up to eighty miles an hour.

Out of nowhere, a BMW i8 came from behind, sped in front and cut him off. Alex swerved to avoid hitting the rear of the sports car. He lost control and flew into a curb. Everything went black.

The chase lasted six and a half minutes from start to finish.

The aftermath of a chase gone wrong can be measured in months and years, not minutes and seconds.

Thousands of police chases had occurred since Alex joined the Motorcycle Section. They abandoned some, or they petered out. Many concluded with arrests, and some resulted in serious injury or death. There had been one hundred deaths in the previous five years.

Those police chases resulted in tyre-streaked roads, yellow tape, and emergency service vehicles. They meant drivers, passengers and pedestrians were killed. Partners and relatives left behind.

Who were these people the police chased? Most had mental health issues. Or they were young men who distrusted authority.

What was the crime the driver had committed? Possession of marijuana with the intent to supply. Did the BMW driver act in the manner he did because he was associated with the criminal? Did he think it was clever stopping the police from catching someone who was a total stranger? Alex had learned the other car just kept driving.

Nobody identified the driver. The i8 carried false plates.

They would never know. Maybe it was simply an accident.

Within hours of his crash, police referred it to the Independent Office for Police Conduct, which started an independent investigation. They took statements and downloaded dashcams and CCTV footage. They cleared Alex of any wrongdoing.

The chase can become a heightened, erratic thing with unpredictable events. Maybe no police chase is routine. Refined guidelines helped reduce risks. The policing manual reminded officers to assess and reassess. Had the dangers of continuing this particular chase outweighed the reason for starting it in the first place?

Alex asked himself that same question every day since the thirtieth of October 2017.

As a pursuit rider, he needed to radio the control room constantly. He described circumstantial detail from the road and other risk factors. He had to get permission to continue. If control said stop, he had to stop. The control room decision depended almost entirely on Alex's accurate verbal description of the chase to make its decision.

Did he give them the right level of detail? Could he have ended the chase?

Alex remembered coming round after the accident. He had no clue how long he'd been unconscious. He lay on his back in the road. Alex saw familiar faces around him. Colleagues from Gablecross, the Swindon HQ, the first responder paramedics he'd chatted to on previous shouts.

Things started to blur when they lifted him onto the stretcher. Then he was pushed towards a helicopter. Alex flew to Great Western Hospital, where he went straight into surgery.

Alex didn't understand what had happened. Why am I

not moving; why can't I move my legs? Why am I here? Why is this happening?

Even as the helicopter hovered above the helipad, those thoughts became: -

This can't be real. I'll wake up in a minute, and it will be a bad dream.

As the hours passed, that became: -

Was this reality? How will I continue working? What's the point if I can't ride again?

Alex received injuries to both his legs. His left femur required nailing inside the bone, so they put a metal rod down the centre and bolts in the knee. They inserted bolts in the upper hip and at the top of the femur of his right leg. He broke his thumbs, and both wrists were damaged.

He would be a nightmare for airport security.

His lungs collapsed, and he had two chest drains inserted to keep them inflated. Once safe to move, he went for a scan to assess the damage. It was touch and go whether he would live. Alex knew nothing of this, but his family had arrived when he returned to the ward.

Alex's parents, and his younger sister, Paula, sat by his bedside when he next awoke.

They were noticeably distressed at seeing him in his bed-ridden state. Alex felt their dejection. There had been dark days and even darker nights. His physical wounds slowly healed, and the pain levels eased. Alex was never a religious man, but he gave thanks to whatever superior being was responsible for his paralysis being temporary. Even if it meant he knew how bloody painful his legs felt.

When family and colleagues visited, he started to sense a more positive vibe. He must be making progress, even if he couldn't let himself believe it. The mental wounds could have burrowed deep inside his head if those positive vibes hadn't encouraged him. He recognised there was a way back. It would be a long, hard road, but he resolved to follow that road to the end. Even if the motorcycle pursuit role were out of the question, he would make it back to a desk in CID. His brain remained sharp. His skills as a detective were in high demand.

It had been a slow process, but he learnt to walk again. Alex suffered from blurred vision for a while and became nauseous whenever he attempted to sit upright. His muscles had wasted away with the enforced inactivity of the previous weeks. A full recovery was always his primary goal. When he transferred to the rehabilitation unit at the hospital four weeks later, he worked harder than most at the exercises given to him by the physiotherapists.

His road to recovery had been long and slow, just as he had imagined. He was frustrated at being off work and unable to do the simplest tasks. Until recently, he only had full use of one arm and one leg. His trips to the gym, plus his physio, paid dividends. The day he could be fully mobile was close enough to touch.

When he went home for the first time, Alex's family and friends had renovated his flat to make it more wheelchair accessible. The first thing he did was to get the flat valued. Someone with a greater need than him should have it, he thought. That flat would go on the market as soon as he could walk unaided.

"HOW FAR HAVE YOU GOT, NEIL?" asked Lydia. "I've finished pinning the murder scene photos and the area map onto the boards."

Alex wheeled his chair across to join his two colleagues.

"These aren't in any order, you understand," said Neil, "but here's my list, for what it's worth."

Neil turned his screen so they could see the names he had included.

James Bosworth was thirty years old at the time of the murder and a self-employed electrician.

Now forty-five years old, married with three sons. His wife's name is Sammie, twenty-eight years old, and a mobile hairdresser. James still runs his own business. He lives on the Westbourne Estate.

Krystal Warner, twenty-four when Trudi died. Unmarried. Krystal has got her name over the door at the Ring O'Bells. She's been running it for twelve years. She's thirty-nine now — another one who is easy enough to find.

Trudi's parents are Ray and Kath. Her Dad turns sixty this year, and her Mum's three years younger. Ray works as a gas fitter, and Kath stacks shelves in a supermarket on the outskirts of town. They live on the Westbourne Estate.

The taxi firm that took Bosworth and Warner home went out of business in 2008, and its owner retired to Lyme Regis. The original file listed the driver's name as Saeed Gill. He was fifty-five years old back then. Now retired, Gill lives in Swindon with his family.

Amy Hobbs was the girl in the office. I found her details tucked away in the murder file. They never interviewed her without any reason supplied. Amy was twenty, an unmarried mother of an eight-month-old son. She's married now, and her son has an eight-year-old sister. Amy Pollock lives on the Greenwood Estate.

Gary, the bar manager at the Ring O'Bells; his surname was Smith. No idea why they didn't include that in the stuff we've seen so far. He died in 2011 from — a heart attack. His wife, Maggie Smith, is now sixty-six, suffering from lung cancer. A heavy smoker for fifty years. Stage Two at present. One of the main reasons she and Gary pulled out of the pub trade was the smoking ban. She couldn't hack it.

Steve Li and his wife Mary are retired from the restaurant business now. Both are in their early seventies. They came here from Hong Kong in the late Sixties and opened the Imperial Dragon. They anglicised their first names to fit in with the locals when they arrived in the country. The place has always been popular, and Steve's son Jason runs the restaurant now. They still live in the same house at the posh end of town. There must be money in spring rolls.

Tony and Tristram Virgo, fifty-two and fifty, respectively, moved to Benidorm in 2016. They sold their hairdressing salon when Tony hit fifty. Both are semi-retired, working three days a week out of a mobile home on a massive ex-pats caravan site next to their place. I think they call that 'living the dream.' They've got six Yorkies now. Bubble and Squeak have gone to the pet cemetery. There's no information on names for the current brood.

Alex and Lydia listened intently to Neil's commentary on what they saw on the screen.

"I wonder who will go to Benidorm to interview them?" asked Lydia.

"Fat chance," said Neil, "Tony only found the body the next morning. So I can't see how he can help us. Tristram was at home. There was no indication either of them even knew Trudi. They weren't her type. But, to be honest, I was desperate to add a few names to the list."

"We can face time them," said Alex, "maybe they picked up something useful in the salon after the murder. I understand it's a great place for gossip."

"Viewing the problem with hindsight gave us the breakthrough last week," said Lydia, "maybe something they say will offer us another lead?"

"Lightning doesn't often strike twice," said Gus. He'd finished chasing camera installers on the phone. A Bristol firm promised he'd be safe and secure by the weekend. Gus again had his eyes focused on the case; next week, he could also have his eyes on the bungalow via his smartphone.

"Neil, have you sent any requests for assistance to the Hub yet?" he asked.

"Not so far, guv. Have I missed something obvious?"

"Well, we know Lewington didn't do it. The original investigation concentrated at the outset on the people I see you've listed. They learned little from them except where Trudi had been that night and her character. Do we believe a name from that list raped and stabbed her? If not, then who might attack Trudi like that? Valuable time was lost in identifying the real culprit when everything focused on pinning the crime on Lewington."

"We could use a list of known sex offenders living in the region back then," said Alex.

"That will be a start," said Gus, "work your way through that to see if anyone hasn't got an alibi. I haven't got a clue what I did fifteen weeks ago, let alone fifteen years, but you never know. It's not the top priority. We'll try to prioritise those interviewed originally, then dig deeper if needed."

"This could have been a revenge attack," said Lydia, "what about former lovers?"

"That might be a long list," said Neil, "who knows the answer to that one? Krystal Warner might be a help. No doubt there were plenty before they met. If you were one of her conquests, would you come forward this long after her death to volunteer information?"

"Nobody said this case would be easy, Neil," said Gus, "Lydia's right, though. We can't discount a former boyfriend or a one-night stand. When I said to think outside the box, Neil, that can be what you uncover. A million questions with no guarantee of an answer. Let's put these initial witnesses in order."

"I suggest we start with Krystal Warner," said Neil, "we can check her recollections of the whole day of the murder. She has to be our best bet for the most likely ex-lovers with a grudge."

"Okay, Neil, let's make her our first appointment. If you can arrange that, Alex and I will visit her. The Ring O'Bells is wheelchair-friendly."

"James Bosworth should be next, guv," said Alex, "his story didn't gel with Krystal's, and he might have a different angle to offer on the ex-lovers."

"What's your thinking behind that, Alex?" queried Gus.

"Krystal and Trudi were great mates, guv. Some of those sexual relationships were shared. Her assessment of whether the guy involved might look for revenge could be coloured by how she felt about him. Bosworth was a recent boyfriend of Krystal's, but he's local. So, he might have a more impartial view on who Trudi fell out with and why."

"I take your point, Alex. Remember that point when we compile a set of questions for him. I'm interested in the timeline on the night. As you said, Bosworth and Warner's versions of what happened didn't match, did they?"

"Maggie Smith should be your third interview, guv," suggested Lydia. "So much of Trudi's social life centred on the pub. Nobody believed Gary Smith was ever involved with her, but Maggie might have thought differently. Even if Gary showed no interest, Maggie would have spent hundreds of hours behind the bar people-watching. She would have picked up the vibes of ill-feeling between one of her customers and her barmaid."

"Exactly," said Alex, "and she would have said something too. Either to Gary, Trudi, or the bloke responsible, because she and Gary employed Trudi purely for her busty barmaid attributes. She kept the punters rolling in and helped them to part with their hard-earned cash. So the last thing they wanted was Trudi to walk out because an ex-lover was bugging her. Or bad-mouthing her every time he came in for a pint."

"We have another potential category to look for," said Gus. "Had Trudi attracted a stalker? What if the guy we're looking for wasn't an ex-lover? What if they were a sad case who fancied her, but Trudi never gave him the time of day? We need to add another line of enquiry for the Hub to pursue. Was anyone cautioned or charged with stalking or similar offences around the time of the murder? Let's spread the net to five years on either side."

"On it, guv," said Neil, "what about the taxi driver next, Saeed Gill?"

"Let's leave him until after Lydia and I talk with Amy, the girl in the office that night. She's still young; she may remember a minor detail that will help. Amy Pollock, is that right?"

"Yes, guv," said Neil. "I guess that leaves us with the three couples on the list. Does it matter what order we interview them? The Li's, the boys from Benidorm, and Trudi's parents."

"Not really; their input will be minimal. Okay, the order's agreed," said Gus. "Get the meetings scheduled as soon as possible. Keep your fingers crossed that a genuine lead comes from those interviews. If not, we'll be up to our neck in sex offenders and former lovers until Christmas."

"Never a dull moment here, is it," said Lydia.

"*Boredom is the root of all evil*," said Gus.

"Was that from your philosopher friend again, guv?" asked Neil.

"Correct, Neil. He would have reminded you that the man responsible for this brutal killing is human. Never lose sight of that. Lists of sex offenders or stalkers aren't inanimate objects; they're real people. He once wrote - *when boredom advances, evil spreads. This can be traced to the very beginning of the world. The gods were bored; therefore, they created human beings.*"

Chapter Six

GUS LEFT WORK at five o'clock on the dot. The team were still hard at it. They were updating the Freeman files and logging interview dates for the diary. He had decided to vary his trips to and from work, both the times and the routes, wherever possible, to confuse those tailing him.

He was eager to hear from Suzie Ferris. Gus hoped it wouldn't feel awkward after last night and the note she'd left. As much as their relationship interested and excited him, his safety being at stake concerned him the most.

Gus noticed the car in his rear-view mirror as soon as he left town. It had joined the main road from Crook's Way. Gus hoped they would have been more discreet if it related to yesterday's break-in.

Suzie Ferris must have gotten the ACC to agree to share his protection duty with the town's officers. Gus gave the driver a wave. His shadow flicked his headlights on and off.

Gus made a mental note to suggest to the ACC that escorts needed more lessons on running covert surveillance.

No nasty surprises awaited him when he got home. He

planned to cook, eat, and clear away his dinner things before the glazier arrived at six-thirty. Suzie Ferris was calling sometime this evening.

At around twenty-past-six, Gus wandered out of the bungalow and crossed over the lane to the car that tailed him home. He knocked on the window. The driver was reading the newspaper.

"A van with 'Glazier' or something similar on the side will pull in here in the next ten minutes. Don't panic; he's coming to fix a panel in my back door."

"Thanks, Sir. I'm being relieved at ten this evening. Are any other visitors expected later?"

Cheeky sod, Gus thought. Whoever was on duty last night didn't waste any time spreading that little titbit of gossip.

"If you spot any unfamiliar faces in the lane under cover of darkness, I hope you or your replacement will be alert enough to take the necessary action. I would hate to be taking a bullet indoors while you're struggling with 15 Down."

The driver folded his newspaper and sat up straighter in his seat. Gus walked back inside the bungalow. Almost as soon as he closed the front door, he heard the gravel crunch under the wheels of a new arrival.

It was the glazier and his bottle-green van. Gus hoped the driver could still read the small print on the back door that fixing windows was their speciality.

Gus would have loved to wander along to his allotment. The weather was still warm and sunny, but he had to stay until the glazier had fixed that back door panel. He looked at his watch; he realised it was a few minutes before seven. How long did it take to fit a piece of glass, anyway?

At a quarter past seven, he had the answer.

Gordon the glazier proudly showed him his completed handiwork, and Gus handed over the agreed sum. Gordon laughed when Gus commented that it seemed a lot for forty minutes of work. He laughed even louder when Gus reminded him to put it through the books. Gus wondered whether he would have been so cheery if he knew his client was still associated with the police. After all, tax evasion had been the downfall of Al Capone. Daylight robbery appeared to be alive and well and working out of Devizes.

The green minivan soon made its way into the lane, and Gus was alone. As he closed the front door, he spotted his bodyguard noting the number plate on Gordon's van. Gus had just made it into the lounge when the phone rang.

"Hi there, how has your day been?" Suzie asked.

"Oh, you know, notes to be read and cameras to source. Then there are glaziers to haggle with; in other words, a typical Tuesday."

"I have news," she said, "do you want the good news or the bad news?"

"Will I be able to tell the difference?" he asked.

Suzie sighed.

"I wish I could get over there. You sound as if you need cheering up. Alas, there isn't any particularly good news. I met with the ACC this morning. He wants to see you in the morning first thing. That's ten o'clock for Kenneth Truelove. So, you get a lie-in."

"You're right; that's not good news. If you could have come over, of course…."

"My staying last night seemed the right thing to do. The odd comment I've heard today suggests people think there was more to it. I didn't mean to tarnish your reputation."

"It was your reputation I was more concerned about

when my escort asked whether I expected late-night visitors tonight. He seemed miffed when I said no."

"I should have had the courage of my convictions last night. They would have something to gossip about."

"Don't let the bastards get at you. Tell me what Truelove thought of my break-in and who was behind it."

"The ACC confirmed it's Organised Crime Task Force watching the shed above Cambrai Terrace. As for who Monty Jennings got mixed up with, they're Albanians."

"Shit, they're a nasty bunch. The message makes more sense if you speak it with an Eastern European accent."

"That's not funny, Gus," said Suzie, sounding concerned. "I've impressed upon the ACC that the OCTF needs to answer for Frank North's death. He's not keen to rock the boat, as you can imagine. I hope you can pressure him tomorrow to make the right decision."

"Will it be just me and the ACC?" Gus asked.

"No, Geoff Mercer and I will be there. Truelove was waiting to hear from the OCTF to learn if they will send a representative to update us on their progress."

"We don't want to hear what they've done so far; we need to see this business brought to a swift conclusion," said Gus.

"See you in the morning," said Suzie, "what have you got planned this evening?"

"I thought of spending an hour on my allotment. To check what Bert's managed to do today. I could read for a while and enjoy this lovely weather. It will be sunset by eight, though, and if I'm wandering in the semi-dark lane, I might stumble upon an Albanian."

"You had better stay indoors. I'm off out tonight. I can't ride to your rescue this time."

"Another time, perhaps?"

"Goodnight, Gus."

Suzie had gone. Gus was thankful for one thing; she hadn't wished him sweet dreams.

Gus wondered what Terry Davis was doing; it was early in the evening in Marbella.

If only he had his number. He'd warned Neil not to get in touch with his father, but the team needed to know some things. Not just what went on in 2003 but why.

He rang the Davis landline. Melody answered.

"Is Neil there?" Gus asked.

"Who's that?"

"It's Gus Freeman, his boss."

"Oh, hello. No, Neil's gone out to watch the football on the big screen in a pub in town."

"Do you know Terry's number? I must have misplaced it."

Gus waited while Melody searched for the number.

"I avoid using it if I can," she said when she picked up the phone again, "he's not a nice man."

Gus took note of the phone number Melody relayed to him.

"Did you ever fly out to Spain to stay with him?" he asked.

"Terry couldn't put us up at his place. It's only a bedsit. He and Neil's Mum split up years ago. So we flew over on a package holiday and stayed in a hotel."

"Terry's not living the high life, then?"

"Far from it," she scoffed. "Terry works as a bouncer on the door at a nightclub in Marbella to make ends meet."

"Has he ever come back to see his family or old friends in the force?"

"I don't know what Neil has told you, Mr Freeman, but

Terry has kept quiet in Spain for the past six years for a reason."

"We realise the wrong man went to prison for murder, Melody. It was headline news for a few days back in 2013. No one can condone what he did, but it's five years since the truth came out. If he landed at Bristol airport with a weekend bag, I can't imagine they'd arrest him as soon as his feet touched the tarmac. They didn't charge him at the time."

"I told you he wasn't a nice man, Mr Freeman. He spent years as a Detective Sergeant. Terry Davis was a bitter man. He got passed over so many times for promotion. Maybe he found other ways to line his pockets. Neil will always stand up for his Dad. But Terry turned a blind eye to bad stuff while he worked at that police station where you're based."

"Do me a favour, Melody, don't mention to Neil that I rang. He'll think I'm senile if he learns I've lost Terry's number."

"Neil won't be home until I've gone to bed, and I'll forget you called by the morning," said Melody.

"That's my girl. Take care, Melody. Thanks for your help."

Gus ended the call and dialled the number she'd given him.

"Davis," came the gruff reply.

"Terry Davis," said Gus, "my name is Gus Freeman. I was a DI in Salisbury while you worked in West Wiltshire. Our paths never crossed. I recently came out of retirement to work with a Crime Review Team to revisit cold cases."

"I heard," said Davis.

"So, you know your son Neil works with my unit. He had to have impressed the top brass."

"I ain't spoken to Neil in weeks, mate. Friends keep me informed. I've heard you've got yourself a spot of bother."

Gus wondered who might tell Terry Davis about the Cambrai Terrace business. That was worth knowing. Even if Terry wasn't forthcoming on the case the team was working on, at least the phone call threw up one little gem of knowledge. There was someone in the area keeping watch.

"Nothing we can't handle," said Gus. "It was another matter I wanted to discuss. The Trudi Villiers case from 2003. What can you tell me?"

"Not my finest moment."

"Was there nobody you fancied for the murder before the series of attacks by Lewington appeared on your radar?"

"It's a long time ago."

"There's still time to review your handling of the case. Look at Operation Yewtree. They dug back forty years to find dirt. The Lewington business was only fifteen years ago."

"I don't like threats, Freeman, and I doubt you did either. Those Albanians don't mess around. You could be six feet under before they could extradite me to the UK."

"I'm not a bloke who enjoys people pushing me around. Give me something to work with, Terry,"

"Culverhouse knew Trudi Villiers," said Terry, "but you never heard that from me. I know you earned a reputation as a straight arrow. I don't think you would follow through on the threat of dragging my name into this business. Dominic Culverhouse would, though, in a heartbeat; he's got more to lose."

"Are you saying Culverhouse told you to off-load the

murder onto Lewington to avoid any chance his liaison with Trudi Villiers got out?"

"Trudi was a slapper," said Terry, "why he got mixed up with her, heaven knows. Perhaps she offered something he couldn't get at home. It wasn't still going on, mind you, when she died. The liaison started when he was a young DC. Someone keeled over at the care home, and we investigated it because the relatives suspected foul play. That happened a couple of years after the Beverley Allitt case; the media thought everyone employed psychopaths for a while. Trudi was sixteen, straight from school. She'd started young, so Culverhouse wasn't her first. Fifty-first, maybe."

"Their relationship started in 1993, or thereabouts?"

"That sounds right. I got partnered with Culverhouse back then. We never found anything incriminating at the care home. The bloke who died was in his late eighties, and pneumonia took him off to dreamland. We found many things wrong with the place, but no serial killers making the beds."

"How long did they see one another, any idea?"

"They never went out as boyfriend and girlfriend. Culverhouse was too precious over his career for that. He picked her up in his car from wherever she worked. That stopped when she began working at the Ring O'Bells. Too many people in town knew Culverhouse. They would recognise the car. I can't prove it, but she flew out to be with him for one week in Majorca. That might have been the last time. Trudi had only been working in the pub for a month then."

"Krystal Warner started not long after that."

"Exactly. Krystal and Trudi hunted in pairs then. Culverhouse was out of his league. I realised she had given him his marching orders when he changed his car."

Terry Davis gave a dry laugh.

"Go on," said Gus, "why was that significant?"

"Culverhouse always drove saloon cars with roomy back seats. He traded the latest one for a two-seater MG because it suited him better. He was moving up the ladder. I got stuck at DS level, and he passed me like a sports car passes a milk float."

"Can you give me anything on the witnesses we've got? Did anyone strike you as having the potential to be a killer?"

"I told you. It was a long time ago. Culverhouse told me who to interview. I followed orders. It was hard graft trying to come up with names of people with a motive. I remember that. As soon as a name cropped up, they produced an alibi. I wanted to dig deeper because there's always something you don't see on the first pass. Culverhouse heard a whisper on the Mason's grapevine about Minehead. I went to Portishead with instructions to bring the case back to Wiltshire. He told me to use any means necessary. You know the rest."

Gus got the impression there was little more that Terry Davis wished to add.

"Some of what you told me could prove useful, Terry. Thanks for that. Sorry to take up so much of your time."

"I hope you won't make a habit of calling, Freeman. I'm retired, and so should you be. If you keep sticking your nose in other people's business, you will permanently retire. A little advice. If you've got any sense, you'll walk away, get back to your gardening, live a little."

Gus heard the sound that told him Terry Davis had ended the call.

Melody had been right. He wasn't a nice man, but he'd given him a loose thread he could tug on to see what was on the other end.

Wednesday, 18 April 2018

GUS TOOK advantage of the extra half an hour in bed. A leisurely breakfast. Two minutes extra in the shower. He smiled when he walked outside and the sun's warmth hit him. Days such as this made you glad to be alive.

Before he got into the Ford Focus, he checked for his security blanket. The officer who came on shift at ten last night was the same one who had accompanied him into town yesterday morning. Gus gave him a friendly wave. He got no response, and they drove into Devizes in convoy.

Today, Gus confused his escort by turning right and heading for the London Road HQ. Gus could see the cogs turning as consternation spread over the young face he saw in his rear-view mirror.

Gus found a space in front of the main building as his companion drove onto the pool car compound. A glance along the line showed Geoff Mercer, Suzie Ferris, and Vera Jennings were already hard at work.

Gus couldn't recall what the ACC drove at present. It had to be something big and shiny, as bright as the medals on his uniform. The registration on the car at the end appeared to be from somewhere further east of this rural patch.

Once inside the building, he signed in and made his way upstairs. On the landing, he looked for a familiar face. Kassie Trotter waved from her desk but did not attempt to speak. That was a first.

Gus heard voices. Geoff Mercer and Suzie Ferris appeared from the gloomy corridor at the rear of the building. They both wore their Sunday-best uniforms. This meeting must be important. Thank goodness he'd worn a clean shirt. Gus shone his shoes on the back of his trousers. A little can often go a long way.

"Is the ACC ready for us?" asked Gus.

"Truelove has company," Geoff replied, "a senior guy from the Organised Crime Task Force is here to tell us what we can and can't do."

That explained the unfamiliar car registration, Gus thought.

Geoff Mercer knocked on the ACC's door and led the way inside when the ACC called, "Enter."

Gus knew where the ACC would be, so he ignored the window and studied the other man. Mid-fifties, distinguished-looking, wearing a suit that cost a month's wages and handmade shoes. The tie belonged to a club Gus would never be allowed to join nor had any wish to visit. Nevertheless, this encounter promised to be riveting.

"Good morning," said the ACC, "Brendan Curran is from OCTF. He's here to bring us up to speed regarding the operation they've been carrying out. Unfortunately, we inadvertently stumbled upon one of the components of that operation. As a result, we've agreed to step away."

Gus wondered whether Wiltshire Police received a choice in the matter. Also, what rank did this guy hold? Curran looked to be high up the food chain by his appearance. He wasn't in a rush to give much away on that score — no introductions, straight to business. As soon as the ACC's bottom hit his chair, Brendan Curran, the mystery man, stood and addressed the four seated officers from the side of the ACC's desk.

"Thousands of Albanians arrived in the UK from the late 1990s onwards during a refugee crisis. Many claimed to be from Kosovo, particularly a group of war-hardened criminals keen to make their mark. They did that in the capital, starting as door staff in Soho, the heart of the sex and vice trade. They had soon taken over the prostitution rackets. It wasn't long before they came to the notice of the authorities. The violence and brutality against women they had trafficked shook police officers on the ground. Over the years, officers became accustomed to seeing how pimps beat their women. The bruises are confined to areas of the body covered by clothing or stockings. The Albanians handed out beatings over the body and face. This hardened band of men weren't on a power trip; they tested the method to see if they could replicate it in other crime areas. Their next move was into narcotics. The gangs traded on their reputation as veterans of the Balkans Wars and moved from smuggling women into the UK to trading weapons and drugs. Across the Channel, they joined with the Turks and the Italians. They operated as enforcers for gangs trafficking heroin from Afghanistan. Then they began dealing cannabis by growing potent strains of the drug, using slave labour."

Gus thought that none of this was news to either of the officers he was speaking to. They were in a one-way conversation. More akin to a history lesson. So far, this brand of menace hadn't threatened the Shires in the same way it had blighted many areas of the major cities since the turn of the century. The free movement of citizens throughout mainland Europe heralded a new dawn by creating an inclusive community. Unfortunately, nobody had bothered to calculate what advantages that new beginning offered criminals.

Gus Freeman wasn't against immigration. On the contrary, he'd enjoyed the influx of new cuisine, music and fashion in the Sixties and Seventies. The UK was a brighter and better place for it. Although integration had taken longer than hoped, things had mellowed by the Nineties. It was far from perfect, but nothing as grim as the mess they faced today.

A bright spark opened the floodgates, and they didn't think what the extra numbers would do to the delicate balance achieved through several decades of strife. Austerity cuts only made matters worse. Border control personnel didn't have the resources to check who they allowed through; an honest bloke with a skill required in the country or a vicious thug who would slit your throat for the price of a good meal.

The police had lost control of crime in the capital well before midnight on December the thirty-first, 1999. Moreover, it wasn't only the Albanians who set up or strengthened their criminal networks in the past twenty years. The Turks, Vietnamese, Bangladeshis, Greeks, Serbs, Jews, Russians, Pakistanis, and Tamils came in numbers. Not to mention the Cosa Nostra, Yardies, Triads and the IRA.

Gus counted the number in his head, wondering if he'd offended anyone by leaving them out. It didn't matter if he had. Without a robust police force supported by a judiciary that delivered true justice, then his former colleagues were pissing in the wind.

Brendan Curran could explain how we came to be up to our neck in it until the end of next year. Gus wanted to hear what he planned to do to rid the country of the bastards responsible.

"Have the Albanians converted Monty Jennings's shed into a marijuana factory without his knowledge?" asked the ACC.

Gus could tell from Curran's face he deemed the question facile and parochial. He waited for Geoff to come to Truelove's rescue. Geoff stared out of the window. Suzie Ferris shuffled uncomfortably in her chair.

Gus realised they hoped he'd say something. He had less to lose as a mere consultant. Curran would suggest to the Chief Constable it might be kinder to allow the dinosaur to spend his remaining days out to pasture.

"If that's what they're doing up there," he heard himself say, "I don't think it matters whether or not Monty knew. The gang could afford to pay him enough to give them free rein from the profits of their sordid trade. Monty needed money fast. We assumed it was another of his get-rich-quick schemes. With his parlous financial state and an impending divorce, he would have taken the money regardless of what they planned to do with the building."

Brendan Curran looked bored. He was keen to get back to his script. Gus wasn't letting OCTF off the hook.

"Forget Monty Jennings," Gus continued, "it's Frank North that concerns me. How long have you been aware of this gang and what they used the building for?"

"I couldn't possibly comment on matters relating to ongoing operations."

"Well, perhaps you might comment on this," said Gus. "Could you have prevented Frank North's death by snatching him out of harm's way when your people first saw him nosing around? I'll remind you if it's not in your briefing notes. He told me to watch out for something odd on the hillside on the twenty-seventh of last month. How long before that he first went to investigate, I don't know, but it's reasonable to assume a month elapsed between his first and last visits."

"The operation could have been compromised if we had broken cover a month ago. OCTF had too much time invested in this complex investigation. We are close to eliminating a major supply route to every city and town in the

West Country. A business worth one hundred and twenty-five million pounds a year."

"Oh, I get it now," said Gus, "the kudos for the OCTF trumpeting a success of that magnitude far outweighs a human life."

"When you put it that way," said Curran, spreading his hands wide.

Suzi Ferris grabbed Gus by the arm. He was halfway up from his chair.

"Don't give him the satisfaction, Gus," she implored.

The death stare she gave the ACC and Geoff Mercer let them know what she thought of their lack of support. Suzie had expressed her fears to Gus earlier; OCTF would tell them they needed to consider the bigger picture.

"If I may continue," said Curran, "when they began dealing in cannabis, the Albanians were very much whole-salers. More of their fellow compatriots arrived and have now created a network across the country. The cannabis business lends itself to retail supply. Few groups that OCTF encounters do an end-to-end supply. There's a disconnect somewhere along the line. They can make even more money through street price mark-ups by controlling the whole supply chain. London-based criminals commute to rural counties to sell hard drugs and often take over the homes of vulnerable users. The term county lines has been bandied around for a few years now, and traditionally the gangs centred on heroin and crack cocaine. They started an expansion into supplying cannabis because there are ten times as many users. A much larger proportion of people come up against organised crime gangs who use weapons and intimidation as routine tools in their criminal enter-prise. We must stop this expansion."

"That's the only sensible comment you've made," said

Gus. "How close are you to eliminating this outfit for good?"

"We were days away before Mr North's unfortunate intrusion," said Curran. "We have undercover officers inside the operation in the capital and their regional centre in Swindon. Their lives would have been at risk if we had moved before we could get a message to them."

"I think we've covered enough for now, Brendan," said the ACC, "we appreciate you coming to explain matters. As you can tell, we are very interested in what's happening above Cambrai Terrace. We look forward to your endeavours resulting in a successful conclusion."

Gus shook his head. What a climb-down. He'll be tugging his forelock next. The bloke's not royalty.

"However," said Geoff Mercer, suddenly finding his voice, "we wish to register our concerns in the strongest terms possible. OCTF has been running an investigation on a minimum of two Wiltshire sites for several months. We were kept totally in the dark. We could have acted on Frank North's suspicions and screwed the whole operation for you. That isn't the way we should operate. I hope you will give us a heads-up in the future."

"Duly noted," said Brendan Curran.

Gus noticed he hadn't said they would cooperate or share intelligence. Instead, he had just recognised that Wiltshire was unhappy with how OCTF had run things.

"You say you were days away from acting against this gang last Saturday when they murdered Frank North," said Suzie Ferris. "Nothing has happened since then. Why?"

"We had to reassess our strategy," said Curran, "we have more components in the chain. OCTF teams must strike at each one simultaneously to achieve the maximum effect."

"Mr Freeman has been very patient," she said. "Are you aware he received a death threat within twenty-four hours of Frank North's murder?"

"That was unfortunate," said Curran, getting to his feet.

Gus wasn't sure whether he was preparing to run or setting himself ready for an attack.

"I would be collateral damage, the same as Frank North," said Gus. "After all, it's a one hundred and twenty-five million pounds business. Don't concern yourself, Mr Curran. I can take care of myself. I'd be more concerned about how secret this operation of yours is. A conversation yesterday evening with a former copper living in Marbella revealed that someone knew all about the Albanians; and that I'd had a visit. Perhaps there's a leak in your organisation? I would check on the safety of your undercover officers. We don't want more collateral damage. That would be most unfortunate, wouldn't it?"

That made Curran blink.

"I think that's enough," said the ACC.

Curran shook the ACC by the hand, wished them good morning and swept out of the office.

Gus heard Kassie Trotter call after him as he disappeared to Reception.

"It's a pity you're not staying for coffee. I've baked muffins."

Brendan Curran struck Gus as a muesli man. Muffins would be far too common.

"I'll see the three of you in my office at two o'clock this afternoon," said the ACC. "We have other matters to discuss."

They weren't getting a coffee, let alone a taste of Kassie's muffins.

Chapter Seven

GUS, Geoff and Suzie filed out of the ACC's office.

Geoff Mercer nodded towards his office.

He wanted to discuss what had just happened.

"This needs to be brief," he said once they were behind closed doors, "I've got another meeting. I'm sure you both have other things that need your attention."

"Can we organise a search party?" asked Gus.

"Sorry, what for exactly?" asked Geoff.

"The ACC's backbone."

"This guy Curran must have serious clout to get that subservient reaction from Truelove," said Suzie Ferris.

"I never had any dealings with OCTF while serving full-time," said Gus. "Just as well, I would have lost my pension. Thanks for stopping me from getting claret on his Savile Row suit, Suzie."

"Right, let's get serious," said Geoff, "why did you call Terry Davis in Marbella last night?"

"It was a legitimate line of enquiry in the Trudi Villiers case. He was involved in the stitch-up of Dennis Lewington.

I wanted to know why he needed to quit searching for evidence that would lead to a genuine suspect."

"I'm not fussed whether or not it was legitimate, Gus. You heard the ACC. He wants to see us this afternoon. You've opened a can of worms. The last thing the top brass want is for matters surrounding the Lewington debacle to surface."

"When Gus and his team solve the case, it will be impossible to keep Lewington out of it. Together with this force's mistakes fifteen years ago," said Suzie Ferris.

Gus thought Suzie was optimistic, considering his team's lack of progress so far. Perhaps she viewed him through rose-coloured spectacles because she was attracted to him.

"You're missing Geoff's point, Suzie," said Gus. He was reluctant to stop thinking of moving their relationship to another level. Work had to come first. He gave himself a mental slap on the wrist.

"That's because you don't know what Terry Davis told me last night. The ACC was aware that the DI in charge knew Trudi Villiers."

"In the biblical sense," added Geoff.

"Gosh," said Suzie.

"It wasn't common knowledge, but one or two senior officers learned the couple had had an inappropriate liaison early in his career."

"The relationship was over before the murder," said Gus, "but Terry Davis had to look for a quick fix. He shoe-horned Lewington into the frame. Then it was a case of, nothing to see here, move on. Culverhouse has continued to get promoted. They forgave him that early slip. He's Assistant Chief Constable with Avon & Somerset at Portishead, destined for further advancement. He has friends in high places and fellow travellers. The ACC will want to sweep this part of the investigation under the carpet. He won't want to upset anyone, not at this career stage. That Curran bloke got under my skin. I didn't think what I was saying."

"What's done is done, Gus," said Geoff, "we three need to be united in how we respond to the ACC this afternoon."

"Are you suggesting we pursue the case wherever it leads?" asked Suzie.

"We must tread carefully if that's the case," said Gus, "I've side-lined Neil Davis from any interviews. Culverhouse's supporters will first accuse Neil of trying to switch attention away from his father's role."

"That could backfire, surely?" said Suzie. "Culverhouse could face questions about Terry Davis's actions and why they were never the subject of an internal investigation."

"He had disappeared to Spain twelve months before they freed Lewington," said Geoff. "Whether he received a tip-off or it was fortuitous, who knows?"

"I wonder why Lewington's lawyers didn't encourage him to file a complaint through the Independent Police Complaints Commission?" asked Suzie.

"This case is throwing up far more questions than answers," said Gus. "It's time for me to address that issue. I'll get back to my team. See you this afternoon."

"The ACC will want to discuss the death threat you received," warned Geoff, "please tell me you don't plan on wandering past Monty's shed again soon?"

"Not on your life," said Gus, "although the visible protection may do more harm than good. The Albanians will reduce their activities above Cambrai Terrace until the heat's off. I hope the covert surveillance of the cannabis farm run by OCTF is of a higher standard. I'll miss my escorts in my rear-view mirror, but enough is enough. It would be foolish to antagonise these thugs, and I'm capable of keeping a weather eye on strangers."

There was a knock on the door. It was Kassie with coffee and a tray of muffins.

"I have to love you and leave you," said Gus, grabbing two as he dashed through the door, "I'll be back this afternoon."

"If you're not watching your waistline, I've got choco-late eclairs," called Kassie.

Gus was already in Reception, heading for the car park.

Gus drove out of Devizes, keeping an eye out for anyone tailing him. There was no one. He reached the Old Police Station and went upstairs to the CRT office.

"Good to see you're working hard," he said, "My meeting with the ACC could have gone better. Our VIP guest from OCTF went off in a huff, and I missed a coffee. If I'm getting myself one, is anyone else thirsty?"

Three hands shot in the air.

They sat around the main whiteboard ten minutes later to recap their progress.

"We've got our first interviews scheduled," said Neil, "the list is in the Freeman file. The landlady of the Ring O'Bells is up first. Krystal Warner's expecting you and Alex tomorrow morning at half-past nine."

"I planned to eat there on Thursday evening after work," said Gus, "it might be wise to switch venue, regard-less of what we learn tomorrow. She'll wonder why we've suddenly started to frequent her place."

"We, guv?" asked Lydia. "Are you treating us to a meal out?"

"Not on this occasion. I'm meeting a friend."

"So, last Friday at the Waggon & Horses wasn't a one-off," said Neil.

"Who's next on the list?" asked Gus, not missing the shared glances between his team members.

"Bosworth is working away this week," said Alex. "Most of his work relies on repeat business from a client base he's grown over the past twenty years. However, times were as tough for tradespeople during the austerity years as they were for many others. Over the past three years, Bosworth has taken on contracts with building firms. That means full wiring systems in new builds with severe time restraints and cutthroat prices."

"In my experience, that leads to shoddy workmanship, too," said Neil, "you should see the state of my mates' houses. They couldn't move in and settle straightaway. Instead, they spent the first six to nine months calling one trade or the other back to finish a job or rip it out and start again."

"Did Bosworth agree to fix a time next week?" asked Gus.

"Monday morning, first thing, guv," said Neil, "he spends the day on paperwork. After that, Bosworth has his local guys chase up to see if they're balancing the books. Then, on Tuesday morning, he'll be off to Swindon for another four days graft."

"It sounds Bosworth only keeps his head above water because his wife provides extra income from her mobile hairdressing job," said Lydia.

"It can't be cheap bringing up three young sons," said Neil.

"Okay, we'll worry about Bosworth next week. Who did you promote?"

"I voted for Maggie Smith," said Alex, "her health won't ever improve. The sooner we get her statement, the better."

"Maggie Smith rarely ventures out, guv," said Alex, "we can visit her tomorrow afternoon."

"Why don't you and Lydia visit her? The sooner you get into the swing of things, the better."

Alex was chuffed. At last, someone allowed him to show he could fulfil a useful role in police work. He wouldn't disappoint the boss.

"Right, that will do for starters," said Gus, "I'll check the rest of the schedule on my computer."

"We're waiting on the Hub to provide the results of the search we requested, guv," said Neil.

Gus thanked Neil and returned to his desk. The list of registered sex offenders might prove a time-consuming red herring. The former lovers could raise more potential suspects and, with them, embarrassing questions. He didn't know whether to share the knowledge he had learned from Terry Davis about Culverhouse with the team. The fewer people who knew, the better. He was particularly wary of letting Neil know he'd talked with his father. The way Neil had been with him since he arrived suggested Melody had kept her word.

Oh, what a tangled web, and that was nothing compared to the fifteen-year-old murder case they were tackling. Events over the past few days had left precious little time to mull over the few facts they had. Gus prided himself on spotting weaknesses in witness testimonies, finding scraps of information that nudged him towards the guilty party.

He wasn't sure whether it was the nonsense around him, partly self-inflicted, or just one of those cases. Had Trudi Villiers been killed by a total stranger visiting the town that week? Someone on a contract job. It was food for thought.

Gus wished he had time to spend on his allotment. Not for gardening but to sit and think. This consultancy role was turning out to be far more time-consuming than he'd imagined. He brought the Freeman file up on his computer to check Neil's proposed itinerary.

"Can you spare an hour, Lydia," he asked. An idea had popped into his head.

"Yes, guv, what do you need me to do?"

"Walk with me. I want to get my head around the relative positions of each destination involved on the night of the murder."

Neil was puzzled.

"Destinations, guv, what do you mean?"

"Krystal Warner and James Bosworth travelled by taxi to the place she shared with Trudi Villiers. What direction would they take? Where is it on the estate relative to where Tony and Tristram Virgo lived? Where is it relative to the sloped pathway leaving the estate that leads onto Riverside Walk? What direction would Saeed Gill take to get Bosworth home after he and Krystal had a falling out? Where was that house situated on the opposite side of town? The destinations are important because they determine the timings. Where does Steve Li live? Could he have taken more than one route to get home? Did the rock group travel together to the Ring O'Bells? It wasn't uncommon for bands to pile into a Ford Transit and drive hundreds of miles to gigs in the old days. These days a fraction of venues remain from the Sixties and Seventies. A lot of bands only play local gigs these days. This band came from the Salisbury area. That's a big place. I once lived in Downton. That's six miles on the other side of the city from here. One guy may have lived in Wilton, three or four miles west. As far as Gary Smith was concerned, he was still booking a band from Salisbury. Their destinations after leaving the pub are important. Maybe, one guy drove the van with the kit, and the others travelled by car. I'm looking at the map and the photos from the murder site. I can't see whether any of those I mentioned are ruled out based on an unchecked time factor. Something doesn't add up. I can't put my finger on it yet."

Alex and Neil realised they had a heavy workload on their hands. Time to graft.

"It's a grand day for a walk, guv," said Lydia, striding towards the lift.

"We'll see you two in an hour. Try not to miss us too much," said Gus.

He joined Lydia, and they emerged in the bright sunshine in the car park. Gus had left his jacket and tie in the office. He was still warm. His female companion had taken note of the mild lecture he'd given her last week. Lydia's colour scheme was less bright, with a striped blouse and black skirt. A printed bamboo headband had tamed the explosion of curly hair. She looked stunning, and Gus noticed admiring looks from every sex as they walked along the High Street.

Hark at him; he thought, every sex; it was hard to keep up with the different options available these days. He wondered whether they would identify fifty-seven in his lifetime. Good luck designing something as simple as a public convenience in the future. Unisex toilets solved the issues of space limitations when 'Gents' and 'Ladies' became contentious. He tried to envisage the ultimate one-size-fits-all building. He gave up. There weren't areas the size of a football pitch available in any cities and towns he knew. Something had to give. He hoped he wasn't around, so his bladder needed to cope.

"Penny for them, guv," said Lydia.

"Perfect," said Gus laughing out loud.

Lydia decided it must be an age thing and let it slide.

The pair continued to walk in silence past the Crown pub, into Market Square and beyond until they reached the river bridge. Before the bridge, there were five steps to a walkway, then twenty yards farther on, five more steps brought them onto Riverside Walk.

"How long since we left the Old Police Station," asked Gus.

"Eight minutes," Lydia replied, "but we need to check with Steve Li. Was Trudi strolling along, walking at a steady pace as we were, or was she in a hurry?"

"Well done. Mr Li was the only witness to see whether she was on a mission to get home or in no hurry. Youngsters spend a lot of time wandering with their heads stuck in their phones. Trudi wasn't scrolling through her messages, or catching up with social media, was she? That hadn't exploded yet. A world without Facebook. How did we manage?"

"She could have been speaking with someone. Maybe agreeing to meet them," suggested Lydia.

"Another question for Steve Li," said Gus, warming to the task. "The phone call may have been later after Trudi passed Market Square or here on Riverside Walk. Nobody would have seen or heard her then."

"What a pity the police never found her phone."

"Did anything missing strike you as odd?" asked Gus. "Her skirt, underwear, phone and shoes."

"The police believed she was raped and murdered," said Lydia. "It makes sense that the killer removed her clothing. Her shoes could have come off in the struggle. Mobile phones are always worth a few quid on the black market."

"What was it Mr Spock used to say on Star Trek? It does not compute, Captain?"

"Before my time, guv," said Lydia.

Gus sighed.

"Hang on. I'll come back to that. Is this the exit onto the Greenwood Estate?"

Lydia left the pathway and walked up the slope to the road.

"Yes, guv. There are houses as far as the eye can see. The local primary school is fifty yards to my left."

"I made that five minutes, agreed?"

"Bang on, five minutes by my watch. It's this way, guv,"

Lydia wondered why Gus wasn't joining her.

"Come and join me," called Gus, who was now under the bridge continuing along Riverside Walk.

"Why would Trudi have come this way, guv?" asked Lydia, running to catch him.

"The place Trudi and Krystal shared was on the north end of the Greenwood. In another two minutes, judging by the bridge I can see ahead, we'll have another exit onto the Estate. So, was it easier to access the property from there rather than thread her way through various roads and alleyways? Trudi discovered this pathway was dangerous late at night, but she might have thought there was less risk than among the dark alleyways on that notorious council estate. There's another possibility. Did she meet her attacker on this side of the bridge? Was her body moved to the shrubbery near the slope we'd just passed? Look around you. There are precious few hiding places for a body on this side of the bridge."

Lydia tried to make sense of it. Last week, a stroll through the countryside in Lowden Woods had made things clearer in both their minds. Today, her head was spinning with the new variables her boss added to the mix.

"Do you have the actual address for the two girls?" Gus asked.

"I've read it but can't remember it, sorry."

"Call Neil. Get the street name and the number," said Gus, walking back to the first exit.

Gus wandered across to the shrubbery behind the tree line. The murder site had altered so much in the past fifteen years; it was unrecognisable. They would learn nothing there.

Lydia had received the answer they needed from Neil.

"44A Kingfisher Close," she said.

"I toured the Greenwood with Neil last week," said Gus, "it's well signposted. You go through the roads and alley-ways. I'll take Riverside Walk. Just a steady walk. Time yourself, and we'll compare notes. Remember what I said about what was missing from the body while you were walk-ing? If you haven't solved it, I'll try to explain outside 44A."

Gus found Kingfisher Close as soon as he climbed the slope from Riverside Walk. The even numbers were on his left-hand side as he made his way along the pavement. There was no sign of Lydia.

It had taken him three minutes from the murder site. Gus basked in the sun's heat.

He finally spotted her on the corner of the street and waved. Lydia closed the gap between them.

"Blimey, did you run?" she asked.

"No, a steady walk. Three minutes."

Lydia looked at her watch.

"Eight minutes. I know why that is, guv, and if I lived here, I'd use the Riverside Walk every time. You can't cover the ground through the estate as the crow flies. You head along one street, and an alleyway takes you into the next. The connecting street or alley is never directly opposite. You either head for the main road or continue crisscrossing the estate via the alleys. There are no shortcuts for a stranger."

"That confirms what I thought. Trudi's attacker could have come from town, behind her, or from the two Riverside Walk access points off the Greenwood."

"I've thought about the missing items," said Lydia, "I still can't see how we couldn't explain them as I suggested."

"Oh, they could," said Gus, "but only if there were a series of attackers, and they had different motives."

"You've lost me, guv,"

"Start with our rapist. Let's assume he's local; he knows Trudi and has a grudge. We first know that he must have been in the Ring O'Bells that night. Otherwise, he wouldn't have known Trudi worked late. Our man also knows Trudi's route home if she's walking. He lies in wait far enough away from the Imperial Dragon that Steve Li doesn't see him. Then he follows Trudi to the riverside and attacks her near the first bridge. Trudi loses her shoes. He rips off her underwear and skirt and rapes her. The situation changes, and the rape isn't enough for him. Either during the attack or straight after, he stabs Trudi to death in a frenzied attack."

Lydia had an idea. Was this what Gus meant?

"Why didn't he use a condom?" she asked.

"Good girl. That's one question we should ask," said Gus. "Show me a criminal who doesn't know DNA is the last thing they should leave at a crime scene. Lewington didn't leave many clues. Did he on any of his genuine attacks? If our man's planned this attack, he would have taken every precaution not to get caught. He had no use for the clothes or shoes. He had no use for the purse and mobile phone. So why are they missing?"

"Could the motive have been a robbery?"

"That was one of my hypotheses," said Gus, "a

mugging that went wrong. An addict was looking for cash and a mobile phone to buy their next fix. Again, the shoes may have come off in the initial contact. It doesn't explain the removal of the other items from the scene. Then, I considered whether we have two crimes — a mugger who nicks her purse and phone. Trudi's pissed off but continues to walk home. What option did she have? When she thought her night couldn't get any worse, her killer jumped out from the bushes..."

"Oh, come on, you can't seriously believe that," cried Lydia, "anyway, what about her shoes? Neither of those attackers would take them."

"What size feet does Tony Virgo have? Trudi was a size six. That's a legitimate explanation for the shoes. Maybe he's a drag artist. Nothing in the murder file to suggest otherwise. What's the betting that he and Tristram perform in the clubs over in Benidorm? A few cut-and-blow-dry gigs for pensioners won't balance the books. He grabbed the shoes, thinking someone had discarded them and went to investigate the shape he could see behind the trees. When the emergency services arrived, he could hardly admit he'd stolen the victim's shoes, could he?"

Lydia couldn't believe her ears.

"Are you winding me up, guv? Okay, I'll check when we get back to the office, but far-fetched doesn't cover the scenario you're painting."

"Finally," said Gus, with a grin, "we're on the same page. I said it didn't feel right. There's only one possible scenario that fits. Over the next week, our interviews will tell us whether or not I'm right."

"Tell me what that is," implored Lydia. "I can't imagine how you've worked out the answer from what few real facts we know."

"Don't rush ahead too far. I haven't got *the* answer. We haven't finished fact-gathering yet," said Gus. "Let's walk back into town via the main road through the Greenwood. It's the only route I can find for the taxi to have used that night. Then, when we talk with Amy Pollock, we'll see whether the timings work. If not, it will blow my theory out of the water."

"Do we tell the boys you think you might have cracked the case?"

"Easy, tiger. So far, I've only produced a scenario that fits the facts," said Gus, "I haven't worked out who did it."

"I'm more confused than ever," said Lydia.

"It's always darkest before the dawn," said Gus, "you've done well today. Don't admonish yourself. Do you want another question to answer?"

"Is it a question with only one sensible answer?"

"What happened to the murder weapon?"

"Well, the killer wouldn't have left it at the scene, would he? It was a short-bladed weapon. Easy to conceal in a pocket of his jacket or jeans. A Stanley knife or a screwdriver. Something similar to the weapons Lewington carried to threaten his victims. Even though we know Lewington didn't do it, it's still the most likely type of weapon. The killer would never have left it for the police to find."

"Keep thinking," said Gus, "criminals can often be stupid; it's the simplest mistake that traps them. As you say, the killer wouldn't leave a knife for us to find. Please don't mention my theory to the lads. There's a long way to go before we nail the killer."

"I understand, guv,"

It took them over twenty-five minutes to walk back to the Old Police Station. Gus told Lydia to suggest to Neil and Alex that they take an early lunch. He wanted to drive home. He needed his head clear before this afternoon's meeting with the ACC.

It had been a strange morning.

Gus was unaccompanied on his trip back to Devizes.

He must have caught his escort on the hop. Maybe a consultant was only entitled to be shadowed from five o'clock in the evening; a spur-of-the-moment decision over half a day's holiday confused matters. When he met with the ACC later, he should ask whether he needed a note for permission to skive off early.

Gus recognised there were two upsides to the situation. It meant he wasn't under constant surveillance by his side. Also, the Albanians might have someone ready to pounce if he stepped over the line and entered the lane behind Cambrai Terrace; but he wasn't worth sitting on while he went about his regular duties.

After a quick lunch, Gus walked to his allotment. Bert Penman was working on his own patch today. He stood and admired Bert's efforts.

"Not looking too bad, is it, Mr Freeman?" said Bert, leaning on his fork for a breather.

"You've worked wonders, Bert," he replied.

"Enjoy this next few days of sunshine, Mr Freeman. We'll pay for this. You mark my words. I don't usually have to water my little darlings as early as this. My water butt is only half full. We may have had a bitter spell to finish the winter, but the days of February fill-dyke are long gone."

Gus understood Bert's age-old expression. It was one the old-timers still used, even though similar truisms had become redundant with the rapid progress of climate change. For example, February had traditionally been a month when rain or melting snow filled the watercourses in England.

In the countryside, far from the nearest river, allotment holders had a series of water butts or old dustbins to collect rainwater. Every precious drop was needed to keep their plants alive. With rising summer temperatures, the threat of a hosepipe ban was only a brief dry spell away. At least the various methods they used to collect something from every random shower protected them from that restriction.

"So, you've found a few moments to come here to think. This latest job of yours is tricky, am I right?"

"It is. You know me too well. I wanted to use the time before my next meeting to go over things in my mind."

"Say no more, Mr Freeman. I'll ask one final question, and then I'll leave you to your thinking. Have they found out who killed poor Frank yet?"

"It's something I can't handle, as you know, Bert. I'm always hopeful of an early arrest in cases like Frank North's."

"Fair enough. I only asked because I'm taking vegetables over to Irene later. I just hoped I could give her a piece of good news. She hasn't even been able to set a date for the funeral yet."

"I'm meeting someone later who might tell me when the body will be released. I can't promise I'll be able to update you on the case, though."

Bert nodded. He knew the way the world worked.

Gus watched him return to his labours. His fork turned over the soil with practised ease. Work he'd put into his allotment over the years saw the clod of dirt fall apart into lumps no bigger than breadcrumbs. No wonder his vegetables grew so well. They didn't have to struggle through layers of clay to the surface. This was paradise.

If only he could stay here all afternoon. The conversation with Bert had eaten into his thinking time. Gus went over his ideas about Trudi Villiers's murder. It was a reason-able hypothesis, but everything hinged on the timing. If one of those was out of synch with his proposition, the whole thing collapsed.

The interviews would prove fascinating. Gus reminded himself of Terry Davis and his handling of the case. It was imperative he didn't make the same mistake and tried to make the facts fit his hare-brained ideas.

Lydia had wanted him to share those ideas with Alex and Neil. There was no way he'd do that.

Alex had to go into those interviews with an open mind. Lydia might accompany him on those visits. He needed to reinforce the warning he'd given her this morning. She was still only a raw recruit, even if she showed the potential to become a good detective.

It was time to head for London Road. He only prayed that the ACC let him stay long enough to sample Kassie Trotter's chocolate eclairs.

Chapter Eight

GUS ARRIVED at London Road with several minutes to spare. He had time to sign in, get upstairs to the administration floor and locate Vera Jennings well before his two o'clock meeting.

Vera was chatting with Kassie Trotter. Nothing new there. They both gave him a beaming smile as he approached. A clear sign they had been talking about him and desperately trying to hide the fact.

"Good afternoon, Mr Freeman," said Kassie, "you look stressed. Are you sure you're getting enough sleep?"

Ah, they had been discussing Suzie Ferris and her overnight stay. The rumour mill was in full flow. Suzie had promised what happened on protection duty stayed there and that she didn't tell Vera everything. There was no point stirring up a hornet's nest. Least said, soonest mended.

"I'm getting enough, thanks, Kassie," he replied, then wished he hadn't.

Vera raised an eyebrow on the young girl's behalf. Kassie's sat way up on her forehead already.

Vera steered him away from Kassie's desk.

"I missed you earlier," said Vera, "I hear it was a lively meeting. Suzie thought you were about to punch one of the nation's highest-ranked officers."

"I thought he must be important," said Gus, "but he was still a shit."

"Are we good for tomorrow evening?"

"I wouldn't miss it for the world."

"It's just a meal. Do I detect a problem?"

"Only with the venue. A witness in our latest case is now the landlady at the Ring O'Bells. We're interviewing her tomorrow at half past nine. There's no point in antagonising people by turning up at their place of work only hours after you've interrogated them. They scream harassment and run for a lawyer."

"Leave it with me," said Vera, "I know the couple who run the Ferret at Newton Bridge. It's a quiet country pub that will suit us very well. Good food and not busy midweek in the early evening. We're far less likely to bump into anyone familiar."

"I knew I could trust you to have the answer," said Gus.

"I'll book a table for half-past six. That will give you time to drive home and get showered and changed."

"It's just a meal," he said.

Vera gave him an enigmatic smile and returned to her desk. Gus wondered where the heck he might find Newton Bridge. How did a village he'd never heard of keep springing up out of nowhere?

As he struggled with the geography of this corner of West Wiltshire, two uniformed officers joined him by the ACC's door. Geoff Mercer and Suzie Ferris.

"Will I enjoy this?" Gus asked.

"Take your punishment like a grown-up," said Geoff,

"the ACC's in the same boat as me. Truelove can hardly sack you, can he? Well, he might, but your pension's safe."

Suzie knocked, and the ACC invited them in.

"We have lots to get through," said Kenneth Truelove, "sit yourselves down and let's get on with it."

Gus knew the ACC was flustered because he sat behind his executive desk. There was no one by the window staring out over the visitor's car park. The room seemed off-kilter, somehow.

"First things first, Freeman. I gather you took it upon yourself to call Terry Davis for advice on the Villiers case. That was most unwise. What on earth possessed you?"

"May I remind you I agreed to return to work on the understanding that I ran the CRT without interference? You said DS Mercer was my immediate superior and that he let his staff run their sections how they saw fit. Geoff only got involved if he felt things had gone off-track. I phoned Terry Davis to get background information not included in the murder file. It was a legitimate enquiry...."

"Davis screwed up the investigation," the ACC interrupted, "and they imprisoned an innocent man."

"Lewington was hardly innocent. As for Terry Davis, he claims Culverhouse made him take the shortcuts he did. Perhaps that left the murder file lacking detail."

"Are you suggesting they falsified the file? That's a serious accusation."

"Falsified is a strong word. However, I believe they filtered information, so the misdirection Davis received no longer appeared."

"Tread with care, Freeman."

"Do you know who is feeding Terry Davis information? He knew of the death threat I received and that OCTF conducted surveillance on Monty Jennings's shed. I wonder how many people here at London Road have his phone number in Marbella?"

"I hope that none of them does," said the ACC. "This mole might be a retired officer, someone who Davis worked with even before 2003. Moving on, what were you thinking of this morning? I thought you wanted to assault Brendan Curran."

"Curran didn't care about Frank North's death, nor was he interested in the death threat I received."

"Curran's a man you would do well not to annoy," said the ACC, "he could make your life very awkward. However, he's not blind to your situation. The gangster who broke into your bungalow is Eron Dushka. He's an Albanian who came to this country under the guise of being a Kosovan refugee. When this case moves to its natural conclusion, they will arrest Dushka."

"Did he tell you this before we arrived this morning, Sir?" asked Suzie Ferris.

The ACC looked most indignant. Suzie suggested he had known the burglar's identity while Gus and Curran went head to head.

"Of course not," said Truelove, "Brendan called me thirty minutes ago from London. He updated us on the investigation's current status. I can't divulge any details; the information is hush-hush for the next forty-eight hours."

That was good news, Gus thought. The ACC would never make a poker player. He tells us he can't tell us a thing, and then he says we only have to wait two days. So, unless something went pear-shaped between now and Friday afternoon to damage a link in the chain, OCTF would wrap up the whole business. Gus had an idea. He would share it with Geoff Mercer when a convenient opportunity arose.

"I'm sure we wish Brendan and OCTF good luck," said the ACC. "Meanwhile, when will you see real progress with the Villiers case, Freeman?"

"Interviews start in the morning, Sir. We'll have a better picture once we've analysed those results. Neil Davis has put a request into the Hub for the registered sex offenders in the area at the time of the murder. Neil's waiting to receive that."

"Good to learn you're utilising their excellent facilities, Freeman."

Gus had only mentioned it because he knew the ACC believed it to be the answer to a maiden's prayer.

"I'm surprised Neil Davis is involved. Is that wise?"

"I've discussed the matter with my immediate superior, and he agrees that I've taken the right action. I restricted Davis to office duties from the outset. DS Hardy and Lydia Logan Barre will assist me in the field."

"How are they both shaping up?"

"Lydia is a quick learner, very astute. She has the makings of a fine detective if handled well. She has much to learn yet, though. Ask me again in twelve months. DS Hardy and DS Davis are excellent officers. You wouldn't have selected them for CRT otherwise. Neil's father was guilty of laziness rather than real malice. Terry got passed over for promotion so often he got pissed off with trying his best. He had one DI who got the best out of him. When Hounsell left for pastures new in London, Terry Davis was side-lined by Culverhouse. He had cultivated the perfect patsy when the need arose for someone to take the fall."

"You are on dangerous ground, Freeman," warned the ACC.

"Look, you aren't a fellow traveller. None of us ever joined the Masons. The brotherhood protects Saint

Dominic, but if he's guilty of perverting the course of justice, we should pursue him, regardless."

"The evidence needs to be iron-clad," said Geoff Mercer. "Unless we bring Terry Davis back from Marbella to testify against him, I'm not sure how we'd get the CPS to move forward with a prosecution. Culverhouse's supporters would want Davis to face a similar charge. Even if we persuaded a jury that coercion led Davis into doctoring the evidence, he'd serve jail time. They buried the Lewington case. There won't be an appetite for it to resurface."

"This goes no further than these four walls," said Kenneth Truelove, "I wish I could support you in this matter. It doesn't surprise me that Culverhouse had skeletons in the cupboard. I retire in fifteen months."

"Understood," said Gus, "you have too much to lose."

"No, you misunderstand me," said the ACC. "If we can gather the evidence, then as soon as I'm pensioned off and booked on my first cruise, I'll add my name to any initiative you put forward. As long as I'm sensible between now and then, having my name attached to it should count for something."

"I can think of nothing worse than being on a big boat with a thousand strangers," said Gus. "I didn't have you tagged as a fan of cruising."

"My wife is the fan, Freeman. She's been looking at brochures since I reached fifty. I prefer to spend my time volunteering with underprivileged and abused kids."

"The tea trolley is outside," said Gus, "I reckon one of your successes will breeze in here in a second."

There was a loud knock at the door, and Kassie Trotter entered the room.

"Cups of coffee and chocolate eclairs, as promised; I always deliver."

"Thank you, Kassie," said the ACC.

As she leaned over the trolley to hand him his cup of coffee, Gus noticed she had added another tattoo. The blue-bird now had a mate. A lonely heart lay on the other breast.

"Still no boyfriend, Kassie?" he whispered.

"No idea how you do it, Mr Freeman. Sherlock Holmes had nothing on you."

"Remember what Soren Kierkegaard advised," he whispered.

"Did he star in one of those Scandinavian thrillers I never watched?"

Gus shook his head.

"No, Kassie, he said, '*don't forget to love yourself*'."

Kassie giggled.

"That's saucy, Mr Freeman," she said. Then she turned and saw the others tucking into their chocolate eclairs.

"It's catching," she said as she wheeled her trolley out of the room.

"No idea what that meant," said Geoff Mercer, wiping chocolate and cream from his chin with a serviette.

"Not to worry," said Gus.

After getting through their refreshments without mishap, the ACC looked ready to bring the meeting to a close.

"I've got two matters to raise, Sir," said Gus, "I didn't have anyone riding shotgun when I returned here at lunchtime. You asked me to attend, so I assumed you noti-fied the people concerned. I left earlier than necessary to reach here for two. Are they still searching for me, or has the threat gone?"

"I had forgotten to arrange it and was about to remedy matters when Brendan rang. I didn't realise you had already left. In the light of his call, I decided the escort wasn't vital."

"Let's hope your confidence isn't misplaced, Sir," said Suzie Ferris, "Gus will be impossible to replace. Will someone be on watch this evening and overnight?"

"The existing schedule remains in place until further notice," the ACC confirmed.

"Until after Friday," said Gus.

The mortified expression on the ACC's face told Gus he hadn't realised his error.

"One last thing," Gus said, "when will Irene North be able to bury her late husband? How much longer do forensics intend to hang on to him?"

"I understand the body went to the coroner this morning," said the ACC, "they have better facilities for storage than the police. The coroner will go through the necessary procedures. I don't foresee any problems. Mrs North will be free to arrange her husband's funeral in a week to ten days."

"I'll pass the message on," said Gus, "that's it. Can I be on my way?"

"Yes, Freeman. Remember what I said. Tread with care. The CRT is still in its infancy. If you start rattling cages, people higher up the ladder than me will end your operation without a moment's notice."

"Message received and understood."

Gus headed for the door, and Geoff Mercer and Suzie Ferris joined him outside.

"Are you heading back to the office?" Suzie asked.

"Plenty can be achieved in an hour,"

"I'll bear that in mind," she replied, "enjoy your meal tomorrow night."

"We might be busy on Friday if your supposition is correct," said Geoff, "if not, I suggest we meet up for a pint again."

"If you can tear yourself away, that would be great,"

Gus said, "but I may need to call you before then. I've got a suggestion you might enjoy. It will be just like old times."

"That sounds intriguing," said Geoff.

Gus said his goodbyes and gave Kassie a friendly wave. He couldn't see Vera Jennings anywhere, but tomorrow would arrive soon enough. As he pushed through the front door, the mid-afternoon heat hit him like a ton of bricks.

Air conditioning in offices had been a fantastic invention, but Gus knew the interior would be as hot as hell when he opened his car door. Of course, he would have loved to have opened the windows, but that was a considerable risk. They would either have stuck halfway or dropped, never to rise again.

The school run ended, and traffic inched through the town centre; everything was designed to make his journey as excruciating as possible. When he reached the car park at the rear of the Old Police Station, he was in meltdown.

Gus reached the blessed relief of the cool interior of the CRT office.

"What have we learned this afternoon?" he asked.

"I've finalised the interview date with Steve Li and his wife. Trudi Villiers's parents are getting back to me tomorrow. If we want to Skype Tony Virgo and his husband early next week, they're available on Monday or Tuesday morning."

"Thanks, Neil," said Gus.

"It will have to be late on Monday morning, guv," Neil continued.

"Sunday night is cabaret night," said Lydia, with a big grin on her face.

"Tony the Tigress and Tristram Dacunha are big in Benidorm," said Neil.

Gus didn't pass comment. He hoped Lydia had kept her mouth shut about the shoes.

"The Hub has promised to send the registered sex-offenders list over to us in the morning," said Alex. "Neil and Lydia can start work on it while we interview Krystal Warner."

"Are you set for the morning, Alex?"

"Yes, guv. We don't see Krystal until half-past nine, so I'll come up here as normal, and then we can scoot over the road to the pub to see Krystal. The pub has wheelchair access. I won't need this chair much longer if my rehab continues to go well. So does my diet, thanks to helpful hints from Lydia. I put weight on after the accident just sitting around. The more I can shift before I retire from this wheel-chair, the less time I'll need to support my weight using crutches."

"That's great, Alex. Don't rush it and set yourself back another six months. Make sure the move from sitting to standing is permanent."

"Don't worry, guv, we're keeping on top of it," said Lydia.

Gus wondered just how much time those two spent together. Should he worry? A relationship between his team would be another arrow in the quiver of those people the ACC mentioned who wanted an excuse to close the unit.

Gus didn't fundamentally object to Lydia and Alex being an item. They would be separated once it became public knowledge. That was the way it had always been since women joined the force. He could ill afford to lose either of them.

For now, Gus decided to keep a watching brief and updated the Freeman file on his computer. A quick skim through everything they had gathered so far occupied him for the rest of the afternoon. At five o'clock, he joined the others in the lift, and once in the car park, the team went their different ways.

Lydia's red Mini turned right onto High Street and sped away. Alex and Neil's cars turned left. His own ageing Ford Focus still felt like sitting inside an oven. As he joined the traffic flow heading out of town, he saw his escort file in behind him off Crook Way. Normal service had been resumed.

Gus dropped by the allotments on his way home. Not to confuse the driver in the car behind but to see whether Bert Penman had left. He spotted him sitting outside his shed, cleaning his tools. If Gus had been ten minutes later, he would have missed him.

"Afternoon, Mr Freeman," said Bert, "twice in one day. Who's your friend?"

"Oh, just a colleague, Bert. I have news for Irene North; the coroner should release Frank's body by the end of next week. She can make the funeral arrangements. Does Irene have anyone staying with her at present?"

"Someone in the family paid a visit, but I can't say if anyone stopped there."

"That's a shame. Neither had a big family. Irene said those still alive lived a distance away. When you take those vegetables over to her, tell her we're thinking of her. Let me know when the funeral is, and I'll make sure we spread the word."

"Right you are, Mr Freeman."

Gus turned to leave. He wanted to tell Bert the other news he'd heard. Irene deserved closure. Village life being what it was, though, a word in Bert or Irene's ear now would be common knowledge over a six-mile radius before the ten o'clock news. Moreover, it might jeopardise the OCTF operation.

Gus returned to his car and drove up the lane to the bungalow. His escort parked in the layby opposite and settled in for what they both hoped would be a quiet evening. Gus headed for the shower as soon as he got indoors. It had been a hot, sticky day — time to freshen up.

Gus heard the phone as he stood under a cool jet of water.

Whoever had called could wait. Perhaps, it was that lady searching for Dorothy? He hadn't heard from her for a while, which pleased him. She had entertained him with her bridge club messages and ignored his insistence that she had dialled the wrong number.

When he had towelled himself dry, he wandered through to the lounge with the towel tied around his waist. The number looked familiar. He listened to the brief message.

'Our representative will visit you tomorrow between noon and six pm.'

The immediate panic for security cameras might be over, but needs must. It was a sensible move to increase the level of security on the place. There was no point in inviting burglars to make you a target. Even if the cameras were just for show, they could prove enough of a deterrent for all but the desperate criminal. Gus hoped there weren't too many of those deep in the Wiltshire countryside.

Another half-day. Alex and Lydia would interview Maggie Smith in the afternoon. He could brief them on what they needed to learn from that conversation in the morning.

Gus felt hungry, but he didn't fancy adding to the heat in the bungalow by cooking. He decided on a takeaway. As he picked up the phone, he paused. That poor chap sat outside in a stuffy pool car wouldn't eat until after ten when his replacement arrived.

Gus returned to his bedroom to find something suitable to wear. He strolled out to the car in his t-shirt and shorts. Tess had always told him that with his legs, he should be excused from shorts. He had always thought that harsh. Tonight, it was too warm to care.

"Chinese or Indian?" he asked.

"Pizza would be kinder, Sir. They don't stink the car up so much. The other drivers who use this car won't thank me."

"I'm ordering a large Hawaiian. We can manage half each, can't we?"

"If I don't finish it, I can always leave a slice for my mate. That's great, thanks."

Gus returned indoors and made the call. He selected a classical album and listened to the first side. Almost as the final notes sounded, the doorbell rang. Perfect timing.

Gus cut the pizza in half and slid his portion onto a plate. After he delivered the box to his new friend, he tucked into his meal. Still only a quarter to seven. How best to spend the rest of the evening?

He called Geoff Mercer; his wife, Christine, answered. Geoff was at work. She promised to get her husband to ring back if he got home at a reasonable time. Christine didn't sound confident. Gus assumed they were organising support for the OCTF raid on Monty's shed.

Gus turned over the album and listened to the other side. Another excellent piece of timing. When the phone rang, he had just finished a long cool glass of orange juice.

"You wanted to speak to me urgently, Gus," said Geoff.

"It wasn't life or death. I take it they've rushed you off your feet this evening?"

"Curran rang the ACC an hour after you left. OCTF are panicking over the undercover guy in the Swindon gang. They haven't been able to contact him. So to warn him, the raids commence at dawn on Friday."

"What did the ACC agree to do?"

"They're switching people from the Cambrai Terrace raid to lift him before he risks being exposed. We're supplying bodies to assist in the raid on Monty Jennings's building."

"Please tell me that you're leading that operation?"

"Yes, but why do I sense that makes you happy? It could be a nightmare. Those guys are armed and dangerous."

"Remember the old days, when we didn't get on as well as we do today. I want you to turn the clock back and stick it to Brendan Curran."

Geoff laughed.

"You are a devious sod, Gus Freeman. If I get the chance to get in front of a TV camera, I will."

"Remember to take care of yourself, Geoff. I'll let you spend quality time with Christine."

"Cheeky beggar. Would she fall for it, though? Imagine we're in the trenches, darling, and at dawn, we go over the top...."

"Goodnight, Geoff."

"Whatever."

Thursday, 19 April 2018

THERE WAS no change to the weather when he opened his eyes and peeked through the curtains.

Gus hadn't slept well. He couldn't decide who or what to blame. Was it because it had been the warmest night of the year so far? Did it have to do with the fact he was seeing Vera tonight? The imminent raid on the drug farm on the hillside was never far from his thoughts nor the death threat he'd received.

What troubled him most was his cold case seemed to be at the bottom of a long list. He could only spend this morning trying to test his theory. Another afternoon was occupied sorting out trivial matters. Today, it was where his CCTV cameras were to be sited and agreeing on the instal-lation date.

No matter how sensible the move might be, it still posed an unwelcome interruption. Gus missed Tess at times like this.

Tess would have been available to pick up these loose ends. Her shift pattern had meant she was home far more often than him, which was never. Tess would have dealt with the glazier and the security consultant with a smile on her face. Gus saw these obstacles preventing him from doing what he did best - solve crimes.

He could imagine what these visitors said when they got home or back to base. 'Miserable old git. You wouldn't think we're doing him a favour.'

Gus started the day with a fried breakfast. He needed something to cheer him up, even if it lay heavy on his stomach on a warm morning. Life was just a bowl of poisoned cherries some days.

Gus stepped outside the front door a minute before half-past eight. He needed the traffic light on the roads this morning to beat the rest of his team into the office.

Gus drove through the gateway and into the lane. His overnight protection officer was already moving forward to follow him from the nearby layby. Gus wondered whether he had found a slice of pizza. There was no sign of a discarded box, so credit to whichever driver now had it. It was destined for recycling and not thrown into the undergrowth by the roadside.

As they passed the gateway to the allotments, Gus thought of Bert Penman. He wondered what Irene made of the produce he had delivered to her last evening. He hoped she was taking care of herself. He could discuss that with Bert and the others from the allotments. Irene's family wouldn't be around much after the funeral, by the sound of things. So the village community should ensure she doesn't get lonely or stop bothering to feed herself. They had to be subtle about how they offered a helping hand. He could imagine Irene bristling at too many visitors and telling them she didn't need charity.

A car sped past him at the widest point in the lane. He had been distracted, and the black Mercedes missed him by inches. Gus braked hard. What was this guy doing? The driver leapt out, and Gus saw the gun.

The escort driver reacted as soon as he saw Gus's taillights. He sprang out of the car and drew his weapon.

Gus took evasive action and dived to his left across the passenger seat. The windscreen shattered half a second later.

He heard the protection officer shout a warning to his assailant. Then two shots rang out. Gus held his breath. He felt every one of his sixty-one years. "I'm getting too old for this," he sighed.

"Are you alright, Sir?"

It was the escort driver calling him. Gus slid back into the driving seat.

He saw the gunman on the ground behind the Mercedes through the broken windscreen. He was alive but wounded. The young officer who had just saved his life stood over him, gun in hand.

"Fine, thanks to you. I never saw the car coming. Where did he appear from?"

"He shot out of the car park behind the pub, Sir. He's taken a bullet to the shoulder and another to the stomach. The latter might give him more of a problem if he's to see out the day. Can you call the cavalry while I secure him and try to stem the blood flow?"

Gus retrieved his mobile phone and dialled 999. While they waited for their colleagues and the ambulance crew, he looked at his beloved Ford Focus.

"Where are the bullets, Sir?"

"In the bloody headrest," said Gus.

Gus leaned against the bonnet of his car, unsure whether his legs would hold him. He shook like a leaf.

If he'd moved a split second later, he would have been a dead man.

Chapter Nine

THE PROTECTION OFFICER tended to the man on the ground.

The shoulder wound looked painful, but the bullet had missed anything vital. The officer dragged the man's leather jacket down his arms to restrict his movements. Neither police officer understood what the gunman said. It didn't sound complimentary. The bullet in the gut had taken most of the fight out of him.

"Stay quiet and let me press this cloth on this hole, mate," he said, "you're not going anywhere. If I have to, I'll handcuff you to the back of your Merc and leave you to bleed out."

Another volley of abuse spewed at him

"Who do we have here, anyway?" Gus asked.

"He wasn't carrying any papers in his leather jacket. His driving licence looks dodgy, even if the photo looks like him from ten years ago. I doubt he's called Erik Drago."

They heard the sounds of sirens in the distance.

"So, this must be Eron Dushka," said Gus, "the bastard

who broke into my bungalow and maybe murdered Frank North."

"The gun is on the grass verge,"

"Don't tempt me," said Gus. "Okay, I'll ensure the cavalry does not trample on it. Forensics can check if it's the same gun. You concentrate on keeping him alive."

Gus looked up and down the lane. His escort's car had parked at an angle of forty-five degrees across the road when he exited the driver's door and prepared to fire, which had offered him maximum protection. Thank goodness he knew what he was doing.

"Have you seen anyone driving this way from the village?" Gus asked.

"Two cars and a van. The excitement ended in seconds. They didn't arrive until afterwards. I reckon they thought there had been a road accident. They turned around in the widest stretch we passed back and headed away from us."

"I haven't seen anyone coming this way from Devizes except these vehicles just arriving. We can persuade them to keep this quiet."

"I think I can see where you're going with this, Sir. It's a quiet spot. There weren't many cars passing to keep me from falling asleep outside your bungalow the last few nights."

"I don't even know your name," said Gus.

"DS Luke Sherman, Sir,"

"Call me Gus, for crying out loud. I'm glad you were here, Luke."

"It's why we do the job. Rick Chalmers told me you were a decent bloke, so we agreed to do our best," said Luke with a brief smile. He struggled to cope with Dushka's wound. It looked serious, and the swearing was less frequent.

"I had the chance to chat with Rick last evening."

"Rick told me when he handed over last night that you treated him to pizza."

"Did he leave you a slice?"

"Don't be daft. Rick scoffed the lot."

"That sounds like him."

Gus wandered away to view the overall scene.

The Merc was parked across the lane, blocking access for any vehicles. Gus realised that between these high hedges on either side, they had a minimum of a sixty-yard stretch where they could paint the picture that suited their purpose.

It might have been quiet in the lane, except for a few Albanian swear words. But the activity ramped up several notches as an ambulance crew and several police officers threaded their way past the Merc and approached him.

"Who have we got here?" asked the officer in charge.

It was a young Detective Inspector Gus hadn't met. Maybe the same age as Suzie Ferris. Luke Sherman knew him. He described what had happened.

The DI put his hand on Luke's shoulder. If Gus had needed a description of the word condescending, this was it.

"You know the drill, Sherman. The world and his wife will want to talk with you after this. To ensure you carried it out per...."

"What, like this animal did with Frank North?" said Gus. "Give the guy a break. Luke saved my life. Give him a medal, don't grill him for hours and offer him counselling."

"Ex-DI Freeman, I presume?"

The little sod emphasised the 'ex'. It was hard to believe, but he looked shorter than Geoff Mercer.

Gus took an instant dislike to him, and this wasn't the time for the touchy-feely approach to modern policing that so many of his peers displayed. It was time to think on your feet and take decisive action in minutes. If not quicker.

"Forget bloody standard procedures and use your brain. Block this road with 'Police Accident' signs to prevent anyone from approaching the scene by car or foot. We're in a cocoon here, thanks to where the planned attack took place. News of this incident must *not* reach the shooter's associates. So get onto Wiltshire Radio, Heart FM, and anyone who can spread these words. *Car accident. Head-on collision. The road is closed until further notice.* Do you think you can remember that?"

"Why would we do that? I don't follow."

"That's because you aren't in the loop," said Gus. "But, if we don't keep a lid on this for twenty-four hours, you can expect to watch your balls being run up the flagpole at London Road."

Gus and Luke would swear on a stack of Bibles the young DI winced.

"I need to ring HQ for guidance," he muttered.

"Insist on talking to DS Mercer. That's M-E-R-C-E-R. Tell him Gus Freeman asked him to explain the word 'misinformation' to you."

The young detective scuttled away.

"Luke, when you went through his jacket pockets, did you find a mobile phone on Dushka?"

"I grabbed it along with his driver's licence and several receipts for petrol and snacks. There was a bunch of keys on the car fob too. One of them will be for the shed, no doubt."

"Terrific. We need to get this to someone immediately. If my guess is correct, Dushka was the muscle in charge of the drug farm team. He wouldn't have been there twenty-four-seven. Otherwise, this Merc would have been spotted at the weekend when DI Ferris and I were up there."

"That visit prompted the break-in the following day, I guess?"

Gus nodded.

The ambulance crew were ready to transport Dushka to the hospital. They had stabilised his condition, but the look on their faces couldn't hide the fact his chances weren't good.

The DI assigned a uniformed officer to travel with the ambulance. As it moved off, two large white vans approached from the Devizes turning.

"Here come the forensic experts," said Luke, "it will soon be as busy as Times Square on New Year's Eve. Carry on with what you were saying."

"We need to get inside this phone to find details for other gang members Dushka contacts. It will help the team Geoff Mercer is leading tomorrow morning. Once they learn how this guy communicated with his superiors, HQ needs to locate a translator."

"This attack wasn't random," said Luke, following Gus's reasoning, "therefore, they will hope to hear Dushka succeeded in his mission. If HQ sends a text confirming the hit in a manner that doesn't raise suspicion, we might buy the time you say DS Mercer needs."

"I don't know how much you have heard, Luke. This morning isn't just about the death threat Dushka left me or today's attack. Nor is it only about the Cambrai Terrace cannabis farm. It's part of a far bigger operation timed for dawn tomorrow."

"So, you need to disappear for a while, am I right?"

"The misinformation I mentioned to the muppet we talked to just now is vital. We have to build on that. I can rely on you to convey the details to London Road. I need to go into hiding. We must keep the news of Dushka being in the hospital with serious injuries under wraps. The ambulance will have taken him to Swindon. His identity must not appear in any official records. If he survives that stomach wound, he must have round-the-clock security."

"Understood, Gus," said Luke.

"If the gang hear news of the 'accident', they will assume it's a smokescreen to hide the truth. The gang will expect the police to be crawling over West Wiltshire hunting an assassin. It won't be unreasonable not to have had further contact with their man if he's gone to ground. The last place Dushka would run to is the shed. We may save the day if we buy just a few hours before they get suspicious."

"What about you, Gus?"

Gus was thinking about how to prevent this from turning into a shitstorm.

He was due at an interview with Krystal Warner ten miles away in fifteen minutes.

He had an appointment this afternoon and a dinner date this evening. His car was out of action for the immediate future; things could hardly get any worse.

Except for being dead, and that had almost happened.

"As soon as they release you, Luke, give me a shout. In the meantime, I need to lay false trails."

Luke ran off to liaise with the DI, and Gus found a calm spot to make his calls. Thank goodness he'd forced himself to have that fried breakfast, he thought. At least he wasn't hungry.

IN THE CRT office at Old Police Station, Alex was getting nervous. Where the heck was the guvnor? Gus was never late. He hadn't called to report anything was delaying him. Neil wanted to phone the local hospitals.

Alex's phone rang. It was their boss; he sounded stressed.

"Alex, it's me. Sorry, you'll have to interview Krystal Warner with Lydia. I've hit a problem. It's too long a story to bother with now. Remember to concentrate on the timings, Alex. Get her talking about everything that happened the day of the murder. Take special note of who was where and when."

"Got it, guv; I can tell Neil to stop panicking and ringing the hospitals now, can I?"

"If he did and heard a rumour, someone came in with gunshot wounds. It wasn't me."

"Blimey, we miss out on the fun up here."

"It wasn't much fun. I can assure you. It might be Monday before I'm back in touch. Have a good weekend."

"Righto, guv," said Alex. He wanted to ask more questions, but Gus had gone.

Alex took a deep breath, then told the others what Gus had told him.

"Never a dull moment," said Neil.

"Come on, Lydia," said Alex. "we've got to get over to the Ring O'Bells for half-past. Neil, have we received that file from the Hub yet?"

Neil nodded. He had a fun morning ahead, checking alibis for men guilty of a wide-ranging variety of deviant behaviour. If only he'd studied harder at school.

AT THE WILTSHIRE Police HQ in Devizes, Vera Jennings faced yet another day as PA to ACC Kenneth Truelove. No two days were ever the same. The ACC always kept her busy.

There were days when frantic described how he appeared, and on other days he was mellow. Vera had learned to go with the flow, but today Truelove was frantic. Something was on the boil. The news hadn't broken yet, but she'd seen this behaviour from him before.

Vera was excited, nervous, and looking forward to her dinner date with Gus Freeman. The phone rang.

"Vera, it's me. Sorry, I need you to do something for me. Please don't ask me to explain. I was hoping you could go to the Ferret this evening as arranged. I won't turn up, I'm afraid. You can appear as annoyed or upset as you wish. The more people notice you, the better."

"Gus, what the heck is happening? You're worrying me. Are you alright?"

"Only just, you'll hear soon enough. I'm lying low for the time being. I need people around me to help with the deception."

"Do your team know?"

"I've kept them informed and asked them to cover for me until it's safe to resurface. Tonight is a postponement, not a cancellation. Events took me by surprise this morning on my way to work. I'm doing my utmost not to let it screw up things Geoff Mercer's handling."

"Geoff's been acting oddly since yesterday. So has the ACC. You get used to it after you've worked here for a while. It's one of three things. They're getting the sack, being promoted, or told to keep a secret."

"Vera, you're very astute. Do you read other people's behaviour with such accuracy?"

"I can't say I can read you very well yet. However, it will

undoubtedly make sense when I learn what this cloak and dagger stuff is for."

"I'll be in touch as soon as I can. I promise."

Vera sighed.

"Just take care of yourself, wherever you are, Gus Freeman."

"I'll try. Thanks."

Gus ended the call. He had decided not to cancel the security camera firm visit. It would annoy the guy to have had a wasted trip this afternoon, but he'd get over it. It wouldn't hurt if Dushka's associates checked the bungalow and spotted a visitor who expected Gus to be home. One more tick in the box of persuading the gang the hit had gone to plan.

His next job was to leave this lane and reach a place of safety.

Gus called Suzie Ferris.

"Gus," she said, "I've just left Geoff's office. He's been tearing a strip off Gareth Francis, the DI who attended your ambush this morning. Are you okay?"

"Fine. I need your help. Can you get me a lift to your parents' farm? It will be a good place to lie low during daylight hours. I'm guessing there's good visibility of the surrounding area?"

"Nobody can get within half a mile of the farmhouse without someone noticing. We're a long way from the main road. Dad's got registered shotguns if required. Where are you?"

"Two hundred yards past the gateway into the allotments. On a stretch of the lane with trees and hedges on both sides."

"I know where you are. If you go fifty yards farther along the lane towards the Devizes turning, there's a gate.

Get into that field and wait. Your lift should be with you in thirty minutes."

Gus did as instructed. Suzie didn't question his motives. She just did the necessary. The young woman impressed Gus more every time they met. If only some of that rubbed off on this prat Gareth Francis.

Gus was leaving when he spotted Luke Sherman running towards him.

"I'm okay to head for London Road. Do you want a lift anywhere?"

"Sorted, thanks, Luke. I know I've thanked you already...."

"Don't worry about it. I'm only thankful it turned out okay."

"The whole thing was textbook. Credit to whoever trained you."

Luke smiled.

"It was my first time, Gus. I did the training, but I've never faced a situation with live ammunition before. I hit Dushka in the left shoulder and the stomach, low on the right-hand side. I aimed centre mass, middle of the chest."

"You hit him, Luke. It stopped him from finishing what he had started. Dushka jumped out of the Merc, ran around the car and fired two shots with only a second to steady himself. The bullets hit my headrest an inch apart. One on top of the other. He wouldn't have missed again."

"I'm okay to take the phone and the gun to HQ," said Luke. "DI Francis has got things moving on the misdirection, and DS Mercer is expecting me. It's been an honour to work with you, Gus. Good luck."

With that, the young DS ran back through the crowd of police personnel to his car. He would soon take the quickest alternative route out of the village to Devizes. Gus wished he was going with him. He wanted to see this thing through to a conclusion. He also wanted to be somewhere; he could learn how his team was coping without him.

It was time to disappear, so Gus made his way to the gate and climbed into the field. He had twenty-five minutes to wait. The sun was high in the sky. He heard voices in the lane as the various disciplines continued to work. On this side of the hedge, the sheer beauty of the field was beyond words. It was pasture land with little to break the monotony, but it felt great to be alive.

Gus sat on the grass and waited. He listened for a Land Rover or the unmistakable sound of a tractor. He wondered who Suzie would send to fetch him.

Twenty minutes later, he groaned.

In the distance, he saw two horses. He stood and watched as the rider drew near.

"Gus Freeman, I presume?"

"You must be Suzie's father. She told me you had retired from point to point. I should have known you continued to ride."

"I'm John Ferris, too old to compete these days. Never too old to hack around the countryside, though. There's a helmet on the saddle of the spare horse. She's very calm. We're not in any hurry; I'll go at your pace. Suzie tells me we must keep you safe until she gets home from work."

Gus donned the helmet. That was the easy part. John Ferris jumped down and helped him clamber into the saddle. God, it felt a long way off the ground.

"I won't trouble you any longer than necessary, John. I want to sleep in my bed tonight. If I can get dropped off at my bungalow after darkness falls, that should end the disruption for both of us."

"Suzie hasn't told us why you need to be incommunicado. None of our business. She tells us you're a good bloke. That'll do for us. We must be around the same age, am I right?"

It promised to be a long ride for Gus. He was trapped on the back of an animal he had no idea how to control, with a father asking probing questions about his relationship with his daughter. First on the agenda - is the age difference. Then, he wondered how many more questions lay ahead as they crossed the fields between Urchfont and Worton. Gus wasn't sure he had the answers.

ALEX AND LYDIA had reached the side door of the Ring O'Bells just before half-past nine. Lydia rang the bell.

They could both hear the click-clack of high-heeled shoes on the parquet floor.

Krystal Warner, the landlady, had put on a few pounds since 2003. That shattered Alex's image of the younger of the two busty barmaids from the murder file.

"Police?" asked Krystal, already looking bored. The day had hardly begun.

"My name's DS Alex Hardy, and this is Lydia Logan Barre," said Alex, "we have questions about the murder of your friend, Trudi Villiers."

"Why's that then? Nobody's mentioned the case for years. Nobody came to see me even when they let that bloke out of prison. They didn't seem to care who killed Trudi."

"No murder case is ever closed, Ms Warner. We're part of a cold case review team stationed across the road at the Old Police Station. We're taking a fresh crack at the case. Can we find somewhere more suitable to continue this conversation? What do you use this for; a skittle alley or a dance hall?"

"Both," said Krystal as she slouched beside Alex's wheelchair.

Lydia trailed behind. She'd noticed the look Krystal had given her. Since her looks had faded, Krystal Warner hated greeting anyone better-looking than her. Lydia hoped her mixed-race colouring didn't play a part in how Krystal dismissed her with a glance, but you never could tell.

They had reached the lounge now. The seating was tired but comfortable-looking. Krystal flopped onto a velour-covered bench and waited for Alex to position his wheelchair facing her. Lydia walked to the other side of the table between the two and sat. Krystal showed no inclination to move along the bench to make room for her.

Lydia studied the other woman. The landlady was just the right side of forty. Three, maybe four stones overweight. Her hair colour had once been brunette, if the roots were a clue. Lydia had cursed her Scottish genes when growing up. Schoolchildren could be so cruel to kids with red hair. Now her biggest problem was taming its wild nature. Krystal tried to stave off the ravages of time with a bottle-blonde hairstyle that did her few favours after a week or two's growth.

As for that short skirt. Why wear something that needed tugging every few minutes? It only drew more attention to the legs. Fifteen years on, trousers might have been kinder.

"Take us through that Saturday, Krystal," said Alex, "we want to understand what led up to the murder. Maybe they missed something important in the original investigation."

"I should think so," scoffed Krystal, "they charged a bloke for her murder before they had time to do any real detective work. That bloke was nowhere near this town. The cops talked to James and me, but nothing more."

Alex ignored her relationship with James Bosworth for the time being. They were aware he had married someone else. Krystal didn't appear to have a partner. If she did, it was unlikely he was more relevant than Sammie, Bosworth's wife.

"What time did you start work that day?" asked Alex.

"We never did the lunchtimes," said Krystal, "we started at six in the evening and worked to closing. The pubs didn't open all day back then. That changed two years later."

"Did you spend much time together away from work?" asked Lydia. "What did you do that day before you got behind the bar here at six?"

"We lived in the same flat," sneered Krystal, "do you think we didn't get on or something? We shared the rent and the housekeeping, and as often as not, we shared the blokes, especially on holiday. We flew out to one of the Costas or the islands in the Med. It was the heyday of those Club18-30 holidays. We overindulged on sun, booze and men. Trudi had an appetite for sex you wouldn't believe."

"You were choosier, would you say?" asked Alex.

"I wish I had been," said Krystal, "no, we spent a lot of time together. As for that Saturday, I think we went to the Spar to buy ready meals, did the washing, and tidied the place. You know, the things normal people do at weekends. We caught up on a few hours' sleep, then got ready for work."

"How did you get here?" asked Lydia.

"We always took a taxi," said Krystal.

"You smiled when you said that," said Alex, "what amused you?"

"We used the same firm all the time. Four or five drivers were, you know, younger."

"Saeed Gill was a driver, wasn't he?" asked Lydia.

"I didn't mean that old lech. We wouldn't have helped him out."

"What do you mean, helped out," asked Alex.

"Trudi went with them in the back of the cab the first time they brought us home. Sometimes we took them indoors for a threesome. They never charged us the fares they should have after that, even when we travelled after midnight. She was a crafty one. If she could use her body to save a few quid for another holiday, she would."

"Are any of those drivers around now?" asked Alex.

"The firm closed. I can't say I've seen any of them in town for years, to be honest. The drivers were young Indians or Pakistanis. I never knew which. They move around, don't they? Might have returned home, who knows?"

"Was it busy for a Saturday night?"

"What, when we got here? Not for the first two or three hours. The band started playing at nine. On for an hour, a half-hour break, and then they played for another hour. That was how Gary had it set up every week. On a night when the place was heaving, he'd turn a blind eye if they kept playing for an extra fifteen minutes. As long as they finished by a quarter to midnight, the law wouldn't be knocking on the doors. Anything to sell a few more drinks."

"So, who came into the bar early in the evening? Who were your regulars? Did you have any strangers around that night?"

"You want a lot, don't you?" Alex sensed Krystal was reluctant to share too much detail.

"We are certain whoever killed Trudi visited the Ring O'Bells that night. You must have seen them. Maybe you served them their drinks. Perhaps you even chatted with them."

Krystal got the message and took her time remembering the regulars. Alex took notes of names. Mick, Vinny, Dodger, Gramps. Good luck trying to identify them from what little detail Krystal remembered.

Alex looked to the heavens.

Krystal leaned forward and gave him both barrels: -

"If you come here tonight for a drink, I'll ask you what you're having. Names don't come into it. Come back every night for a week, and I'll have a glass of your favourite tipple poured before you reach the bar. I still don't need your name. I've got people coming in here in an hour who have used this pub every day for twenty years. All I know is a first name or a nickname. The only surnames back then were blokes I'd gone to school with that I'd slept with, and not every one of them if I'm honest."

"Were any of Trudi's ex-boyfriends in the bar?" asked Lydia. "Someone she had a row with when they finished?"

"Are you for real?" asked Krystal. "There were a dozen or more blokes on the other side of the bar with whom she'd had sex. Five of them were in the band. Even the roadie pulled her one night. Was it always sweetness and light when they got thrown on the scrap heap? Not likely. Trudi used them for as long as she wanted, then tossed them aside like yesterday's newspapers. That's how she was."

"And yet you remained good friends," said Lydia.

Alex gave her a stern glance. They weren't here to judge; they needed information.

"When you're best friends," Krystal replied, as if she hadn't noticed, "you stick together no matter what. We wanted to have a good time. It's what being young's meant for; anyway, we never hurt anyone."

"What time did James arrive? Had you two been dating long?" asked Alex.

"James always got there by eight on a Saturday. We could chat until it got busier. I started seeing him regularly after returning from Ibiza at the end of August."

"Does regular suggest the relationship had started earlier?"

"He wasn't a taxi driver or in a band if that's what you mean. James had been drinking in the Ring O'Bells since he was eighteen. I'd seen him around town. We got together once or twice, just casual, and then he asked if we could go out on proper dates."

"Did Trudi ever do that?"

Krystal laughed and shook her head.

"How did she react to you having a steady boyfriend?"

"Trudi thought I was mad; I must be getting old before my time. She worried I would stop going on holiday with her. We booked to return to Ibiza in the Spring. James wasn't keen on me returning because he knew what Trudi would get me doing."

"Did the band play for that bit longer that night? Can you recall?"

"When we arrived, Trudi chatted with Gary while I restocked the bottle shelves. She wanted to stay on for an hour to earn extra cash for the holiday fund. Gary put the bar clock forward ten minutes. He wasn't too happy about a late night. Maggie told him to forget, asking her to help. It was a long enough week without tagging on another hour."

"So, when the band finished playing, and Gary called last orders, nobody complained it was early?"

"They were too pissed to notice or didn't want to get on the wrong side of Maggie. She gave them the rough side of her tongue if they got lippy. I called time that night. Then I told James to get us a taxi."

"Because you wanted to take advantage of an early night, too?" asked Lydia.

"More fool me. James was all over me in the back of the taxi. That pervert, Gill, never looked at the road; he stared up my skirt in the rear-view mirror. I wanted James to stay the night, but he went home. That was it. I wasn't as keen after that. He hung around until after Trudi's funeral, and then we drifted apart."

"How long before the taxi arrived to collect you?" asked Alex.

"We stood outside for a while. Gary and Trudi didn't want us hanging around inside while they worked. The band moved their kit out of that door you came through. It could have been ten minutes. Why?"

"We just need to fix the timeline in our heads," said Alex. "If Gary moved the clock forward ten minutes, it meant that when you left here, it was ten to twelve, not midnight. So you got picked up by Saeed Gill at midnight. So how long did it take to drive from here to your flat on Kingfisher Close?"

"It should take five minutes, but James and Gill argued over the fare. The firm upped the rate after twelve. James said he'd booked the taxi well before midnight, and it wasn't his fault it had taken Gill so long to reach us. He thought he was trying it on. In the end, it was a quarter past when we got to our old place. Then the other arguments started."

"Over James staying the night?"

"Yeah. We were kissing and fooling around on the pavement. Gill called out. He wanted James to pay the fare to get back into town and earn more money. Finally, James decided he didn't want to stay for an hour until Trudi got back. So, he jumped in the taxi, and Gill drove him across town."

"What time did he leave?"

"Twenty past, maybe? I was pissed. After they'd gone, I went indoors and went to bed. You know what happened on Sunday after they found Trudi. I had no idea she wasn't home. Her bedroom door was closed, as usual. I let her sleep."

"Did you try to contact James after he'd gone home? Did he phone you?"

"James didn't call me until Sunday afternoon. He couldn't believe the girl we'd left, the life and soul in the Ring O'Bells, was dead. I shed a few tears that day, I can tell you."

"Sunday afternoon was the first time you spoke after he got into the taxi?"

"Yeah. I was mad as hell when he left. I wanted to have sex with him, but staying for breakfast was a commitment. Trudi wouldn't have liked it; she didn't want James and me going steady. I slept through until ten. Then I made a coffee and waited for James to call. I hoped he'd apologise. I was working Sunday night too, so I planned to make it up to him."

"The next few days must have been tough," said Lydia, "are you saying James didn't come over to comfort you?"

"This place closed lunchtime out of respect. Maggie called to tell me to take the night off. Maggie and Gary held the fort, but I don't think they had many customers. The police came on Monday morning to talk to me. They went to see James at lunchtime, and he called me in the afternoon. I came to work in the evening. That was weird. Nobody knew what to say."

"Did you and James see one another that week?" asked Alex.

"He came in most nights after work. Things were never

the same after Trudi died. Well, I suppose it changed after we argued before she died."

"I think that's it for now, Ms Warner. Thanks for your time. If we think of anything else, we'll pop back."

"I'm always here," said Krystal, "if I'm not working, I'm usually upstairs in my flat."

The landlady made her way to the side door. Lydia and Alex followed her. When they stood outside, Krystal shut the door without a word.

As they waited for a gap in traffic to cross the road, they listened to the click-clack of her high heels on the parquet floor fading into the distance.

Chapter Ten

ONCE THEY RETURNED to the CRT office, Alex and Lydia made themselves a coffee.

"We didn't get offered a cuppa in the pub, did we? Nor anything stronger," said Alex.

"No, she wasn't a happy bunny, was she? Sorry, Alex. I can't imagine what Trudi was like, but Krystal is a nasty piece of work. It just slipped out."

"You need to be careful what you say, Lydia. We can't be judgemental. In many situations, the circumstances we meet in people's lives are alien to normal people. We must see through their baggage and keep seeking the truth."

"You sounded like the guvnor then. Are we any further forward, do you reckon?"

"Gus asked me to concentrate on timings. There weren't many to make a note of, and Krystal's timings matched what we already knew. They match her earlier statement, as far as I can tell. Perhaps we have to compare them with others later. Gus thinks something will materialise. He doesn't ask for something without good reason."

"I hope he's okay. What do you think happened to him? It must have had something to do with that break-in he had on Monday."

Lydia was glad she'd boobed when they were in the pub. Alex was right to give her a dressing-down, but it had reminded her to watch what she said. At least she hadn't discovered that Gus had a theory on who killed Trudi. She wondered whether any of those disgruntled ex-lovers in the bar that night matched a name thrown up by these timings Gus enjoyed mentioning.

"Gus said he might not be back until Monday. So we should keep up with things here this morning, then interview Maggie Smith after lunch."

"Coffee break over then?" said Neil as they emerged from the restroom. "It's okay; I had one earlier."

Neil soon put them to work trawling through the sex offenders listing. There were around four hundred names of offenders within the county borders between 1998 and 2008. The Hub had highlighted those in prison or on remand. There were many instances where police discovered indecent images on home computers, and nothing suggested these men were interested in someone as old as twenty-six.

"I feel grubby," said Neil. "The only good thing to come out of what I've done so far is the list of possible offenders is getting smaller and smaller. If you can stomach two hours analysing the rest of these characters with me, we can break the back of this job today."

The team grafted for two hours, then broke for lunch. However, their thoughts never strayed far from their boss. They had received no word since his phone call.

"No news is good news," said Neil.

"Usually," said Alex.

"Stay positive, guys," said Lydia, "we can keep busy this afternoon to take our minds off fretting. After we finish at five, I vote we call him."

"That's crazy," said Neil, "if it goes to voicemail or just rings out, we'll worry all weekend."

"Lydia's got the right idea," said Alex, "if we can't get hold of him, we'll call his DI friend, Suzie Ferris. Did anyone get that older lady's number from last Friday night? Vera Jennings? Anyway, we can ring London Road before we leave here. Catch one of them before they leave work."

"That sounds sensible. Don't forget to be on time to see Maggie Smith."

"If we leave now, my Mini will get us to her house before two o'clock," said Lydia.

"Do you keep your eyes closed when she's driving, Alex?" asked Neil.

"Enjoy the rest of the afternoon, Neil. We'll be back in a couple of hours," said Alex as he scooted across the carpet to the lift. Lydia joined him, and they descended to the car park. Alex knew better than to question Lydia's driving skills.

The former landlady of the Ring O'Bells lived in a quiet cul-de-sac of council maisonettes. Maggie had lung cancer and was virtually housebound. It made no sense for the council to house her on the first floor, but there you are, a typical example of joined-up thinking that had failed. Lydia rang the bell.

"The door is open,"

True enough, they could push the door open and enter. Alex found the hallway a tight squeeze to negotiate in his chair. These 60s maisonettes hadn't included wheelchairs in their design. They probably hadn't expected to cope with a sixty-six-year-old cancer patient who needed oxygen to get through the day either.

Maggie Smith did not look well.

"Are you the police who called?" she gasped.

"That's right, Mrs Smith. I'm DS Alex Hardy, and my colleague is Lydia Logan Barre. We're from the Crime Review Team in town. We're taking a fresh look at the murder of Trudi Villiers fifteen years ago. You and your late husband Gary ran the Ring O'Bells back then, do you remember?"

"Nothing wrong with my memory. Just my lungs."

"We'll keep this as brief as possible, Mrs Smith. Trudi started work at six o'clock that Saturday. Is that right?"

"Both her and Krystal, yes,"

"Trudi and Gary worked late that night, I believe?"

"The cleaners got stroppy. Trudi thought it would help if they cleaned up before going home."

"What time did you go upstairs to bed?"

"At midnight. The band had finished. Krystal had called last orders. I was tired."

"Did you go to bed straight away?"

"I had a drink and smoked a fag, while I watched TV. Then, finally, I got in bed before half-past midnight. Gary was downstairs. I never heard a thing after that."

"Did anything odd strike you that evening? Any strangers in the bar? Any arguments? Did Trudi behave herself with the customers?"

"Nothing different that night to any other we had. Except for what happened later."

Maggie Smith stopped to catch her breath. This conversation was painful for Alex and Lydia too. They didn't enjoy watching the poor woman suffer. She hadn't given them enough to warrant putting her through this.

"Gary was never the same after that night," Maggie said.

"How do you mean?"

"The smoking ban was the beginning of the end. Opening all day made it harder to make a living. Things were even worse with supermarkets flogging cheap alcohol. Trudi and Krystal had become our best draw. As soon as she died, lots of our regulars stopped coming. Krystal wasn't as popular, and she was miserable after she split with her lover boy. Gary just gave up trying."

"You mean James Bosworth? We understood they drifted apart after Trudi's death."

"Pretty much straight after that weekend. It surprised me James went for Krystal in the first place. You see plenty when you're in a pub every day. I watched him chatting up plenty of the single women that came in before he got together with Krystal. If you had asked me, I would have bet good money he would have caught Trudi's eye first."

"Thanks, Maggie. We're sorry to have put you through that. You've done well. My colleague and I will leave you in peace."

Alex and Lydia made their way into the hallway. As they stood by the door, Maggie waved a bony hand.

"James never came to the pub much after that weekend. If he did, he ignored Krystal. Gary told me he asked on the quiet one evening if he'd ensure one of us served his drinks."

"Interesting," said Lydia when they sat outside in her Mini. "Krystal gave me the impression there was something between them. At least until after the funeral. That would have been a few weeks, surely? Maybe Gus didn't want us to note just times from the night in question. We should ask Bosworth next week when the relationship ended."

"I'm struggling to understand why it matters," said Alex, as Lydia set off towards the town centre. "Krystal was angry and upset. She lashed out at Bosworth, leaving bruises and scratches on his cheek and forearms. Bosworth was frustrated at what he saw as her lack of commitment. Think of the holiday in San Antonio Trudi had booked; that was six months away. Krystal did whatever Trudi told her. Bosworth realised he faced months where he battled with the thoughts of what they got up to on holiday. I don't blame him for walking away from a relationship of that nature. Everything points to him wanting them to go steady and be faithful to one another. He's now settled down with a wife and three sons, a family man. Krystal has no one, as far as we can tell. If Trudi hadn't died, where would she be today? I bet both names would be over the door at the Ring O'Bells. Nothing would have changed except fewer blokes interested in them."

"We need to dig deeper with Bosworth," said Lydia, "there's something I read in the original murder file. I can't remember the wording. I'll check when we get back to the office."

Neil looked unhappy in his work.

"Please tell me you've broken this case," he pleaded, "these guys didn't follow a life of crime; more a life of grime."

"Maggie Smith was sicker than I imagined," said Lydia, "it wasn't fun trying to tease out of her what she remembered."

"We finally got something to chew on," said Alex, "she was adamant Krystal and James broke up after that

Saturday night. They may have talked after Trudi's body was found, and he attended the funeral, but it had ended."

"Get everything added to the Freeman file from your interviews today, plus what you contributed to this gruesome task of mine. Then we'll have a go at finding out what happened to the boss."

"Got it," said Lydia, "and what you said, Neil. Here we are; the WPC who helped interview Bosworth commented that 'his dark-brown eyes and designer stubble gave him a good look, even if it held a hint of danger'. He might not be the clean-living, faithful family man you imagine, Alex. Maggie Smith said he'd played the field with attractive women before he homed in on Krystal."

"Let's just park that for now," said Alex, "and wait until next Monday when we interview him. We must approach that meeting with an open mind. Maybe it will be best if Gus is back with us. We can let him read our Freeman file notes and plan his line of questioning."

"I haven't done any of the interviews for obvious reasons," said Neil, "but it isn't straightforward. Are we any closer to finding a suspect yet?"

"Blowed if I know," said Alex, "we're running out of witnesses. If we don't find a name from this list of yours, we might have to put surnames on a few of the ex-lovers Krystal remembered. We will be clutching at straws then."

While Alex and Lydia updated the Freeman file, Neil called the London Road HQ and asked to speak with DI Suzie Ferris.

"Good afternoon, Ma'am. DS Neil Davis from CRT. Have you seen Gus Freeman today?"

"Gus rang you this morning, I believe?"

"He did, Ma'am, and informed us he needed to lie low

for a while. We were concerned about his safety and how his absence affected us here in the office."

"He's in a place of safety. My understanding is he could be in the clear by noon tomorrow. You three must feel like a ship without a rudder at present. I'm sorry I can't offer you anything other than suggest you keep working on the case you're investigating."

"Thank you, Ma'am," said Neil. Suzie Ferris had ended the call.

"The boss is okay, then?" asked Alex.

"It sounds like it, doesn't it? We've got to keep busy tomorrow. Gus may turn up if the threat is over. Something big is happening. DI Ferris didn't give much away. It's one of those need-to-know situations where we don't need to know."

The three of them were just relieved at the more positive news. The team finished work at five o'clock and drove home. Tomorrow was another day.

VERA JENNINGS HAD SPOKEN to Suzie Ferris before she left London Road. Gus Freeman owed both of them a few favours after tonight. Vera drove home and spent over an hour preparing for her supposed night out. She went to Newton Bridge and the Ferret, keeping an eye on the cars behind her to see if she was followed. She spotted no one.

The small bar was sparsely populated when she entered. That had been what she anticipated when she suggested it to Gus as a suitable venue for their second date. She knew Bob, the landlord, and he came around the bar to reward her with a welcome hug.

"Welcome back, Vera. It's been too long. Is this an early

celebration of getting rid of that waste of space, Monty?" he asked, showing her to a corner table.

"Another two weeks yet, Bob. No, just a quiet meal with a close friend. I hoped to see him here by now."

"Let me get you a drink while you're waiting. I'll bring the menus over in a tick. Plenty of time if he's late. We're not busy on Thursday evenings."

Vera ordered a soft drink and relaxed as she watched Bob and his two young waitresses flit to and from the bar and the kitchen. She resigned herself to people-watching. Bob kept looking across, and Vera smiled sweetly. After an hour, she got up and placed her empty glass on the bar.

"If a chap called Gus Freeman comes in here later looking for me, tell him not to bother. I get dressed up, and he can't even bother to call to say he's changed his mind."

"He doesn't know what he's missing, Vera," said Bob.

Vera stomped out of the bar. She was pleased that every one of the Ferret's dozen customers watched her make her dramatic exit. Then, standing by her Alfa Romeo in the car park, she called Suzie Ferris. Part two of the plan needed to swing into action.

"Suzie? Can you help me? I'm worried about Gus Freeman. Meet me at his bungalow. You know where he lives."

Vera drove to Urchfont and found a police car with its lights flashing in the driveway of Gus's place. The two women walked to the front door and rang the bell. Suzie went to peer through the lounge window.

A dark saloon car slowed as it passed by the gateway and carried on along the lane.

Suzie Ferris soon communicated with a colleague parked a short distance from the bungalow.

"Dark saloon, carrying a 17 plate. A lone male driver is heading your way. Follow but do not intercept."

Suzie made a second call. This time for a Crime Scenes Investigation van.

Vera and Suzie waited in the driveway, looking suitably concerned.

"I hope this acting masterclass is necessary," said Vera, "I'm freezing standing out here in this skimpy dress."

"You certainly dressed to impress. I'm sure Gus will try not to get shot at in the future."

A white van pulled into the driveway several minutes later. Suzie checked the lane in both directions, but there was no sign of the dark saloon. When she reached the house, the forensic team had already moved indoors.

"Can I get anyone coffee while you continue to appear to be working," asked Gus, removing the white overalls that covered his clothing.

"We'll be alerted if that car comes back," said Suzie, "the team can look busy for another thirty to forty-five minutes. You're home now; you can sleep in your bed. At dawn tomorrow, the planned strikes go ahead across the gang's operations. Geoff agreed Vera's concern over your non-arrival for a date justified us, ensuring you hadn't suffered an accident or taken ill. Geoff sent the CSI van to collect you from the farm. It added to the picture that nobody knew you had been missing since early this morning. Fingers crossed, the gang members in the shed won't panic when they don't hear from Dushka and abandon the building above Cambrai Terrace."

"How is Dushka?" asked Gus.

"He died on the way to the hospital," said Suzie.

"I must give Luke Sherman a call," said Gus, "it was his first rodeo. He did the right thing. Dushka didn't leave him any choice."

Half an hour later, as darkness fell, the actual CSI

members left the bungalow and drove away. Vera and Suzie watched them go. Time for them to leave.

"Thank your mother and father for the hospitality," said Gus.

"They said they enjoyed your company," said Suzie.

"Sleep well tonight," said Vera, kissing him on the cheek.

"I'll be fine," said Gus, "as long as I sleep on my stomach."

Suzie looked at Vera. They burst out laughing.

"Hilarious," said Gus, "now, you two had better get your serious faces on before you leave here. All this hard work will be for nothing if someone spots you with big grins on your faces."

"In other circumstances, it wouldn't harm your reputation, " Vera said.

Vera and Suzie left, slamming the door locked behind them. Gus was alone in his kitchen in the dark. What a day.

Friday, 20 April 2018

OCTF COULDN'T HAVE PICKED A BETTER day for it. Five in the morning, and Gus had been awake for fifteen minutes. He wasn't involved in the operation but couldn't stay in bed with everything kicking off.

Gus showered and dressed for work. Smart casual today. He'd had enough of wearing a suit during this hot spell. He wondered where Luke Sherman was today. No doubt, providing cover for those officers drafted onto the operation above Cambrai Terrace. If everything went to plan, he'd seen the last of Luke and his mate, Rick Chalmers.

Gus wolfed down two slices of toast for breakfast. Too early for a fry-up. Too early and too warm. Without his faithful car, he had no choice but to walk to the allotment for a better view of the hillside. From this distance, everything looked quiet. There could have been a dozen vehicles in the lane behind the houses, and he wouldn't have seen them.

Gus opened his shed and fetched his father's field glasses. He spotted movement on the hillside; it was precisely six o'clock, and the operation had begun. The sound of several sharp cracks carried across the valley. Then silence. The team had met resistance, but it was mercifully brief. He prayed there were no casualties.

Gus didn't expect to bump into anyone before he headed to work. It was far too early. Geoff Mercer and OCTF would struggle throughout the day with whatever was hidden from view. He wondered how involved Monty Jennings had been.

Gus hoped it was only a rental agreement. Something which wouldn't cause the guy too much aggravation if he held his hands up and said he wished he'd done due diligence. In truth, he wasn't as concerned about Monty as how it affected his relationship with Vera.

Gus focused his glasses on the hillside for the next thirty minutes.

There was no point wishing he could be up there, running around with the youngsters. His body was telling him he was too old for new adventures. John Ferris had been riding since he stopped wearing nappies. Gus had wished he'd had several pairs available yesterday to soften the blows.

He eased himself up and returned his chair and field glasses to the shed.

As he strolled back to the bungalow to make himself a cup of coffee, he wondered when Neil Davis got out of bed. He needed a lift, and Neil lived closest.

Melody answered on the fifth ring.

"Sorry, I didn't wake you, did I? Is Neil there?"

"He's in the shower," she replied, "that's Mr Freeman, isn't it?"

"That's right. Don't disturb Neil. Please ask him to pick me up on his way to work. I'll be ready and waiting."

Neil arrived at half-past eight. Gus got into the passenger seat.

"Morning, guv, are you okay?"

"Better than at the same time yesterday when some bugger tried to put two extra holes in my head. We'll pass the spot in a minute. My Ford Focus is in the garage. I told them it only needed a new headrest and a front windscreen. You know what they're like, plenty of rubbing of chins and shaking of heads. It's only ten years old. Years of life in it yet."

"The threat you received wasn't an empty one, then. What happened to the bloke who got shot?"

"He died on the way to the hospital."

"What a shame."

"Did you notice increased traffic on the roads when you came to collect me?"

"Not this side of the village, guv. Has the balloon gone up?"

"On the hillside. It might be over bar the shouting by now. I hope it was a total success."

"If so, we can expect you bright-eyed and bushy-tailed on Monday morning, guv."

"I sincerely hope so, Neil. What progress have you made so far?"

Neil told Gus the basics and confirmed that the Freeman files were updated.

"Terrific. I can familiarise myself with everything before we meet Amy Pollock. I'll give Alex a rest and take Lydia with me. She's got a knack for the younger women. They talk to her more readily."

"Maybe she knows the right questions to ask, guv?"

"You may be right. The attack occurred here, Neil. Dushka overtook me on this wide stretch, and in seconds it was over."

"There's no evidence of anything happening there, guv. No skid marks, blood, broken glass - nothing."

"That prat DI Francis did his job well in the end. All someone has to do now is collect the 'Police Accident' notices."

It was ten to nine when they reached the first floor of the Old Police Station. Alex and Lydia arrived only two minutes behind them.

"Welcome back, guv," said Alex, "you had us worried for a while yesterday."

"Glad to be back. I'll interview Amy Pollock with Lydia in an hour. First, I need to read through everything you've added since I was here, which feels like a lifetime ago."

"Fair enough, guv. Neil and I will continue vetting the last few sex offenders from the list the Hub provided."

Gus was confident the killer wouldn't be on that list. He hadn't altered his theory since he had visited Kingfisher Drive and the murder site.

Gus told Lydia he was ready by ten minutes to ten, and they headed for the lift.

"You're driving. My car is in the garage," said Gus, "remember, I'm almost a senior citizen. So take it steady."

Lydia got them to Amy Pollock's house on the Greenwood Estate at just after ten o'clock. Gus had been gripping the seat so hard he wasn't sure his hand would ever open again.

Amy Pollock, formerly Hodges, was tall with long blonde hair and dazzling blue eyes.

"Hello, you must be the police people I was expecting."

"My name's Freeman. I'm a consultant with the Crime Review Team. We are checking details from a murder case fifteen years ago. My colleague here is Ms Logan Barre. Can we come in?"

"Of course, what was I thinking? Come through to the lounge. Coffee?"

"I'll get it," said Lydia, "you sit and chat with Mr Freeman."

"Did you know Trudi Villiers?" asked Gus.

"Not at all. I worked for the taxi firm as a dispatcher, I suppose you'd call it. I had an eight-month-old baby. The job was something to fill in while I tried to get into full-time employment. Childcare is so expensive. We had trips to and from her place, but I never met her."

"How did you get on with Saeed Gill?"

Amy paused before answering.

"You don't think he had anything to do with the murder, do you?

"I don't think anything, Amy."

"Saeed could be a bit of a creep. Most of the lads they had driving for them were decent enough, though. Saeed wouldn't have hurt anyone. He was all talk."

Lydia returned from the kitchen with three coffees.

"What time did you start work that night?" asked Gus.

"Eight o'clock. I did six hours on a Friday, six on Saturday, and four on Sunday. I needed to keep the hours low to protect my benefits. Although my main aim was to get off benefits and return to what I did before I got pregnant."

"What was that?" asked Lydia.

"Training to be a primary school teacher."

"Did you make it?" asked Lydia.

"No, but I've been a Teaching Assistant for fourteen years. I took a maternity break when I had my youngest. She's eight now, and her big brother is nearly sixteen. I married a maths teacher."

"I appreciate it was a long time ago," said Gus, "but can you recall anything of the Saturday night in question? Can you recall the events leading up to midnight and beyond?"

"I remember Saeed calling me. He was having a heated discussion with a passenger."

"What time was that?"

"At midnight. Saeed had collected the other girl we ferried to and from the pub. Krystal had her boyfriend with her. He accused Saeed of deliberately hanging around on the taxi rank in Market Square. This boyfriend reckoned he rang at twenty to twelve, and there was no way it should have taken twenty minutes to drive two hundred yards. Saeed asked me to check my log. I had it logged at eight minutes to twelve. I called for any driver free to pick up from the Ring O'Bells. Saeed said he would do it but had just returned from the Westbourne Estate. He needed to clean out the fast-food cartons and drink cans the previous lot had discarded."

"When did Saeed contact you next?"

"I expected him to call sooner to say he could do another fare. It was always manic around that time of night. The bloke kept arguing over the fare. It took fifteen minutes, at least, before he called back again."

"Was he ready to accept another fare by this time?"

"No, Saeed said the couple was still on the pavement, arguing and fighting. So I told him to forget it and come on back to town. He could make up his money with tips from my other jobs in the queue."

"What did he say to that?"

"I heard him shouting at the bloke to get in the cab if he still wanted to be taken home. If not, pay him the fare, and he'd leave. Next thing I know, I hear the door slam, and Saeed tells me he's heading for the Westbourne."

"What time did he drop the boyfriend home?"

"He called back a minute after they left Kingfisher Close."

"Excuse me?"

That made Gus sit up and take note.

"Saeed called to say he was ready for another job; I asked what happened to the last one. Saeed said the boyfriend was searching in his jeans and his jacket. He realised he didn't have enough cash on him. He was pissed, ranting and raving about his girlfriend, saying what slags Krystal and her mate were. Saeed stopped the taxi and told him that he had to walk home if he couldn't pay. The bloke gave Saeed a mouthful of abuse and told him he would visit a cashpoint and get a ride home with another firm."

"Did Saeed see the bloke again that night, do you know?"

"I don't, I'm afraid. Saeed never mentioned it. I quit a year later. The firm closed a few years after that. I reckon it's ten years since he stopped driving. He lives in Swindon but had a stroke a few months ago. So he won't be much use to you now."

"We'll try not to trouble him," said Gus, "what you have told us has been very useful. For some strange reason, nobody came to talk to you earlier. It could have saved an awful lot of bother."

"Glad I could help," said Amy, walking them to the door.

Gus and Lydia said their goodbyes and headed for the Mini.

"Wow, that was amazing," said Lydia, "the case has been blown wide open. James Bosworth lied. He said he took a taxi home. Now we know differently. He could have been in town when Trudi left the pub."

"Odd that Steve Li didn't mention him, don't you think?" said Gus.

"Have I jumped in too soon again, guv?"

"Possibly. We won't be able to verify whether Bosworth used an ATM that night. Banks need to keep records for seven years, but certainly not fifteen. We need a witness who saw Bosworth between leaving the taxi on the Greenwood Estate and arriving home on the Westbourne. We don't know what time he reached there. Let's say between half-past twelve and half-past one."

"Did Neil say what Bosworth was doing this weekend?" asked Lydia.

"I need to apply for overtime if you're thinking of grabbing him tomorrow."

"I can do it if you need me,"

"It's important enough to bring the interview forward. I don't know whether Geoff Mercer will be available. Blow it. We'll work tomorrow morning, regardless."

"You have put your life on the line for them this week, guv. They should be grateful you still want to do it."

Gus laughed.

"I'll tell you what. When we return to the office, try to bring the other appointments forward. You and Alex can visit Steve Li and his wife. Trudi's parents, too, if they can spare an hour this afternoon. We'll scrap Saeed Gill. Amy told us far more than he could have done, even before he had his stroke. Tony and Tristram can have as many late nights as they wish in Benidorm; we won't need their statements."

"What will you be doing this afternoon?" asked Lydia as she parked the car.

"I intend to go to the security camera firm to get someone to help site my cameras. Then, I'm off to my allotment. I deserve a spot of 'me' time."

Chapter Eleven

GUS UPDATED his computer file with the new evidence Amy Pollock had provided. Lydia passed the details on to Alex and Neil. The office was buzzing. There was a light at the end of what had appeared to be a very dark tunnel.

Neil arranged for Alex and Lydia to interview Steve and Mary Li at two o'clock.

Ray Villiers worked until half-past four. Kath had just finished a shift at the supermarket when Neil called. He suggested to Alex that he and Lydia arrive at four to talk with Trudi's mother first. Even though their daughter had been dead for fifteen years, Kath might still have a few secrets about her only daughter she had withheld from Ray.

"We can't be blasé with these final interviews," he said. "We must ask the same searching questions we wanted to before you learned what you did this morning."

"Well done, Neil," said Gus, "that's correct. We mustn't assume these couples will merely cement the opinions we may have formed so far on who was responsible. Amy

Pollock asked me this morning if Saeed Gill was involved. That reaction was because she thought he was a creep. I had asked how she got on with him. It is a simple enough question, but people respond in various ways depending on their relationship with the person involved."

"Are there any specific things you want us to ask, guv?" asked Alex.

"Timings will still be important, as far as the Li's are concerned. Also, we need to check whether Steve Li saw James Bosworth that night. How many ATMs did the town have available back then? Check that, Neil. We won't learn until tomorrow which one Bosworth used to withdraw cash. If, indeed, he did. Another thing to check is which taxi firms had cabs on the rank in Market Square that night. A long shot, but would one of their drivers recall taking Bosworth up to the Westbourne at a quarter to one or later?"

"Do we need to ask Trudi's parents more about her teenage years, guv?" asked Alex.

"I'd just let Kath Villiers chat to begin with," said Gus, "then use your common sense. If a potential line of enquiry presents itself, jump in with follow-up questions. Think on your feet. You'll know when to quit and let her witter on again with stories of their little girl."

Gus tidied his desk and thought about how he might pass the afternoon. He knew much of what he had asked his team to do was pointless, but they were still raw recruits at this game. It was good practice. These tactics would stand them in good stead for cases that lay ahead.

"When Ray Villiers arrives home, make sure he knows Kath has been very helpful," he said as an idea struck him. "It may prompt an admission from him tension existed between him and Trudi. Mum and Dad may have been ravers in their day, and Trudi followed in their footsteps. Or was it something between father and daughter that caused her to go off the rails? Is Ray religious or a strict disciplinarian? That could have been a trigger. I consider myself broad-minded, but a daughter like Trudi would have tested my patience. The way she behaved would have horrified me."

"I've made a note of those things, guv," said Alex.

"Go with the flow. Sometimes witnesses give answers to questions you haven't dreamed of asking."

Alex wasn't sure whether or not that made sense, but he nodded in agreement. The boss knew best.

"Right, I'm off," said Gus, "get Neil to tell you where my place is, Lydia. You can pick me up after ten. We'll camp outside his place on the Westbourne until James Bosworth can chat. No excuses. I'll ask the custody suite up the road if he gets stroppy to send an officer to arrest him."

Gus left the team with enough interviews and information-gathering to fill the afternoon. He took a taxi home and prepared lunch. The security camera representative arrived at three o'clock. As soon as he had got rid of him, Gus planned to spend until seven this evening on his beloved allotment. The thermometer had read twenty-six degrees centigrade when he parked in the driveway at one o'clock. Gus couldn't remember an April day as warm as this. Time to enjoy it.

STEVE AND MARY LI had done well out of the restaurant and take away business. Their detached house on the town's outskirts looked pristine inside and out. The double garage probably housed Steve's more modern Jaguar. Alex wondered whether they had extended the garage when Jason still lived at home.

Alex and Lydia parked outside on the main road. Lydia retrieved Alex's chair from the back seat of her Mini. He manoeuvred himself from the passenger seat and sat in his chair.

"Not long now, Lydia," he said, "I'll be on crutches by the end of the month."

"You've done brilliantly to come as far as you have, Alex," she replied. "Mary Li is watching us from her lounge window, by the way."

The front door opened, and a diminutive Chinese lady skipped onto the gravel path. She pointed to the pathway at the side of the house.

"This way, please," she said.

Mary showed them into the sunroom at the rear of the house. Steve sat reading a book and stood when Lydia reversed Alex's chair and lifted it over the door sill.

"Welcome," said Steve Li.

He stood five foot, six inches tall, and Mary only came up to his shoulder. She hovered as the two police personnel made themselves comfortable.

"You want tea?" she asked when they had settled.

"No, thank you, Mrs Li," said Alex.

Mary Li was already halfway through the door into the house. Alex nodded to Lydia. She followed Mary inside to ask questions to confirm what her husband had told the detectives in 2003.

"You are aware why we asked to speak with you, Mr Li," said Alex.

"Call me Steve, please. Everyone does,"

"Okay, Steve, I work with a cold case review team. My

name is DS Alex Hardy. We're looking into the death of Trudi Villiers fifteen years ago."

"They make a mistake back then. I remember."

"Yes, they did. We're hoping to get the right person this time. Remind me what you saw that night, Steve."

"We were busy. My son dealt with the takeaways until half-past ten. Jason joined us in the restaurant after that. Our last customers left after midnight. Ten past, not later."

"What did you do then?"

"Jason brought Mary home. I helped my kitchen staff clear everything away. My chef was last to leave at ten to one. We discussed changing menus and prices. I locked the shutter doors at the front of the restaurant when I saw that girl."

"Did you know her?"

"I remember Trudi from when she was a schoolgirl. Thirteen or fourteen. She was always with boys when she came into the takeaway — bad girl. Trudi got served in the pubs in town before she was old enough. Mary refused to serve her many times because she was drunk. Trudi's father came to collect her when I rang him. He was ashamed of her, I think."

"What time did you see her that night?"

"One o'clock, I told the man before at one o'clock. I get in my car and drive home. I never saw her again."

"Was she in a rush, would you say?"

"No, just walking. Girls can't run in high heels."

"Anyone else in the street when you drove home? Not just near Market Square. Who did you meet on the road leading out of town?"

"Nobody followed that girl," said Steve Li, shaking his head. "Between the restaurant and here, I see two couples.

A few cars, taxis mostly. Same as every other weekend night. Lots of taxis after one o'clock."

"You don't remember a man walking alone, perhaps coming into town to use a cash machine?"

"No machines. Not on my way home. Before they closed the banks, they were in Market Square. Those places were not visible from my restaurant. There was no man alone across the street, only that girl."

"Thanks, Steve. I don't think there's any more I can ask. You've been very helpful."

"Will I rescue your friend from Mary now?" asked Steve with a smile.

Alex paused as he turned his chair towards the door.

"Mary loves having a young girl to talk with; she wanted a daughter after Jason was born. Nothing happened."

Steve called his wife. Mary and Lydia came through to the sunroom.

"If you need more, just come back," she said, squeezing Lydia's hand.

"We will," said Lydia as she walked beside Alex to the doorway.

Steve Li and his wife followed along the pathway and waved them off before returning indoors.

"What a lovely home," said Lydia, "she's got great taste in art and ceramics."

"Steve's not your average Chinese restaurant owner. Did you clock the book he was reading? 'The Unfinished Revolution' about Sun Yat Sen came out last year."

"Mary confirmed Steve got home at around ten past one. Her son, Jason, drove her home after the restaurant closed. I asked if she knew Trudi. Mary had trouble with her in the takeaway when she worked on the counter. She did that for years before Jason was old enough to take charge. Mary got Steve to ring Ray Villiers to fetch Trudi when she came in, falling down drunk. She said Trudi was only fifteen, and she had several boys tagging along whenever she came in."

"Steve and Mary told us the same story," said Alex, "oddly, neither mentioned Trudi after the age of sixteen. Krystal didn't get a mention either."

"How old is Jason, mid-forties now? Maybe, we should talk to him. Steve and Mary likely dealt with just the restaurant customers after he took over the takeaway section."

"Good idea. Jason will be in the Imperial Dragon every day now Steve and Mary have retired. We'll check with Gus. We'll have to go for a meal if he thinks it's worth pursuing."

"On a date, you mean?"

"We can call it a fact-finding mission if you prefer," said Alex.

"No, we can call it a date if we split the bill," said Lydia.

Alex thought he could live with that.

"We'll have a coffee when we get back to the office," he said.

"Why didn't you want that cup of tea earlier?" asked Lydia.

"Mary seemed traditional. I worried we might not make our appointment with Kath Villiers at four."

"Daft beggar, I know a proper tea ceremony takes four hours. Mary would have used the tea bags on her Italian marble worktop in the kitchen."

"How did it go?" asked Neil when they returned to the office.

"The timings didn't change. We clarified the details surrounding what Steve Li saw and did. We learned more background on Trudi. It may be worth talking to the son,

Jason Li. Trudi spent more time in the takeaway section than in the restaurant. Jason served her more often than his parents after she reached sixteen."

"I've seen Jason Li's photo in the local paper. He sponsors the town football team. Jason buys the match ball for Home games and stuff like that. Good publicity. He must have been a year or two above Trudi at school."

"A lot of the boys she hung out with were older than her. You don't think…?" asked Lydia.

"I can't see Steve and Mary allowing Jason to mix with Trudi Villiers," said Alex, "and there was no hint of Steve keeping anything from me. Maybe we should add him to our list for Monday. He might be someone of interest to Gus."

"I located the cash machines available in 2003 after you left," said Neil.

"The Big Four banks in the Market Square, plus the out-of-town supermarket," said Alex.

"You missed one, smartass. The garage on the other side of the river bridge had one, but it wasn't free to use."

"Steve Li said the banks were too far from his restaurant to know whether anyone had used them at one o'clock. Did you have any joy with the taxis?"

"Not much. There were two other firms in town. Both are still in business. As for the drivers working that night, they haven't got a clue who they were or where they might be now. So that looks like a dead end. You had better get off to interview Trudi's parents. Better luck with them."

"We'll see you on Monday then, Neil," said Lydia as they prepared to leave, "have a good weekend."

"I vote we try getting another team night out next week," said Neil.

"Married life is getting boring, is it, mate?" joked Alex.

"A laugh a minute," said Neil, "Melody says she's late."

"That's great news, Neil. You're right; a night out would be in order if she's expecting and we crack this bloody case."

"We could make it three things to celebrate if you beat your target of losing that chair by a week," said Lydia, ruffling Alex's hair.

Neil hoped the others bought the beers when they next went out together. He reckoned money might be tight in the Davis household if Melody was right.

Lydia drove on the speed limit, crossing town to where Ray and Kath Villiers lived. Kath answered the door. She was a grey-haired, late fifties, a tired-looking lady dressed in a navy blue blouse, cardigan and skirt.

Kath led them into the living room and sat by a giant fish tank.

Alex and Lydia sat side by side. Alex in his chair, Lydia on a leatherette settee. She was terrified to move in case it made an unpleasant noise. Alex told Kath why they had come.

"I don't know what I can tell you," she shrugged.

"Can you think of anyone capable of killing your daughter?" asked Alex.

"Raped and stabbed to death," said Kath, "she was raped and stabbed to death."

"You're right. It was a terrible crime. So, was there anyone Trudi mixed with you suspected?"

"You know how she behaved. We couldn't control her. She had no control over herself."

"What was she like as a young girl," asked Lydia.

"A lovely child, look," Kath stood and fetched a photo-graph. There were four images. Trudi at six months, two years, five years and ten or eleven years old. Happy and smiling throughout and smartly dressed in the final image where she wore her school uniform.

Lydia looked around for more recent photographs.

"Do you have any pictures of Trudi at sixteen? Her eighteenth birthday, say?"

Kath Villiers shook her head. She fought back the tears.

"Ray wouldn't keep them in the house after she died. He only kept ones before she grew older."

"Trudi caused you more problems once she hit puberty?" asked Alex.

"Trudi was nothing but trouble from thirteen to sixteen. Ray had enough when she left school with no qualifications. He threw her on the street. When he was at work, I went looking for her and waited for her up at Gracelands when she worked there. Trudi visited me just for a chat. When Ray found out I'd been seeing her, he blew his top. Trudi never came here again after that. I kept in touch with her, though, in secret."

"When was the last time you talked with her before she died?" asked Alex.

"On Wednesday. I didn't work that day. We met in town, in a café. We had coffee and cake and chatted for an hour. She was still my little girl, even though she was a tearaway. I used to tell her to find someone, get married, and cut out this nonsense. Trudi said there was plenty of time to settle down when she was dead. She wanted to live life to the full, regardless of who she hurt. It was Trudi, Trudi, Trudi. Nobody else mattered."

"Not even Krystal?"

Kath laughed.

"Krystal followed our Trudi around like a lost sheep. If Trudi said 'jump', Krystal jumped. I was surprised she had the initiative to run the pub independently. That was the first time she surprised me."

"Was Trudi ever in a relationship with a boy where you thought it might lead to something permanent?"

"In her first year at secondary school, hardly twelve, she walked home with a smart-looking lad. He had dark hair and brown eyes and was tall for his age. I spotted them on the corner. I thought it was sweet. She looked up into his eyes; you know, it was the first time anyone had kissed her, I bet. All I can describe it as is a look of wonder. It sounds daft now. Within a year, she was having sex with half the school."

"What happened to the lad?"

"Ray came home and found them. He was spitting feathers. I'd never seen him so angry. Let's say he told the lad to disappear. He said Trudi was too young to be messing with boys."

"Did you learn his name?" asked Lydia.

"I don't think Trudi mentioned his name. He was older than her. You know what kids are at that age. He may have got ribbed at school for cradle-snatching or Ray giving him such a rocket in public. They might have taken it out on Trudi too."

Had that been the trigger Gus sought? Could she make an educated guess who the tall, dark-haired, brown-eyed boy had been?

Alex heard a door slam outside.

Ray Villiers burst into the house and threw his coat onto the floor in the hallway.

"Who the hell are you? Why are you talking to my wife without me being here?"

"We're from the police, Mr Villiers. The Crime Review Team. Our colleague contacted you earlier in the week to say we were taking another look into your daughter's murder. My name is DS Hardy; here's my identification."

Lydia stepped forward and showed Ray Villiers her card too.

"Kath has been very helpful," she said, "other interviews finished earlier than we had expected. It made sense to meet you as soon as possible. Kath said you would be home later this afternoon. We've only been here for thirty minutes."

"I'm sure you want us to have the best information available," said Alex, "to help us solve this case.

"You were supposed to interview us together," Ray insisted, "Kath will fill your heads with rubbish. Trudi was a bad lot. We did everything for her, but she just threw it back in our faces. Do you know how it feels to have your neighbours, work colleagues, and shop assistants sneering down their noses at you for years? No, of course, you don't. Do you know how I felt when they told us they had found her body? Relieved. That's no way for a father to be feeling."

"Why don't Kath and I get us a cup of tea or coffee," said Lydia, "you've just finished work. Sit and chat with Alex. We're only looking for background on Trudi. Little details might point to people who could have held a grudge against her for years. Whatever you can offer will be useful."

Ray Villiers began to relax. Alex wondered whether he was intimidated by Lydia. She had a presence. It wasn't just her physical appearance; her voice oozed calm.

Kath Villiers and Lydia left the two men alone and went to the kitchen.

"We tried everything," said Ray, slumping into a chair next to Alex, "when Trudi reached thirteen, her personality changed. You read in the papers of celebrities going into clinics to get treated for sex addiction, don't you? Well, that was what it resembled. As if she needed it all the time, yet she was never satisfied. She moved from boy to boy, searching for something, for someone. There was nothing Kath or I could do to stop her. So finally, we had no choice but to get her to the doctor. Trudi was on birth control pills earlier than any kid in town. There was no chance we could risk waiting until she reached sixteen. How she never fell pregnant was a miracle."

"She left home at sixteen, I believe?" asked Alex.

"I told her to go," said Ray. "I would have crawled a hundred miles over broken glass to help her understand what damage she was doing to herself, the boys she used, and her mother. Finally, I couldn't stand it any longer."

"Kath kept in touch with her?"

"We had blazing rows every time I found out she'd seen Trudi behind my back. I'm not proud of how I acted back then, but the only way I could cope was to shut her out of our lives. I could pretend it wasn't happening that way. Fat chance of that, though, when people in town never let us forget it."

"Kath met her in the week before she died. What did you two do on that Saturday?"

"Did she? I never knew that. We did nothing unusual; we watched TV in the evening and went to bed around eleven. I fetched the Sunday papers at nine in the morning. We were getting lunch when the police came."

"Did anyone from those early teenage years keep reappearing in Trudi's life? Someone you might have thought might pose a threat?"

"Did I think one of them might kill her, do you mean? No, nobody I knew. I didn't see enough of her in the last ten years of her life to know what she did. I just wanted it to stop. As I said, I was relieved it was over when they said someone had killed her."

Kath and Lydia returned with the drinks and passed them to Alex and Ray.

"People don't sneer at me in the street now," said Ray, "it's more a look of pity. That's never going to change. Even if you finally work out who did it."

"Ray doesn't talk about it if he can help it," said Kath. "When you first got here, you referred to it as a killing. I said a man raped and stabbed Trudi; that's what happened. Someone was capable of that, someone she knew. It could have been anyone. They might walk past us in the street tomorrow and know they took our only child from us. We'll never be rid of those thoughts whether you catch him or not."

There was little Alex could think might add to what they had learned.

Kath and Ray Villiers had suffered enough already.

"Thank you both for being so open with us," he said, "I hope we can bring you closure by finding the person responsible. It sounds empty to say we're sorry for your loss, but we're glad to have seen parts of Trudi's life where she was innocent, happy and smiling. Those photos are something to treasure."

Alex and Lydia left Trudi's parents to their nightmares.

Saturday, 21 April 2018

GUS AWOKE to the sound of the dawn chorus. Yesterday afternoon had panned out as he had hoped. He had agreed on positioning the security cameras, negotiated a price and pencilled in an installation date. He would have preferred not to wait two weeks, but many people needed protection, it seemed.

He had then worked on his allotment for the first time in over a week. His visits were restricted by working with the CRT or interference from foreign gangsters. But, while digging, weeding and planting, he had glanced up to the hillside to catch a sight of police activity.

Without a car, there was no way he was walking up there to check. He wouldn't be welcome if he had. Consultants aren't involved in ongoing cases. Geoff Mercer might have made an exception because someone had tried to shoot him, but OCTF wasn't an organisation to make exceptions.

Who had been in charge of the operation? He was itching to find out.

Gus had set his alarm for seven o'clock. He succumbed to the temptation of an hour's lie-in until the ringing clock roused him.

Gus looked at his options for breakfast. The disruption caused by the attempt on his life had left him short on provisions. It was his fault, he supposed; he could have gone shopping yesterday. However, time alone offered the opportunity to mull over the Trudi Villiers case. Gus had most of the steps involved worked out in his mind.

There was nothing for it; he must call Lydia. He needed to find out what they learned yesterday afternoon in his absence. If she drove over to collect him earlier than agreed, they could drop into the office before visiting James Bosworth.

Lydia was not an early bird by the sound of it.

"Is it Saturday already?" she said, "you said after ten.

Does my clock say seven-thirty? Heavens, that's the middle of the night."

"Look, I need to get up to speed with the interviews you did yesterday. Have you added your notes to the Freeman file?"

"Yes, we both did that before we finished yesterday. Alex and I worked until six. I could drop into the office on my way to collect you. If I print off what we included from the Li's and the Villiers's, you can read everything before we catch up with Bosworth."

"That will have to do," said Gus, "although it doesn't solve my immediate problem."

"No transport?" asked Lydia.

"No, hunger," said Gus, "can you pick up croissants for me to munch as we drive to the Westbourne Estate? I can make a flask of coffee to tide us over until lunchtime."

"Will do, guv. I'll get there as soon as I can."

Lydia decided it was out of the question to sneak another thirty minutes in bed. Gus had been through the mill in the past forty-eight hours. The least she could do was fetch his breakfast.

She reached the Old Police Station by half-past eight, collected a copy of the pertinent items and headed for Devizes. A quick stop to buy her boss a healthy snack at the Community Shop in his village, and she stood on the doorstep of his bungalow before nine.

Gus opened the door and came straight out, carrying a large thermos flask.

"Are those still warm?" he asked, pointing to the paper bag she carried.

"Yes," she replied, "I bought them in the shop, along the lane."

"I never realised they stocked them," said Gus, grabbing the bag, "cheers, let's get going."

Twenty-five minutes later, they threaded their way through parked cars and vans on the Westbourne Estate. Gus had devoured his pastries. The notes Lydia had given him now bore buttery finger marks.

"Should we talk with Jason Li, guv?" asked Lydia.

"You can ask him to recommend a good wine to go with your Kung Pao Chicken,"

"Oh, can't he add new information to the investigation?"

"One step at a time, Lydia. Ask me again after we've spoken with James Bosworth."

"This is where he lives. The van that has his name on the side gives it away. But, at least, it suggests he's home."

Gus and Lydia approached the van on the drive. Three boisterous young boys played on the pavement; they stopped and stared.

"Those must be the Bosworth boys," said Lydia.

The front door opened. Gus and Lydia knew Sammie Bosworth was twenty-eight and a mobile hairdresser; they didn't expect her to be plump, plain and short.

"We ain't interested in buying whatever you're selling," she said, still holding the door.

"We're not selling a thing," said Gus, whipping out his identity card. "It's James we came to interview."

"Who's that?" A disembodied voice came from inside the house.

"Coppers," shouted Sammie.

James Bosworth appeared in the doorway, easing his wife to one side. Lydia thought he matched the WPC's description perfectly. Even at forty-five, Bosworth was tall and dark and had that edgy vibe that appealed to many women. Bosworth knew what effect he could have and graced Lydia with one of his smouldering looks.

"When you've finished undressing my colleague with your eyes, perhaps we could get on? My name's Freeman, a consultant with the Crime Review Team reviewing the murder of Trudi Villiers in 2003. You were interviewed at the time; we have further questions."

"Take them indoors," snapped Sammie, "we don't want the neighbours to know the law's here."

Bosworth ignored her, turned on his heel and walked into the house. Gus and Lydia followed him indoors, where they found Bosworth leaning against a unit in the large kitchen. He had positioned himself so the island in the middle of the room lay between them.

"You lied to the police, Mr Bosworth," said Gus.

"Don't know what you mean."

"If you mess me around, we can carry on this conversation at the nick, do you understand? We know what happened after you and Krystal argued and fought. So, where did you go after you left Saeed Gill's taxi?"

Bosworth was shocked; they knew so much.

"I told the slimy git to drop me off so I could use a shortcut. I knew the streets on the Greenwood Estate, so I headed for the garage near the river bridge. My building society had an ATM there. It meant paying two per cent on cash withdrawals, but I was broke. I had no choice. I wanted to draw out twenty quid. Just my luck; the bloody thing was out of order. Then it began to rain when I walked home. I lived a couple of streets further into the estate in those days. So I got soaked by the time I got indoors."

"What time might that have been?"

"A little after one, I guess,"

"You can't be certain?"

"I wasn't interested. I didn't expect someone to ask me fifteen years later. If I'd known, I would have looked at a clock."

"You walked across to Riverside Walk?"

"That's right."

"I'll be generous," said Gus, "it might take fifteen minutes at a slow pace to walk from the point you mentioned to the garage. The taxi firm stated you left Saeed Gill's taxi at twenty-five past twelve at the latest. That puts you on the garage's forecourt at twenty minutes to one."

"If you say so," shrugged Bosworth.

"Talk me through the argument you had with Krystal Warner."

Sammie hovered by the doorway, listening in to their conversation.

Bosworth gave her a different look from the one he had given Lydia earlier. Sammie closed the door.

"I told the truth about that. We hadn't been going together very long. Krystal wasn't the love of my life; let's say that. The sex was good. I wanted to spend the night. She was scared of what Trudi would say if she found me there in the morning. It was pathetic."

"When did you first meet Trudi?"

"At school, why?"

"Oh, I thought you might have mentioned you were her first love when she was twelve years old."

James Bosworth pushed himself away from the unit.

"That's enough," he said, "this isn't happening anymore. I want a solicitor next time we talk."

"That's fine, Mr Bosworth. Why don't you meet us at the new unit on Crook Way this afternoon? Shall we say one o'clock?"

Gus didn't wait for an answer. Sammie was standing outside with her three sons.

"Is he in trouble?" she asked.

"I don't think so," said Gus, "but the sooner he tells us the truth, the quicker he can attend to more serious matters,"

Sammie and the boys trooped indoors.

Lydia drove back towards the town centre.

"I'm more confused than ever, guv," she said, "you had him on the ropes back there. Why didn't you finish him?"

"One step at a time, Lydia. We haven't done talking to him yet. It will be over soon."

Chapter Twelve

GUS SUGGESTED they could use the spare time they had thrown up working in the office.

"Get everything we heard from Bosworth into the Freeman file," he said, "and I'll check with London Road to find out who's available. I realise this eats into your weekend, but there's no point ferrying me back to my place. I'd only need a lift back here in an hour."

"That's fine, guv. I can clean my place another time. Will you need an Inspector present this afternoon, guv?"

"I'll ask when I reach someone at HQ, Lydia. Of course, as Bosworth will have his brief with him, they might insist. However, the ACC knows I've carried out a thousand interviews, and I'm not likely to be tripped up by a silver-tongued solicitor."

Gus got through to Reception. But unfortunately, the officer he spoke with was reticent about who was on-site and what they were doing.

"Look," said Gus, "I'm aware of the operation that took place yesterday. If the ACC, DS Mercer, and the others are attending a debrief, preparing a statement, or interviewing prisoners, that's fine. I don't need the details. All I want to know is can a senior officer attend the custody suite here in town if I need to arrest someone this afternoon?"

Lydia's ears pricked up at that. So terrific, they had got their man. Why hadn't Gus said? He was so frustrating.

Gus remained on hold. Then came a reply.

"Oh, okay. See you at one o'clock. Bye."

"All set, guv?"

"We have the pleasure of the company of Gareth Francis this afternoon."

"Is he a DI, guv? That's a new name to me."

"Francis is a D-I-C-K, Lydia. I permit you to kick him if he steps out of line."

"What else do we need to prepare for this afternoon, guv?"

"Call Krystal Warner. Invite her to attend the custody suite at two o'clock. If she refuses, tell her we will arrest her for obstruction. Then, we'll send uniformed officers to march her out in front of her Saturday afternoon regulars."

"Should Krystal call her solicitor, guv?"

"Absolutely. The more, the merrier."

Lydia made the call. Krystal didn't seem worried or surprised.

"That's sorted, guv. Have we got time for lunch before we drive over to Crook Way?"

"We're running out of places we can go for a bite to eat," said Gus, "ideally, I want a place with a TV. There's due to be an announcement on the local news."

"We can watch it here, guv. Then, I'll pop out for a pizza from that place just past Market Square or fish and chips from the retail park."

"No contest," said Gus, "I'd love a piece of battered cod."

Lydia made her way to the lift, and Gus turned on the TV. They had a while to wait before the regional news broadcast. He wondered how Geoff Mercer had got on yesterday.

Gus checked the murder file and had a chuckle at Lydia's comments. He wondered if she had ever come up with a plausible answer to his question about the items removed from the murder scene.

Lydia returned in next to no time.

"I hope you stayed within the speed limit, young lady," he asked.

"Yes, I flashed my ID card and jumped the queue, telling them this was urgent police business,"

"Very funny," he said.

"The young lad serving me thought so. So he gave us extra chips."

They tucked into their lunch. Time was of the essence. Gus turned the sound up as he saw a reporter standing one hundred yards away from Monty Jennings's shed. Uniformed officers kept the public and the media behind the crime scene tape.

"A sophisticated cannabis farm has been uncovered by Wiltshire Police inside a large shed that stands in this isolated field above the village of Urchfont, near Devizes. When officers forced open the door, they discovered a secondary interior wall. The exterior and interior walls had been insulated to keep the heat in and the stench from leaking out. Behind the interior walls, they found fifteen hundred cannabis plants. Twelve hundred were mature plants, and the rest were seedlings. The plants would have produced over a million pounds of Class B drug."

The reporter stood to one side for the camera to pan down the lane towards the roadway.

"As officers approached the large shed behind me at dawn yesterday morning, they could hear the humming sound of the ventilation system. When they stood outside, waiting for the big red key to force open the door, the smell of the cannabis was minimal. It wouldn't have troubled residents of these nearby houses on Cambrai Terrace. But, of course, the truth of what was happening inside became obvious once the door was forced open. Shots came from within the building. The speed of the surprise attack and the number of armed officers present resulted in a swift conclusion to the action. Officers took five men and two women into custody."

The reporter handed back to the studio.

"Let's join the senior officers involved in this case on the steps outside Wilshire Police Headquarters in Devizes. They are making a statement: -

Gus smiled when he saw the row of faces at the front of the array of police personnel.

A familiar figure stepped forward, and his name appeared on the bottom of the screen. Detective Superintendent Geoff Mercer of Wiltshire Police -

"These men and women will be charged with various drug-related offences and money laundering charges. We will push for sentences that reflect the serious nature of the offences carried out by a sophisticated organised criminal gang. They made huge amounts of money from their operation, stretching from the capital to the Bristol Channel coast. They used false identities. Many had counterfeit documents, which raised questions over border security. How did they get through so easily? Since they joined their fellow countrymen, who had already lived here for ten years, they rented properties. The sole purpose of these properties was to grow cannabis. The appearance of a husband, wife, and child replying to advertisements fooled landlords. These people were not related. The child was returned to his family once the man and woman had installed a sophisticated hydroponics system. This system involves growing plants using sand or gravel and liquid with added nutrients. There was no necessity for soil. If the people in the houses needed help, so-called relatives arrived to tend the crops. The leaders of the gang were brothers Florian and Valmir Rexha. They came to the UK from Albania at the turn of the century, claiming to be Kosovan refugees. Their ages have yet to be proven because the documentation they carried was counterfeit. When arrested today in London, each man had half a dozen passports in their possession. They are between thirty-five and forty-five years old. Wiltshire Police carried out this raid with the Organised Crime Task Force. Early this morning, OCTF raided properties leased by gang members across the South. We seized cannabis worth six million pounds in total, plus three-quarters of a million in cash."

An attractive blonde officer did her future promotion prospects no harm by giving the next statement. The camera loved her.

Gus watched Detective Inspector Suzie Ferris with pride as she said: -

"Several of the defendants we picked up this morning were trafficked. They assert that these criminals forced them to work for them. We will check their IDs and documentation, but we believe their defence will be a pack of lies. It's a tactic the gang have used to avoid detection in many areas of their operation. They leased the building in question from a local businessman. A series of unauthorised alterations had been made to the building to prevent local people from recognising what was happening. These alterations did not have the owner's permission."

Gus continued to have a broad grin as the next face appeared.

Kenneth Truelove, Assistant Chief Constable, told reporters: -

"Wiltshire Police will continue to target the production of cannabis within our county boundaries. It has lasting physical and mental effects on users and negatively affects our communities. Drugs fuel other crimes, and we have to combat that. We need the public to work with us to help tackle drug crime. Please inform us of any suspicious activity. As my officers have stated, this was a sophisticated operation. At its heart was a shed that underwent a conversion without the owner's knowledge and for no known purpose. Strangers drove in the lanes nearby. The clues were there. Be alert to things that feel odd, and give us a ring."

The Police and Crime Commissioner added his bit: -

"We need to send a clear message to those involved in drug crime. We have the tools and the determination to bring down gangs like this. We must thank our colleagues in OCTF for their guidance and cooperation in a successful operation."

ACC Truelove closed by saying, "This gang ran a huge criminal operation across this county and up to six counties beyond our boundaries. We need to leave no stone unturned in the fight against organised crime. I wish to pay tribute to the dedication and effort that has helped bring these gang members to book."

"Brilliant," said Gus, "Geoff Mercer, you are a genius,"

"Wiltshire Police took most of the credit for that job, didn't they, guv?"

"Well, OCTF deserved a kick in the teeth. A man died because of their inaction. I was nearly another victim. Geoff used to make a habit of hogging the limelight when he'd only done ten per cent of the work on a case. So I suggested he do something similar this time. I'm not surprised he could convince the top brass to join him. Their status in the county has just rocketed. The nationals will pick up this regional broadcast. It will knock spots off any statement issued by OCTF. They think they're too special to court publicity. They give the impression they're the secret police. Their faces are always blurred on the screen to protect their identity."

"What happens now, guv?"

"Don't forget what I told you last week. There were unusual circumstances with this one. Muggins here nearly got killed for having the audacity to look for a missing pensioner. I'll keep pressing for an apology from OCTF over Frank North's murder. At the very least, they owe that to Irene North. If it's not forthcoming, I could light a few fires and try to inquire into the matter. What happens next is down to those senior officers still in operational roles and the Crime Prosecution Service. We have nothing to contribute. So move along; nothing to see."

"You love that phrase, don't you?"

"When you've been in this game for as long as I have, you learn to understand acceptance, Lydia. Some things you can change, other things you can't. You view whether what you've done has reached a level where you can live with it. Often it won't matter if you don't like what you see because unchangeable can be just that. If I allow myself to think I can't live with only getting an apology for Frank's death, I could go to my grave a bitter and frustrated man."

Lydia believed Gus would get that apology. She

wouldn't want to be the man who said no to him — time to move on.

"Could you pass me your fish and chip wrappings, please, guv? We should drop these in a bin."

"Let's hit the road, young lady. James Bosworth and his brief await."

DI Gareth Francis was waiting in the custody suite when they arrived. His mood hadn't altered since Thursday morning. He drew himself to his fullest height and stared at Lydia's chest. Not a great start.

"My, what big eyes you've got, Grandma," said Lydia.

Gareth Francis's face turned as red as a beetroot.

"Is our guest here yet?" asked Gus.

DI Francis nodded. He'd decided not opening his mouth meant less chance of putting his foot in it.

Gus entered the interview room, and DI Francis joined him. Lydia seated herself in the viewing room next door. She sat behind a one-way mirror. She could see Little and Large in the interview room, or Gareth and Gus, with Bosworth and a sharp-suited gentleman.

Gus introduced himself and Gareth Francis for the tape. He added that also present were James Bosworth and Neville Purchase, solicitor.

"James," said Gus, "we're here this afternoon at your insistence. When I asked if you had been Trudi Villiers's first love, you decided you wanted to have your lawyer present before answering."

"Has my client been cautioned, Inspector?" asked Neville Purchase.

"No," replied Gareth Francis.

"Why on earth would we caution or charge your client?" said Gus. "Will you answer the question, please, James?"

"No comment," replied Bosworth.

"Fair enough. I'll tell you what I believe happened. Feel free to jump in when I miss something."

Neither Bosworth nor his brief had anything to say.

"Ray Villiers told you in no uncertain terms he didn't want you to see his daughter. Trudi fell for you in a big way. You, on the other hand, were ambivalent."

"I resent that. I've always been straight...."

Gus raised a hand.

"Your brief can explain later. I don't think you've ever fallen heavily for anyone in your life. You've had a succession of girlfriends. Maggie Smith, the landlady from the Ring O'Bells, told us that. Many were attractive enough, but you were keen to settle down and have a family. Krystal Warner fitted your type. I met your wife, Sammie; she's made from the same mould. You didn't want a trophy wife, someone who looked great on your arm but who you worried about every day you spent working away. She had to be servile, the little wifey at your beck and call twenty-four-seven. It would be even better if she provided you with a few bairns running around at home. You told us Krystal wasn't the love of your life. It was time to look elsewhere if she wouldn't spend the night with you."

"Is this leading somewhere, Mr Freeman," asked Purchase.

"Of course, I'm merely showing the true character of your client. He's not a pleasant man. When he left Krystal Warner that night, he didn't travel home by taxi as he told the police at the time. Your client couldn't pay the fare. Instead, he walked across the Greenwood Estate, joined Riverside Walk and headed for the nearby garage. He intended to use the cash machine there. Would you prefer to continue the story, James?"

Bosworth shook his head.

"The machine was out of order. It rained. James says he walked home. That's not true. The rain didn't start to fall until after two o'clock. The murder file showed the police surgeon confirmed this with Lyneham airbase. The Met Office has a weather station there. They tend to be more accurate than the memories of your average electrician. Let's retrace your steps. You left the pub with Krystal with high hopes for a night of sex. According to Saeed Gill, things got started on that front in the taxi. You had been drinking from eight o'clock. You were drunk, angry and sexually frustrated. Who did you blame for this state of affairs? According to Gill, again - Trudi and Krystal were slags. Trudi was the cause of your early night. You knew she walked home via Riverside Walk. The whole point of the extra hour at the Ring O'Bells was to scrounge another tenner out of Gary Smith for the holiday fund. Trudi would never waste that money on a taxi. She might have had to pay the full fare if Saeed Gill had collected her. What did you do for the next fifteen minutes? We can guess. You left the pub at midnight after drinking several pints. I bet you were bursting by the time you reached the garage. So, you stopped along Riverside Walk before you got there to empty your bladder or wandered back after your trip to the cash machine had been unsuccessful. Time flies when you're having fun. A few minutes after one o'clock, you stood by the entrance to Riverside Walk. You met Trudi. Here's a good point to jump in. Did she ask why you and Krystal weren't in bed at their place? Did she offer to help you out, or did she find it funny?"

"Trudi asked me why I didn't still find her attractive."

"She had fallen for you at twelve years old, hadn't she? You weren't as obsessed. Ray told you to leave her alone, and you didn't give a toss. You looked elsewhere. You told Trudi you found her attractive that night, didn't you? It was a lie but guaranteed to get you laid. Finally, the sexual frustration the argument with Krystal had built up would end. You took her onto Riverside Walk, and we know what followed. How long did it last? An hour of sex with a woman who liked it rough. Trudi enjoyed being with you. She was a willing partner. It was fourteen years later than she had hoped, but she finally got what she'd always wanted. I believe your blood type is O-positive. Is that correct?"

"Yes," whispered Bosworth, his head bowed.

"What happened afterwards?"

"Trudi pulled her skirt down and put her knickers in her bag. Then she carried her shoes as she walked from the bushes where we lay. Trudi said her shoes were new and made her feet hurt. I went to kiss her goodnight, but she turned away. I could tell it had meant nothing to her. It was just another screw. She carried on up Riverside Walk past the bridge. I walked home, and I got indoors at half-past two. It was chucking it down with rain by then, as you said. I didn't kill her. I swear on my life."

"We know you didn't," said Gus.

Lydia heard Gareth Francis's sharp intake of breath, even from behind the glass. He was as surprised as she had been.

"What happens now?" asked James Bosworth.

"We won't be able to stop this from coming out once the murder case gets to court, I'm afraid. Sammie and the children will learn of the part you played. You should have come forward immediately to say you and Trudi had been together early on Sunday. The miscarriage of justice would never have occurred. They might have found the real killer far sooner. Whether that carries any legal consequences isn't my problem. Do you mind hanging on for a few minutes, both of you? I'll consult with my colleague next door, and then we'll let you get on with your day."

Lydia jumped out of her seat. What was Gus up to now? Why did he need her when he had the Detective Inspector with him?

"It's okay, Lydia," Gus said when he met her in the corridor, "I'm killing time. Can you bring Krystal through as soon as she arrives, please? I want to keep Bosworth hanging around. It will be interesting to note their reaction when they see one another."

"Do you believe Bosworth, guv? Are you sure he didn't do it?"

Gus smiled.

"You've still got lots to learn, haven't you? So what time do you make it?"

"Five to two," she replied.

"Go to the front desk and see if she's early. Then, I'll finish things in the interview room."

Gus returned to the doorway of the room and found Bosworth and his solicitor preparing to leave.

"Everything's in order, Mr Freeman," said DI Francis, "Mr Bosworth has written and signed a statement."

"Thank you both for coming in," said Gus, "a little late for the truth to come out, but better late than never."

The two men shuffled past him.

"If Bosworth admitted to having sex with Trudi Villiers, he had to be in the frame for her murder," said Gareth Francis after they were gone. "How could you expect the detectives back then to believe he left her at two, then someone appeared out of nowhere to kill her? I don't get it."

"Bosworth explained the missing items to my satisfaction. I hope the officers involved would have had the common sense to see the truth. The first question was what he'd done with her skirt, underwear, purse, and phone. He wouldn't have had a clue. They didn't find them in the river or near the murder scene. That should have suggested they were looking for a second person."

DI Francis shook his head.

"I still don't know how Bosworth dealt with hearing Trudi was dead. Who did he think did it?"

"Patience, we're nearly there," said Gus.

As Bosworth and Purchase reached the end of the corridor, the door opened. Krystal Warner entered, followed by Lydia Logan Barre.

"This way, Ms Warner," called Gus, "so glad you agreed to join us."

Lydia went to sit in the viewing room. Gus shook his head and ushered her and Krystal into the interview room ahead of him.

"You've met Lydia Logan Barre," said Gus, "my name is Freeman. My colleague is DI Francis. We will tape our conversation as this is a formal interview. You decided to attend without a solicitor?"

Krystal Warner seemed calm on the surface.

"I didn't think it necessary."

"We've concluded a long session with James Bosworth, as you witnessed. We have the pertinent facts now in Trudi's murder. Is there anything you wish to tell us?"

Krystal shook her head.

"For the benefit of the tape, could you answer yes or no, please?" said Gareth Francis.

"No, nothing."

"I had several discussions with my colleague, Lydia,

about aspects of this case," said Gus. "She's new to police work. I posed a question. Why were items Trudi had been wearing or carrying removed from the murder scene? What made them significant? What confused me, to begin with, was how often the events of Saturday night and early Sunday morning altered. It wasn't easy to get to the truth. The two main culprits were you and James. We know why he lied on at least two occasions. He had something to hide, but you knew that, didn't you?"

Krystal shifted in her chair. The calm demeanour was slipping.

"When the taxi disappeared, taking James home to the Westbourne Estate, you went indoors. You were angry and upset after arguing and fighting with him. Yet you wanted us to believe you went to bed as soon as you entered your flat and slept through until ten o'clock. That would have been very unusual behaviour. The natural response might be to shed a tear, call his mobile, and beg him to come back. Maybe call your best friend to cry on her shoulder. You might drown your sorrows and wait for her to get home. Trudi would have been with you by twenty-past one. Only an hour to wait. What time did you call her mobile?

"Who says I did?" said Krystal.

"Several things told me that was what happened," said Gus. "I believe you called her at half-past one, maybe later. You knew how long it took to walk home via Riverside Walk. The two of you had done it often enough to save the taxi fares for your holidays. You hadn't gone to bed as you said; you remained fully dressed. After you left Kingfisher Close and entered Riverside Walk by the second bridge, you expected to meet Trudi somewhere along the pathway. You asked yourself, what could have kept her? Did she leave the pub later than planned? Where were you when you heard them talking, Krystal? James told us he left Trudi and didn't look back. He said he had just been another screw to her, a convenient male to satisfy her insatiable hunger for meaningless sex. So when Trudi passed that first bridge and carried on up the pathway, you were lying in wait."

"I knew what they'd done," whispered Krystal, "I could smell the sex on her, the filthy bitch. Strolling, along with her bloody shoes in her hand. We were supposed to be best friends."

"You struggled with Trudi and overpowered her. Did she keep telling you how good it had been with James? Saying what a fool you were for not letting him spend the night? You had to shut her up, didn't you? How ironic that Trudi had been carrying her stilettos. You grabbed one and hit her time after time in the throat to silence her. Then, when she lay there, quiet, barely alive, you stood up and stamped on her chest twice with one of your high heels. What words did you use?"

"Fuck you," said Krystal.

"One of those two blows was the fatal one," said Gus, "what happened next explained the missing items. It was the only logical conclusion to draw. First, you dragged her body from the pathway to the bushes. Second, you removed her skirt to confuse the police and make them believe it was a rape homicide. Her underwear was already in her bag. Third, you removed her shoes from the scene because of the bloodied heel used in the initial assault. Finally, Trudi's mobile phone contained the missed call you made. How long did you hang on to those items before getting rid of them, Krystal?"

"Sunday morning."

"And what did you do with your shoes?"

Krystal stood. She was wearing black stilettos with a four-inch heel.

"I had to have a new heel on the right one because it snapped. I don't wear this pair every day. I keep them for special occasions. They remind me never to trust a man ever again."

"I'll leave you to do the honours, Gareth," said Gus, "nice working with you this time."

Epilogue

GUS LEFT the interview room and walked along the corridor, followed by Lydia. As they passed the front desk, the officer on duty watched a TV news bulletin on a screen high on the wall. It featured the same reporter from the earlier news conference.

"Orges Ahmeti, an Albanian with an outstanding European arrest warrant for GBH, was arrested after he shot at officers when they raided the cannabis farm. He is currently helping us with our enquiries into the murder of Frank North, seventy-one, a pensioner who lived in the village. Mr North went missing last Saturday night. His body was found on Sunday evening. It's believed Mr North became suspicious of improvements to the building. Bernard Jennings's lawyer told us the local entrepreneur rented the field and outbuildings to the Rexha brothers. He hadn't visited the site since the agreement was signed fifteen months ago. So he was unaware of the reported alterations. Mr North had noticed smoke coming from a new chimney and wondered whether people lived in the shed. The smoke came from a wood burner installed to keep the growers warm. Without the Beast from the East we experienced in February, this clue to what lay behind the building's walls may never have surfaced."

"Did Ahmeti shoot Frank North, guv?" asked Lydia.

"Dushka was the assassin in that gang, in my opinion. He wasn't in the shed twenty-four-seven. Ahmeti was just muscle to keep the others in line."

"That poor old man thought he was helping you by checking what was happening."

"Seek not the Devil's work, for it will surely find thee," said Gus.

"Is that Kierkegaard again, guv?"

"No, I made it up to teach me never to listen to gossip."

WHEN THEY WERE outside in the car park, Lydia turned to Gus. She had a frown on her face.

"I'm still in shock, though. How did you know the murder took place that late? Everyone said it was just after one."

"The police surgeon listed the time of death as 'after one o'clock' because he knew that was when Trudi left the pub. Nobody queried whether it might have been two-thirty or even three o'clock. We know the original investigation was flawed, and they chose a time that fitted their rationale. After that, it was hard to get people to consider an alternative. It was simple as soon as I put the timings and missing items together. Two people being involved sounded crazy, but I was right."

"That DI Francis asked an intelligent question," said

Lydia, "what was Bosworth thinking when he learned Trudi died minutes after he'd left her? Did he suspect Krystal?"

"Bosworth's such a rotten character; he might not have given a toss. He knew he didn't do it. Did he think Krystal did it? Maybe. When the police investigation switched to Lewington, that changed everything. He could hardly come forward to say he'd been with Trudi, and he thought his ex-girlfriend did it. He moved on, found Sammie, got married and settled down. Krystal was in a dead-end job in a pub he no longer visited. Why bother raking up the past?"

"I can see how Krystal tried to implicate James by removing the skirt and underwear and hid her involvement by removing the phone. However, when the investigation veered towards Lewington, a total stranger, how could she carry on as if nothing had happened? She continued working in the same pub and even took over the licence. How could anyone do that?"

"Krystal had told the police she went to bed as soon as the taxi left. How could she know where Bosworth was at two that morning? Unless she admitted, she was on the pathway by the river. How would she explain why James didn't even know what was missing, Lydia? She told the police she didn't get up until ten. Someone might have seen her ditch the incriminating evidence if questioned while things were still fresh in their minds. No, she had to keep quiet, just like James. In the end, the whole case hinged on those missing items."

"I still can't get over how creepy that was being in the room when she stood up to parade those shoes in front of us."

"They were killer heels, alright. But it's clear Krystal is a very troubled woman. She is troubled yet calculating. That could have been her first move in convincing people she's unhinged and unfit to stand trial. The CPS will need to be very careful with their next steps. Either way, we know we have found the person responsible for Trudi's murder. That's what the ACC asked the CRT to do. The rest is down to the system."

Lydia started the car and prepared to drive her boss home.

"Neil and Alex won't believe it. We've cracked another case, guv."

"It's been a hectic week," Gus agreed.

Another quote from Kierkegaard slipped into his head:

Life is not a problem to be solved but a reality to be experienced.

Gus Freeman wondered what experiences lay ahead on their next cold case.

Next in The Freeman Files series

vinci-books.com/pressurepoint

In a town cloaked in silence, the truth fights to be heard.

Detective Gus Freeman and his team delve into the murder of twenty-seven-year-old Laura Mallinder, a massage parlor worker, each step bringing them closer to the truth... and deeper into danger.

Turn the page for a free preview…

Pressure Point: Chapter One

Sunday, 12 June 2011

Laura Mallinder prepared to leave for work at half-past five in the evening.

Only a three-hour stint tonight. A typical Sunday. She had her regular clients to see to and perhaps a phone enquiry. With luck, she could earn one hundred pounds. Not a bad rate of pay for three hours. Twice the national average for women.

When she left Bedminster Down Secondary School in 2000 with seven GCSEs, she had no burning ambition to continue studying. University wasn't for the likes of her and other family members. Her Dad worked in a factory, her Mum served dinners at her old school, and her two older brothers worked in the building trade.

Laura wanted something different. Her best friends Mo and JoJo enrolled at the City of Bristol College to gain hair-dressing and beauty therapy qualifications. She followed in their wake as she wasn't ready to commit to a full-time job.

Instead, she studied Business and Professional Services. That seemed ironic now.

When she left the College in the summer of 2002, she landed a job in a solicitor's office. Laura found it boring. She hated seeing the same people every single day.

At her first firm, the partners were all men. A couple had wandering hands. They seemed to think the office junior was there to give them a cheap thrill. Laura complained to one of the older secretaries.

"We've had to put up with that too, Laura. It goes with the territory. Why complain?"

"It's not right," said Laura.

"The partners will be here long after you've gone. So bite your tongue and hope they take on a new girl in a month or two. They're like children with a shiny new toy."

Laura stayed until the end of the month. There was no sign of a new arrival to disrupt the constant harassment. So she signed on at a secretarial agency, and the work took her to dozens of different working environments across Bristol for over three years. Large office blocks with open-plan layouts and hundreds of employees. Offices with plenty of banter to fill the empty gaps in her working day. There were smaller firms too, where she had a room to herself and a boss who rarely visited the office. The work was still dull, but it brought in a living wage.

That was part of the problem. Times were tough for a young girl wanting to leave home and strike out on her own. So, when Mo and JoJo suggested they rent a place together, she jumped at the chance. All three were single. There were plenty of boys in the pubs and clubs they frequented. Times had changed from Mum's day when she met Laura's Dad at the youth club at fourteen and walked up the aisle a virgin at nineteen.

The rented house wasn't a palace; it stood on a large housing estate with its share of social problems. The parties they held were wild. Laura lost track of the number of men who stayed over. Mo and JoJo proved more interested in the late nights, the drinking, dancing and recreational drugs than dealing with the housekeeping. Laura enjoyed the drinking and dancing, but the novelty wore off after three years. The temporary work from the agency was still well-paid and consistent, even if it bored her to tears. How could she break this vicious circle?

Laura recalled the night her life changed as she smoothed her short skirt and checked her stockings were pristine before she began the fifteen-minute walk to work. She had just ended a relationship with a twenty-two-year-old guy from Bradley Stoke. They met in a nightclub and saw one another for several months.

Not long after they broke up, he moved to the Midlands. It was a relief. Laura had wondered whether he was the one for a while, but he got too clingy. Plenty of other fish in the sea.

Her friends had arranged to visit a new wine bar that had opened in Redcliffe. Laura had nothing better to do, so she tagged along. While Mo and JoJo bought the drinks, she guarded a corner table as best she could. Unfortunately, the place was filling up, and soon it would be standing-room-only.

"Laura? Is that you?"

A slim, dark-haired girl had leaned towards her, gripping a large glass of white wine.

"Blimey, Carol Gullis? I haven't seen you since we sat our Geography GCSE."

"I know, what a bleeding disaster. Answer one question from Sections A, B and C. What did we do? Answered both questions in section A and the first in Section B. We couldn't fathom how we only found time to do three of the six questions. Silly mares."

"Are you with someone?" Laura asked.

"No, are you? Can I take the weight off and sit for a while?"

"My housemates are at the bar getting drinks. Please, sit here; it's not a problem. You look great."

She did; Carol's clothes looked to bear designer labels and her hair, which at school had been in bunches secured by elastic bands, now fell over her shoulders.

"You look good yourself. What are you doing these days?" asked Carol.

"I've been with a secretarial agency for just over three years. There is plenty of variety in my place of work when I'm temping around the city, but it's boring as hell. Where did you go after school? The Civil Service, wasn't it?"

"Yeah," Carol sighed, "the treadmill. Nine to five. Week after bloody week in offices out at Filton.

At that moment, her friends returned carrying two rounds of drinks.

"We thought it saved time," said Mo.

"It's heaving in here. So who's this then?" said JoJo.

Laura had made the introductions. Mo and JoJo were on a mission. They wanted to get their drinks down their necks and move on to a nightclub. So they begged Laura and Carol to drink up and accompany them.

"You go, Laura," said Carol, "time for me to get my beauty sleep. Here's my card; slip it in your purse. Call me if you're interested. Maybe we can meet up another time?"

"I'd like that," Laura had replied, taking the card and slipping it into her purse without a second glance. Mo and JoJo stood by the bar door beckoning for her to hurry. The night was a blur now as Laura stood thinking back five years. Too much to drink, a dodgy kebab and a sick day were as much as she could remember.

Laura had found the card in her purse later that week and given Carol a call.

"Cleo's, Amber speaking. How can I help you?"

Laura didn't know what to say. It sounded like her school friend's voice if she was trying to sound sexy. Was she messing around?

"Carol? It's Laura; we bumped into one another the other night in the wine bar. I thought this was your mobile number. Who's Amber?"

"Oh, hi Laura," giggled Carol, "this is what I do now. It pays a helluva lot better than the Civil Service."

"Where are you?" asked Laura.

"Cleopatra's, it's a massage parlour," replied Carol.

"That's gross, Carol," said Laura, "and dangerous, surely? There are many stories about those places being raided by the police because of what goes on."

"I work for a lady called Maggie Monk. She runs a chain of shops across the West. They're not brothels. We give a sensual massage, and there's a price list for extras. Intercourse is forbidden. If you get caught with condoms in your handbag, Maggie will sack you on the spot."

"How can you stand it? I don't know if I could do that," said Laura.

"How many hours a week do you work?" asked Carol. "Thirty-six? What do you take home? Three hundred quid a week? I work twenty-four hours in total over seven days. Depending on the extras my customers want, I can earn six to eight hundred pounds."

"You make it sound so easy," Laura had said.

"It's the same as everything else, sweetheart," Carol replied, "once you get over the first time, it's a breeze."

Laura promised to think about it. Carol begged her to keep in touch even if she turned down the chance to work as a masseuse.

That had been five years ago.

Mo gave Laura the push she needed. Another month had arrived when her friend's housekeeping money was late or non-existent. Laura had found another pile of dirty laundry to clear before she started her own. It was Monday, and the weekend had seen another succession of late nights and partying. Something had to give. She'd kept quiet for long enough.

"I know what you're going to say," sighed Mo when Laura said they needed to talk. Her mate flopped onto the sofa and burst into tears. JoJo wandered through from the kitchen with a coffee. She had just surfaced, too and looked like death.

"Why did you have to upset her?" she moaned, "she's up the duff and can't remember who she was with when it happened."

"Well, things would have had to change," Laura replied, "I can't go on carrying the extra load. I keep making up the housekeeping because you've maxed out your credit cards on clothes, drink and dope. Nothing ever gets done around here unless I do it. So I'm moving back in with my parents until I can find somewhere else to live on my own."

Laura left JoJo comforting Mo on the sofa and went upstairs to pack. Those two deserved one another. Whether they could sort out a future for themselves wasn't clear. Laura doubted it. She'd tried to make it work, but some people think they can keep taking and never give a thing in return — time to move on.

"There's always a place for you here, sweetheart, you know that," her Mum said when Laura rang to check if moving back to her old bedroom was okay. They welcomed her home with open arms.

"Are you still working at the solicitor's office?" her Dad had asked as he carried a case upstairs to her room.

"I've been temping, Dad, but I'm looking for a more permanent position."

"Good. We'd love to see you settled. You're still young, but flitting from job to job doesn't help in the long run."

"You think Mr Right will be more likely to find me if I stay in the same place for forty years like you, eh Dad?"

Her Dad laughed.

"I hope he wouldn't take that long, darling. You're as pretty as a picture. You're always smiling and have a bubbly, outgoing character. Just like your mother did when I met her at the youth club. Love at first sight."

Fate lent a hand two months later. Laura had been temping in Brislington for several months, covering maternity leave. When the boss called her into the office, she had expected it to be news of the date the other girl returned to work. It was far worse. The secretarial agency was bankrupt, and everyone on their books was now a free agent.

Then the boss added that the girl Laura covered for was indeed returning to work next month. Laura was distraught. The firm paid the agency, and she received her salary cheque direct into her bank account on the first Monday of each month. It was unlikely that she would get paid for what she'd worked so far this month. The boss could tell she was upset. He agreed to pay her until the end of the month. Two weeks at the rate he paid the other secretary. Less than the agency charged him, but it was something. Laura told her parents when she got home.

"It may prove to be a blessing," her Dad had said, "this might be your chance to find that more permanent position you spoke of when you moved back home."

"Don't worry about the money, sweetheart," her Mum said, "we can look after you until you find a job. There are a healthy number of vacancies at the moment. So it shouldn't take you long."

Laura had finished the temporary assignment in Brislington. She looked at the parlous state of her bank account and searched through her purse for that business card Carol had given her. She called from home after her parents had left for work.

"Cleo's, Ebony speaking. How can I help you?"

"Is Carol there? Sorry, is Amber working today?"

"Please hold,"

Laura soon realised the girl had her hand over the mouthpiece. The conversation became muffled, but she picked up the gist of it.

"Hey, Amber. It's a woman on the phone asking for you. Do you see female punters?"

"Hello?" Carol replied.

"It's me," said Laura, "and no offence, I don't want to book you. I'm out of work. I need money. Is there any chance of getting an interview with this Maggie Monk?"

"Oh, Laura, I'm so sorry to hear that. Unfortunately, Maggie's not here at present. We've got branches in Bath, Devizes and Swindon that she's visiting today. I'll leave a message for her. Can she call you on this number?"

"God, no, this is my parent's home phone. They can never find out I'm even considering working there. I'll give you my mobile number."

When she ended the call, Laura sat on the hall carpet and wondered what the hell she had just done. It was one thing finding the nerve to make a call to her school friend; how on earth could she steel herself to do the same job as Carol?

She considered the facts; it had been three months since that chance meeting in the wine bar. Carol was working at the same parlour. The place kept busy enough for more than one girl on each shift. The money must still be good. Money was what she needed. What did she have to lose? It was only an interview at this stage.

Maggie Monk called the following day.

"Is that Gem? Amber gave me your number. So I understand you're looking for a job?"

Carol had given her boss a false name. That was quick thinking. If she got cold feet and couldn't go through with it, Maggie Monk would be none the wiser.

"Yes, I'm Gem. I told Amber I needed a change of scene."

"Age?"

"Two months older than Amber,"

"Have you done this line of work before?"

"Never,"

"That's okay. We can train you on the job. Has Amber told you the rules? There's no funny business in any of my places. I intend to keep the doors open. I don't want the law sniffing around every waking hour."

"We know one another well. Amber talked me through the procedures. She thought I could be an asset to your business."

"I'll need to meet you to check if that's true. Amber said that you're a good-looking girl. Can you come to Cleopatra's in Knowle tomorrow morning at ten o'clock?"

Here goes nothing, Laura thought.

Laura found herself in a lounge area as she stepped off

Green Lane and made her way through the black entrance doors. The walls and floor were crimson, and the lighting was harsh and bright. The four-seater black leather sofas on either side of the room looked comfortable and welcoming. There were glass-topped coffee tables, potted plants and magazine racks by each sofa. High on the wall above each sofa hung a large TV screen showing daytime TV. She checked her watch — two minutes to ten.

Just as well, she had worn her watch today; there were no clocks in sight. At the Reception desk stood three women of similar height and build. Laura imagined Ebony was the dusky beauty beaming a smile her way. The two white girls beside her differed in age by at least ten years, maybe more. All three wore crisp white blouses, and as Laura neared the counter, she saw that a black miniskirt completed the branch's outfit. There was no sign of Carol. Maybe this was one of her days off.

"You must be Gem," said Ebony, "Maggie told us you were coming in today. Would you like a coffee?"

"Thanks, that would be great. Is Maggie here yet?"

"She's running late," said Ebony. The other two women giggled.

Laura wondered if that meant it was a regular occurrence.

"I'm supposed to give you the grand tour," the young girl continued. She led Laura along the corridor off the Reception area and into the first room.

"This is where the staff amenities are. Lockers for your belongings during a shift. Tea and coffee-making facilities. How do you take your coffee?"

"White, no sugar, thanks," Laura replied.

While they drank their coffees, Ebony asked if Laura had always lived in Bristol and what she did with her spare time. Ebony's family arrived in St Paul's in the early Sixties from Jamaica. It appeared she was a keen sports fan and watched football, rugby and ice hockey when not working.

As they made their way into the corridor again, Laura noticed mirrors and lights everywhere. It made the place seem far more extensive, and the decorations added to the ambience. But, if she forgot what went on behind each of the five doors, it felt like a pleasant working environment. It was classier than a few offices they had lumbered her with while temping.

"I'm sure Maggie will be here in a few minutes," said Ebony, "we'd better get back to Reception. You can see that none of the five doors is open now. We're open from ten in the morning to ten at night. Janina and Kathy, who you saw earlier, were waiting for their first clients. The other girls were still getting their rooms ready when you arrived."

Ebony had offered to show Laura how to answer the phone and book in the clients. Each girl who worked at the parlour had a card detailing the extras price list. If they hadn't committed the details to memory and destroyed it, that card was the first thing they grabbed in a police raid. They were to collect that before they picked up discarded items of clothing.

"The booking form is basic," Ebony had explained. "The guy's name, the time he arrived, the girl he went with, and the straight massage cost. It's always cash, which goes into the money box here at Reception."

That part seemed straightforward enough, Laura thought.

Ebony continued with the tour.

"Maggie charges us for sundries such as oils, tissues, tea, coffee and milk. That's a standard sum per shift. It varies from parlour to parlour."

"When I answer the phone, what do I say?"

"The name of the parlour, and can I help you? Don't say more than you have to, in case it's a reporter or the law. Just quote the opening times and the cost of a massage. If they ask, tell them who's working today. It's on a list at Reception. When it's a regular calling, they see the girl they ask for unless she's unavailable. After that, we take our turns in alphabetical order. So, I pick up a client before you if you want to use your name."

"I don't suppose Ebony is your real name?"

"Of course not. I ain't telling you what it is either,"

Laura smiled. If Ebony showed caution about revealing too much, then she could follow suit. Carol had kept her real identity secret so far. Why change things?

"I think I'll stick with Gem. I can't risk anyone learning I work here."

"Gem's a cool name. I still earn money before you, though," Ebony grinned.

The telephone rang, and Ebony swung into action. Laura heard footsteps outside the main door. High heels. The middle-aged woman who entered was short, stocky and smartly dressed. She looked every inch a businesswoman. Her hair may have been fair when younger, but it was cut short today, and the ash-blonde colouring gave her a sophisticated look. No way would anyone ever say Maggie Monk was mutton dressed as lamb.

"Are you Amber's friend?" she asked, offering a manicured hand towards Laura. "Has Ebony looked after you? I'm sorry that I'm late. It's my fault for being successful. I won't be in a rush to open another branch for a while."

"You need a massage," said Laura, shaking her hand and smiling. "You've come to the right place if you need to relax."

Ebony had entered the latest customer's details into the book and overheard the comment. This new girl knew how to sweet-talk the boss. They needed to watch Gem. She would steal their regulars if they weren't careful. The girl looked pretty and confident with it.

"I can offer you three shifts to begin with," said Maggie. "Monday, Wednesday and Friday. When can you start?"

"Next Monday," Laura had replied.

"We'll train you here first, then the following week, you'll work at the branch in Bath. I'll study the rotas over there when I visit next week. I'll guarantee there will be the same number of hours total, but the days and the shifts might vary. How does that sound?"

Laura heard herself reply, "It sounds fine," but she felt anything but fine inside. She was as nervous as hell.

Laura Mallinder closed the door of the two-bedroomed terraced house she called home and walked briskly towards the main road. It was a pleasant evening. The afternoon showers had disappeared; tonight promised to be rewarding at Gentle Touch.

She had long since given up on her dream of finding something different to fill her working day. Her life as a masseuse was no different to the treadmill Carol Gullis felt she was on in the Civil Service. The upside was this particular treadmill paid well.

Over the past five years, Laura met men of all ages from all walks of life. That surprised her in the beginning. She had an image in her head of the sad individual forced to pay for any sexual experience. However, her time working for Maggie Monk showed her that it took all sorts, like everything in life.

Maggie had kept her promise. Janina and Kathy helped

her with training in how speed, pressure, and contact were crucial elements in enhancing the customer experience. They also advised her to avoid the pimps that lay in wait to exploit vulnerable girls. Laura followed their tips and tricks to become skilled in her role and avoid the pitfalls. Maggie soon added Gem's name to the list at Cleopatra's in Bath.

Laura moved out of her parent's home within the first year. She bought a modest one-bedroomed flat in Kingswood and worked in the Bath and Bristol parlours. When the Gentle Touch brand name was added to her growing chain of premises at the end of 2007, Maggie asked Laura if she was interested in moving to Swindon. She wanted someone experienced to run the business in Broadgreen day-to-day.

"I want to be less hands-on with these new parlours," she told Laura.

Don't we all, Laura thought, but the money on offer would be better. If she lived in Swindon, she would save the travelling costs backwards and forwards from Kingswood on the bus to the two parlours where she worked.

She sold her flat while the market was high, and although prices plummeted because of the ensuing financial crisis, Laura came through unscathed. Some businesses suffered a recession, but theirs carried on as if nothing had happened.

Broadgreen was a district frequented by streetwalkers when she moved there. There was less evidence of girls loitering on Manchester Road these days. Why kerb crawl when there were the internet and smartphones? The girls did most of their business indoors, not in a car or a back alley.

Laura had never been propositioned on the streets, walking to and from the parlour. She took care to cover the provocative nature of her work clothes as she made frequent visits. Swindon had several volunteer organisations attempting to clean up the streets. They weren't happy about Gentle Touch being in the Broadgreen district, but they had softer targets to strike.

Gentle Touch had never had a raid. There were never any lousy reviews on Trip Advisor, and Maggie's books passed an auditor's scrutiny every April. He was a regular customer in the Knowle parlour, but he was a straight arrow as an accountant.

Laura had arrived at the entrance to the alleyway. The Turkish barber's on the ground floor were closed until tomorrow morning. Maggie had leased the shop to the guy eighteen months ago. Before that, it had been a record shop. Laura unlocked the door halfway along the alleyway and climbed the stairs. Camille would be there soon. Time to get the rooms ready for their first customer.

After Laura had stocked each room with fresh towels, she heard the click-clack of Camille's high heels on the stairs. The Thai woman arrived in the UK twenty years ago. She was married with three children. Laura was unsure how old she was but based on the age of her eldest son; it was unlikely she would see forty again.

The other girls had asked Camille why she worked at the parlour. The tiny woman shrugged and said it was necessary for her and her husband to earn as much as possible. They had a family at home who needed their support. She had no qualifications. A cleaning job only brought in enough to feed her children.

Laura knew her colleague never wasted time on idle chat. Camille turned up for her shift, did what was required and then went home. She found her in the small staff room, checking her hair and make-up in the mirror.

"You look great, Camille,"

Camille nodded and gave Laura a brief smile. Then she rubbed cream into her hands and walked through Reception to await her six o'clock appointment. Laura did the same. Just another Sunday evening.

At half-past seven, both girls took a break. They recorded the details of three satisfied customers for each masseuse and put the cash in the money box. Camille brought two coffees through to Reception. Laura was waiting for Jeff Naylor, one of her regulars, to arrive. Camille was waiting for her last customer this evening.

"Is Maggie coming, Gem?" asked Camille.

"Don't worry. She rang to confirm she would step in to cover for you," said Laura.

"Good. I must get home. My husband is not well. I'm sorry."

"You can't help that, Camille."

Laura had called Maggie to warn her she would be alone when Camille left. Laura worked until nine. Maggie had a strict rule that there were always at least two girls in the parlour on any shift. Although this never became an issue on a weekday, most parlours had five or six girls available throughout the twelve hours opening time.

On a shorter Sunday evening shift, the two girls on duty accepted the odd phone booking. It filled the gaps between their regulars and boosted their earnings. If nobody called, they used their spare time at the end of the shift to get the used towels into the washing machine and give the parlour a general clean.

Laura hoped Maggie didn't mind giving her a helping hand later. An early night would be welcome.

Maggie Monk was running late. That was nothing new. When Gem called to warn of the lack of cover, Maggie had rung several girls to see if they could dash over to help. She couldn't believe how many had their phones switched off — what a bloody nuisance.

Gem caused no bother, though, and the parlour was one of the better-performing businesses in her portfolio. So Maggie could stand the hassle this one time, as long as Gem didn't make a habit of it.

Maggie was far later than intended when she parked outside the barber's shop. She hurried into the alleyway; the door was open. That was odd. Camille would have left ages ago. If Gem booked in a late caller, she should have locked up after he arrived. They didn't encourage walk-ins. They tended to be riff-raff, and Maggie wasn't in business to cater to the likes of them.

The lights were on in Reception and along the corridor; the cash box was in the drawer. Gem and Camille appeared to have been busy tonight.

It was silent now. Maggie checked the rooms; someone was in Room One.

"Gem?" she called. There was no reply.

Maggie couldn't hear a thing. She eased open the door.

Gem lay sprawled, fully clothed, face down on the floor. The room was a mess, with blood everywhere. There must have been a mighty struggle. Maggie closed the door and staggered back to Reception.

What a mess. Why would anyone want to stab Gem to death like that?

Pressure Point: Chapter Two

Tuesday, 24 April 2018

"Another day, another collar, guv," said Neil Davis when Gus Freeman exited the lift in the CRT office. It was ten to nine on the second day of a new week for the Crime Review Team housed in the Old Police Station. The team knew that last week had been full of incidents.

Frank North, the older man with the adjoining allotment to Gus, had been murdered. Gus had escaped an attempt on his life as he drove to work. Those responsible for the violent attacks and operating a cannabis farm behind Cambrai Terrace in the village of Urchfont were either dead or in custody.

On Saturday afternoon, Gus exposed Krystal Warner as the killer of her best friend Trudi Villiers in 2003.

Yesterday, while the team attended a safeguarding briefing at the Police HQ, Gus had retrieved his beloved Ford Focus from the garage. As a result, his ten-year-old car now possessed a new windscreen and driver's headrest.

When Gus returned to work as a civilian consultant, the Krystal Warner item was the only one that should have registered. ACC Kenneth Truelove had convinced the retired detective his old-style methods were just what was needed to solve a series of stubborn cold cases. Gus wondered if he had been wise to accept the challenge. His team wondered how they would keep up their rapid success rate.

"I see you're up to speed, Neil," Gus replied without smiling.

"Sorry, guv," said Lydia, "I resisted the temptation to ring them over the weekend. That was hard enough. I blurted out the news as soon as they arrived yesterday morning."

"Neil and I were sorry to miss the fun, guv," said Alex Hardy, "but it was a team effort. I'm sure you'll pass that on to the top brass in Devizes when you report to them."

"Never fear, Alex. I'm a strong believer in giving credit where it's due. So before I get summoned to attend London Road, I suggest we get everything up to date on the Freeman file. Once that's achieved, we can forward a copy to DS Geoff Mercer."

"He'll still be busy with the Rexha gang and the fallout from their arrest," said Neil. "We may have a few days before we learn what's next on our agenda."

"There was me thinking you arrived early this morning because you were eager to get cracking on another puzzle, not looking for a holiday," said Gus as he looked up from his computer screen.

He could only see the top of three heads beavering away on the task he had just set them. He smiled. There might be an odd bump in the road, but his team was shaping up well. He glanced at a blank space on the far wall. He needed to check the translation.

Torquem alius, alium diem could become their Latin motto. Admittedly, it was a bit presumptuous on the back of only two wins; but if they didn't blow their own trumpet, no other bugger would.

The morning passed quickly as the team removed the Villiers case debris.

Wallboards and flip charts were cleaned or replaced. Paperwork got added to the physical files forwarded to them only a week ago. The Freeman file looked in pristine condition. Every interview was presented in full. No discrepancies in the reports were provided by whichever two officers attended. They had followed every clue or potential lead they unearthed. The conclusions drawn by Gus Freeman from the details gathered by himself and his team could get scrutinised with no doubts harboured of their integrity. The computer file didn't have a padlock, but the case was watertight.

Lydia looked at the only item they hadn't removed. The map of the town. Should it stay in place? Alex saw her hand hover over the first pin.

"Take it down, Lydia. I don't remember another murder in this town in the years I've been a copper. We're off to pastures new, I reckon."

"Variety is the spice of life," said Neil.

The phone rang at one-forty-five pm. Gus guessed who was calling.

"Good afternoon, Sir," he said.

"Sorry? Freeman, is that you? It's Truelove here. Can you drive over for a chat?"

"Certainly, Sir," replied Gus, "do you know what Kassie Trotter has been baking over the weekend?"

"You'll have to wait and see, Freeman. I had to attend meetings this morning with the new Chief Constable. She's eager to meet you."

"Another female in your life, Sir? Where did the Police and Crime Commissioner find this one?"

"In the Midlands, Freeman. Look, this phone conversation is preventing you from reaching my office. Please tell me you're on your way?"

"I apologise, Sir. I hoped to avoid negotiating the heavy traffic on London Road for as long as possible at this time of the afternoon. I'm running to the lift now."

Gus slammed the phone on his desk.

"We'll see you in the morning then, I assume?" said Lydia.

"When you'll be carrying folders with details of our new case," said Neil, rubbing his hands.

"Don't count your chickens, Neil. The PCC has appointed a female Chief Constable. Let's wait until we learn her approach to this team."

Gus had been right about the congested roads. The temporary traffic lights slowed progress to a crawl. If there had been a posse of workmen in sight as he threaded his way through the centre of Devizes, it would have been excusable. The only advantage of not arriving at Wiltshire Police HQ before ten to three was the prospect of teatime.

He was a familiar face in Reception now, and the officer on the desk recognised him. Police officers are another breed of animal that rarely forgets. The young man looked him in the eye as he nodded a silent greeting. Then his gaze descended as he checked for gardening trousers and dirty shoes.

"You're out of luck today," said Gus, resplendent in a short-sleeved blue shirt, black trousers and shiny shoes. He'd stuffed his tie in his pocket, deference to the warm day.

He took the stairs two at a time. The administration area was a hive of activity. Vera Jennings prepared to deliver refreshments to the ACC's office. The delicate bone china cups and saucers he recalled from his first visit were back in service. That meant only one thing. The new Chief Constable really couldn't wait to meet him.

"Good afternoon, Gus," said Vera, "we had almost given up on you. The ACC has been like a cat on hot bricks. When I entered his office earlier, he stood by the window, checking the car park for your arrival."

Gus didn't see why that felt out of the ordinary. Truelove spent most of his working day standing by that window. His executive chair would be in demand when he retired next year. 'As new. One careful owner.'

The Gothic vision that was Kassie Trotter emerged from the dark recesses of the passageway leading to Geoff Mercer's office. The top shelf of her tea trolley lay bare.

"No opportunity for baking this weekend, Kassie?" asked Gus, a trifle concerned.

Kassie nodded towards the ACC's door.

"Blame her," she replied, "her Ladyship's not a fan."

"Vera can slip me a custard cream to satisfy my cravings."

Kassie tapped the side of her nose.

"All is not lost, Mr Freeman. I'm hiding my Chelsea buns under a cloth on the bottom shelf. It will be business as usual when she's not in his room. Today, if you want to sink your teeth into my buns, I can put them in a doggy bag for you when you leave."

"Now there's an offer that's impossible to resist," said

Gus, heading for the ACC's office before things became more surreal. He tapped on the door.

"Enter," came the reply.

Gus crossed the threshold. Vera followed right behind him with the tray.

The ACC sat at his desk. A short, stern-looking woman stood by the window.

"Come along, Freeman," said Truelove, "we haven't got all afternoon. Thank you, Vera. A cup of tea will be most welcome."

Gus remained standing. He knew his place.

Vera was already leaving. The new Chief Constable spoke as soon as the door closed behind her.

"Good afternoon, Mr Freeman. My name is Sandra Plunkett. You're with us on a temporary assignment, I understand?"

"That's correct, Ma'am."

"The Crime Review Team was my initiative," explained the ACC, "we couldn't have hoped for a better start. Two cold cases have been solved since the ninth of the month. I knew Gus Freeman was the best detective for the job."

"I'm not a fan of parachuting retired officers into the workplace. There's usually a good reason for them being retired. It doesn't send the right message to rank-and-file officers struggling to make their way up the chain of command."

Gus picked up his cup and saucer. He didn't feel the need to comment. If this new broom wanted him to scuttle off to his retirement home and the allotment, fine by him, he would miss it now that he was back in the swing of things, but he'd never stay where he wasn't wanted.

"I'm sure we agree that while the CRT produces positive results, we should support them as much as we can," said the ACC. The sweat on his brow owed little to his tea cup's warmth.

"There are various aspects of policing in the county to be reviewed," Sandra Plunkett continued. "Some aspects will require a complete overhaul. Others will disappear. The vision for 2025 sees us move even further away from the service you provided during your time with us, Freeman. Things move far quicker these days."

The bloody traffic through the town centre doesn't, Gus thought.

"Am I to understand my team is under review, Ma'am?" he asked.

"I haven't been in post for enough time to have a timetable yet, Freeman. Let's say; I'll be watching you. Good afternoon."

Sandra Plunkett strutted from the room.

Kenneth Truelove stood and walked to the window; normal service could resume.

"Bloody hell, Freeman. I could have done without that woman becoming my new boss. After last week's coup, I hoped for a honeymoon period, followed by fourteen months of calm waters until my retirement. So sit, man; you're making the place untidy."

"I didn't want to claim the high ground, Sir. Sandra Plunkett and Geoff Mercer could model for the weather house couple."

"From memory, that weather house lady came out when it was sunny and warm. The man's appearance signalled bad weather. I think the roles would reverse if Mercer and Plunkett ever got involved. Our new Chief Constable signals dark clouds ahead. On the other hand, Geoff Mercer seems to be in far better humour since you've been with us."

"I try my best," said Gus.

The ACC was right. Geoff sat firmly in the CRT corner if push came to shove. Provided the ACC kept the Police and Crime Commissioner happy, his team could complete the programme that had tempted him to return.

"What did you want to talk to me about, Sir? Before Ms Plunkett hijacked this meeting. I take it she's not married."

"There's a press release in a file on my desk somewhere. I'll find it before you leave. What I want to discuss is last week's amazing turnaround. When Brendan Curran was here on Wednesday, you were light-years from solving the Villiers case. I have no idea how you kept your cool after the incident the next morning and then came up with the answers. That was awesome."

"Awesome? I'm surprised to hear you use that American term,"

"Blame my grandchildren, Freeman, and the youngsters my wife and I run into at our meeting house. Somehow, on this occasion, it felt the right expression."

"Thank you, Sir. A team effort, as I'm sure you realise. Despite the obvious reservations of the Chief Constable, Wiltshire Police will benefit significantly from my sojourn. However brief that may be. Davis and Hardy will be better detectives, and young Lydia will outshine the lot of us given the right opportunities."

"You lead by example, Freeman. That's good enough for me. The more knowledge you can pass on to those three, the better. All good things must end, though. I keep harping on about my retirement next year, but I anticipated the CRT still being in place when I left. I dreamed of you training a second or even third batch of likely lads and lasses before you finally retired. Sandra Plunkett might put the skids under that."

"Let's not get ahead of ourselves," cautioned Gus, "we've been very fortunate with our first two cold cases. Unfortunately, they remained unsolved because simple questions didn't get asked at the time. We can appreciate the reasons for that. However, things might have been different if the force had the right resources and adopted a more robust approach to serious crime."

"I think someone has expressed this opinion, Freeman. Unfortunately, we have to operate with the system we have, no matter how much we wish it operated otherwise. Things will never return to before 1965."

"Don't worry, Sir. Nobody outside these four walls will hear that comment. I think the new breed of copper would have a touch of the vapours just reading an account of a hanging, let alone attending one. The black cap had been consigned to history a decade before I joined the force. Several old hands in Salisbury worked on cases where a killer received the death sentence. One of my Sergeants said we would rue the day they withdrew the option. He said no matter how brutal the process appears to the public; they would lobby to reverse the decision in a heartbeat if they saw the horrors carried out in killings he witnessed. Far worse murders get committed today than that old Sergeant could ever imagine. There's no going back, as you say, but will society ever move forward while evil exists among us until it dies a natural death?"

"You're a deep thinker, Freeman. No wonder you get a handle on these cold cases. I imagine you would enjoy a change of scene. What do you know about Swindon?"

"I've spent many wasted hours at Crown Court there, Sir. Other than that, they've got an average football team and a Magic Roundabout. Nothing significant comes to mind from the last hundred-odd years. The town's railway history is a distant memory these days. Is that where our next murder occurred?"

"The victim was Laura Mallinder, a twenty-seven-year-old sex worker. Her employer found her body at nine thirty-five on the evening of Sunday, the twelfth of June 2011. The details are in this folder; if I can find them. So here we are, right next to Sandra Plunkett's life story. Get yourself back to the CRT office and have a read of both files. I haven't discussed this latest case with Geoff Mercer yet, but we'll set up the necessary contacts for you to access the proper personnel at Gablecross. The detectives who investigated the murder are still there. You can use interview rooms, have someone accompany you with a warrant card and so forth. I see no reason you can't continue using the Old Police station as your base. Ask Geoff Mercer for help if that proves an obstacle. I encourage you to continue to use the Hub's research facilities."

"I don't know how we'd cope without it, Sir," replied Gus, tongue firmly in his cheek.

Gus took the two files from the ACC.

"Are any of the serving officers likely to cause us a problem, Sir?" he asked.

"It might be best to consult DS Hardy on that matter, Freeman. He will know the lie of the land. Even though he's been on the sidelines for the past eighteen months, his insight will be better than any gossip I've gleaned. Will there be anything else?"

"I realise you have your hands full with the new Chief Constable and last week's organised crime caper. But I want you to press for a response from OCTF over Frank North's murder. His funeral is next Monday afternoon. Two o'clock at the West Wilts Crematorium."

"I'm not sure I can make it, Freeman. However, I'll

ensure a message reaches Mercer and Ferris that suggests they drum up a few officers to attend. We owe the poor chap that much. As for Brendan Curran and his cronies, I can only promise to do my best. But, rest assured, I've not forgotten the matter."

"Thank you, Sir," said Gus. Time to head home. The school run was over; office workers still had an hour to suffer.

There was nothing to gain from rushing. The Mallinder girl had waited seven years for someone to find her killer. Gus hoped she'd forgive him for not getting his team on her case until the morning.

Once back inside his bungalow, Gus organised a schedule for the days ahead. They would spend the remainder of this working week in preparation for this Mallinder case. If he could get to his allotment over the weekend, it would be a chance to get to grips with the chores May might present. Next Monday afternoon was set aside for Frank's funeral. As for the following Friday, the camera installers had left a message yesterday to say they would arrive at nine am. Gus wondered how long it would take him to learn how to access the feed on his smartphone. Progress can be slow for a sixty-one-year-old when technology is involved. Safety was a priority, though; it would be time well spent.

Thoughts of time spent in Swindon during the next few weeks prompted a quick check of his provisions. He mustn't let this increased activity associated with the consultancy role lead him into bad habits. That's why the allotment had become so important. He had to keep that going to provide his fresh fruit and vegetables. He made a note to visit the supermarket one evening after work to stock up on items he couldn't grow himself.

As he knocked up a mushroom omelette for his evening meal, he decided to call Vera Jennings later. He owed her a night out. Vera had played the role of a stood-up date last Thursday evening. The ploy was to convince anyone associated with the Rexha gang that Gus had died in that morning's assassination attempt. That move had bought the Organised Crime Task Force precious hours as it prepared for its widespread dawn strike on Friday morning. But, unfortunately, the gang were none the wiser until too late.

DI Suzie Ferris had helped with that misdirection. She had arranged for Gus to hide on her father's farm for ten hours. He owed Suzie something too, but how to repay that debt was another matter. The younger woman had made clear her feelings toward him.

Gus tried to put those thoughts out of his head as he ate his meal. The background music didn't help. He had chosen an album at random. Eva Cassidy was easy listening on a warm Spring evening, but Suzie had also picked it when she visited him the other day. Eva was another piece of common ground they shared. He dispensed with the musical accompaniment and concentrated on the Sandra Plunkett file.

Gus poured a glass of white wine and sat in his favourite chair in the lounge. With the ACC's file on his lap, he placed his drink on the table next to him. Under the coaster lay a scrap of paper. He didn't need to rescue it to know what it said. It was a quote that touched his heart after Tess's sudden death. The ACC said earlier today he reckoned he was a deep thinker. He had always thought long and hard about the cases he'd handled. Only after his wife's death did he consider other matters to the same degree.

'One must first learn to know himself before knowing anything

else. Not until a man has inwardly understood himself and then sees the course he is to take does his life gain peace and meaning.'

He brushed a finger around the coaster and thought of Tess as he sipped his wine.

What would she make of him today? Time to delve into the madcap world of the stern-looking weather house lady.

'Sandra Plunkett was born in Rugeley, Staffordshire, in 1970. She attended the Abbotts Bromley School, where she developed a passion for the creative and performing arts. After graduating with a degree in Film Studies and Media from Keele University, she joined the Staffordshire Police force as a Constable and worked in Cannock. Sandra got promoted to Sergeant in 1993, Inspector in 1997 and Chief Inspector in 2000. She attended the accelerated promotion course at Bramshill Police College in Hampshire and transferred to West Mercia Police as a Superintendent in 2003. She got promoted to Chief Superintendent in 2005 and was head of Professional Standards at Hindlip Park on the outskirts of Worcester. In 2009 she completed the Strategic Command Course. In June 2011, she returned to Staffordshire as an Assistant Chief Constable in charge of the counter-terrorism unit. She was appointed Chief Constable in September 2014 for the West Midlands. Sandra was awarded the Queen's Police Medal for Distinguished Service in the 2015 New Year Honours. Sandra has lived with her partner, Naomi, in a small village near Lichfield since 1998.'

So that was who they were up against, thought Gus. A formidable woman on every level. Sandra had ticked the right boxes as far as her superiors were concerned. However, he had never flown high enough to be pointed towards the SCC, policing's most senior leadership development programme. It prepared police officers and staff for promotion to the highest ranks in the service. The course was open to Superintendent and Chief Superintendent ranks and staff at equivalent grades from all UK forces who had shown the potential to progress further in their careers. It was a statutory requirement for officers seeking promotion to Assistant Chief Constable and above in UK forces.

The course aimed to develop senior leaders in law enforcement to lead policing operations and organisations locally, regionally and nationally. It offered a unique opportunity to engage in a challenging leadership development programme, which benefitted from the broad range of experience and perspectives shared by others within policing and partner organisations, nationally and internationally.

Gus had never needed a personal development plan to support his continuing professional development. He had reached his limit and was happy with his lot. The problem with these biographies generated by the force's publicity machine was that they remained exclusively positive. He needed to dig deeper for reports on cases screwed on Sandra's watch, even deeper to discover any dirt. Perhaps it wouldn't be necessary. But, if he kept solving these cases, the new Chief Constable would find it hard to prevent the CRT from becoming a permanent fixture.

Gus decided on a change of pace and called Vera Jennings.

"Hello there," she replied, "you left in such a rush this afternoon. Kassie was distraught."

"Yes, I forgot to grab her buns. Can you apologise to her in the morning? So, my highbrow friend was distraught. I take it you weren't that bothered?"

"That would be telling. Anyway, I hoped you would ring tonight."

"Does the FEW have a social outing planned this week?"

"No, my diary is a wasteland. If we plan something, can I be sure you'll turn up this time?"

"I should hope to get shot at proves a once-in-a-lifetime experience. I have every intention of being wherever we agree to meet."

"OK, Friday suits me best. We could eat at the Waggon & Horses. I'll drop by and pick you up around half-past eight. How does that sound?"

"It sounds terrific. Book a table. We know from our last visit it will be lively. If we fancy a boogie after our meal, no doubt, there'll be live music again?"

"Get you," laughed Vera, "don't let Kassie hear you say 'boogie', though. I don't think anyone under seventy uses that term."

"Ouch," said Gus, "it's been so long."

"Until Friday then," said Vera. "Goodnight and…"

"Sweet dreams," replied Gus.

Wednesday, 25 April 2018

As Gus drove through Devizes on his way to work, he thought about the second file he had read through last night. The murder files on the young woman they were to reopen hadn't received national coverage. Laura Mallinder's chosen profession prevented her from receiving the sympathy other victims could expect.

How often had he read reports of sudden death where the victim's family and friends declared they were saints? Yet, whether they died in an accident or got murdered, it never changed the dialogue. Nobody was ever a waste of space, a liar and cheat, someone you crossed the street to avoid.

Yet when a sex worker was involved, the crime drew far less attention. Regardless of the service they provided, they were still human beings. Their family deserved the same closure as any other that lost a son or daughter. Gus hoped the Crime Review Team could find answers the original inquiry failed to uncover.

Gus noticed a flurry of activity on the High Street as he turned into Church Street. The Food Bank had opened for business, and the Cancer Charities staff unloaded furniture items from a van parked outside. The ground floor of the Old Police Station showed no sign of recession.

In his rear-view mirror, he saw the boarded-up windows of the Ring O'Bells. Sadly, the pub Krystal Warner had managed until last weekend got mothballed. The landlords had erred on the side of caution and protected it against vandalism. When it might reopen was anyone's guess. Gus patted his car on the roof as he left it in his parking space at the rear of the Old Police Station. He had no intention of mothballing his old friend. A glance along the line confirmed he was last to arrive — ten minutes to nine. The team had gotten the message. He let them know he had arrived as soon as he exited the lift.

"Right, this is our new task. We'll be knee-deep in the seamier side of Swindon for the foreseeable future."

Three eager faces looked up as Gus breezed into the office.

"Our victim was Laura Mallinder, stabbed to death on the evening of the twelfth of June 2011. Laura worked in a massage parlour in the Broadgreen area of the town. She worked a three-hour shift on Sundays from six until nine.

Her body was found just after half past nine by the owner, Maggie Monk. Our twenty-seven-year-old victim sustained fatal stab wounds to her back. When the original investigation was closed, there were no known suspects."

"I don't remember much about this one, guv," said Alex Hardy, "my guess is DI Theo Hickerton handled it."

"What was he like as a copper?" asked Neil Davis.

"Keen enough," replied Alex, "but under pressure to get a result or move on to the next case on the books."

"Was that due to the sheer volume of cases or the fact it was a sex worker?" asked Lydia Logan Barre.

"The former, Theo, would have asked the right questions," said Alex. "He did things by the book when I knew him. With this killing, it's tough to get people to talk. Which business are we talking about, guv? There are so many these days."

"They weren't shy of advertising what was available on the premises," said Gus, "it closed within weeks of the murder. It traded under Gentle Touch, and Maggie Monk had run it since early 2008 without getting raided."

"Was it above a shop or in a private home?" asked Lydia, "I wouldn't know the first thing to look for."

"Maggie Monk owned the property," said Gus. "A Turkish barber leased the ground floor. The massage parlour on the first floor was accessed through a separate entrance halfway along an alleyway between two adjoining units on the quiet side street."

"If you lived next door, you would soon spot the steady number of male visitors," said Neil. "When it's a holistic spa on the High Street, it resembles any other hairdressing or beauty parlour. Lots of chrome, bright lights and a recognisable price list you can compare with the competition. Businesses such as Gentle Touch have subdued lighting and basic fittings."

"How far did the initial investigation get?" asked Lydia.

"I've had a brief look through the murder file," said Gus. "Despite the detectives' best efforts and numerous appeals to the public for help, nothing concrete surfaced regarding motive. However, the post-mortem examination indicated Laura had been stabbed to death by an unknown attacker as she worked alone."

"It sounds like they've landed us with a locked room mystery to solve, guv,"

"Nobody said all these cold cases would be easy, Neil," said Gus.

Grab your copy...
vinci-books.com/pressurepoint

About the Author

Ted Tayler is the international bestselling indie author of The Freeman Files and The Phoenix series. Ted lives in the English West country, where his stories are based. He was born in 1945 and has been married to Lynne since 1971. They have three children and four grandchildren.

His thought-provoking mysteries appeal to readers of Sally Rigby, Joy Ellis, Pauline Rowson, and Faith Martin. His action-packed thrillers are a must for fans of Mark Dawson and J.C. Ryan.

Gus Freeman's cold case investigations are carried out with reasoned deduction rather than bursts of frantic action. In each of the twenty-four books, unsolved murder is accompanied by romance, humor, and country life. The core message in the twelve Phoenix novels is that criminals should pay for their crimes. Unfortunately, the current system fails to deliver the correct punishment, so Phoenix helps redress the balance.

Acknowledgments

The love and support of my family; without them, this would have been impossible.